THE DEMON WITHIN SERIES
BOOK ONE

The Demonic Savior

LAWRENCE NEWTON

Copyright © 2024 Lawrence Newton
All rights reserved
First Edition

NEWMAN SPRINGS PUBLISHING
320 Broad Street
Red Bank, NJ 07701

First originally published by Newman Springs Publishing 2024

Photo by Natalie Serwan, South Jersey Portraits.
Legal rights to photo owned by the author.

ISBN 979-8-89308-420-7 (Paperback)
ISBN 979-8-89308-421-4 (Digital)

Printed in the United States of America

I wish to dedicate this book to the two people in my life who have ever truly understood to not try and understand me: my mother (posthumously), who always tried her best to nurture me even when I wasn't listening or completely understanding at the time; as well as my wife, who has filled the inspirational and motivational role, thus driving me to provide the best story I possibly can and has stood by me throughout this process.

For the readers of my stories, I have one thing: "Please enjoy. Thank you."

Chapter 1

It's about 10:00 p.m., February 14, and I just spent the last two and half hours on the road. I past Red Arrow Park in my brown Chrysler Town and Country station wagon. Despite the cold, scantily clad women line the streets looking for the next john so they can make a living or just to get the next "score." I creep along eyeing the latest prospects looking for the right one, as if I was shopping for a new outfit. One catches my eye, a lanky blond with scant features. She is cute in a streetwalker kind of way, blond hair, or wig like Farrah Fawcett. I slow to a stop, and she approaches my window, the heat from inside wafting through the barely opened glass.

"You lookin' for something, doll?" she calls in.

"Yes, I think I'd like some company for the night," I reply.

She rattles off the "menu." "Five dollars for a handy, ten dollars for a blow job. After that, it goes up depending on what you're into."

"How about the whole night?" I respond.

"A hundred dollars, and that's just for my time. Everything else is added on. Girl has to make a living, you know." She never missed a beat in her response, like she knew what I wanted.

"Sounds good. Get in."

She opens the passenger door and climbs in.

"I was wondering if you might like to get something to eat. I come here for business often, and I know a good diner nearby," I say.

"The one over on Broadway is good. We can do that. It's your money. Speaking of which…" She's asking for payment so she doesn't get stiffed.

I reach under my Bible on the seat and hand her the cash.

"You religious or something?" she says as she notices the Bible while she counts the cash.

"I'm a pastor, to be honest," I answer.

"You're a dirty one if you're in this neighborhood looking for sexual favors," she retorts.

"Well, that might be true if that was my plan." I lay my hand on her thigh, and a needle attached to a syringe pierces her skin and injects her with a sedative. It provides enough of a kick at the right dosage to keep them quiet and still until I can get them home.

"Hey, what gives?" she exclaims, feeling the needle pierce her skin.

"You see, my aim in life is to rehabilitate and hopefully change your path to one of more purity…" I drone on, ignoring her surprise. As I talk, she falls asleep, deep into la-la land. The next three hours to home, she will rest, and if anyone sees her, she will look like she is my wife, asleep in the car. I topped off before getting here, and I don't plan to stop.

* * * * *

I pull into the drive around 2:00 a.m. It's bitter cold as I head up the quarter-mile drive. Even during daylight, the old house looks ominous; at night, it looks like a monster looming over the land masked by the dense forest that has surrounded it. The headlights strike the wraparound porch, giving it a toothy, sinister grin. I pull to a stop in front, and my rider moans as the car shudders to a stop.

Not able to part with the home my father grew up in, we moved in when I was a child. Mother acquired ownership of the house when my grandmother passed. Oddly enough, though she has been dead for several decades, the house has a musty, mothball smell to it. The outside shows decades of neglect. The paint strains for the air like a trapeze performer reaching for the wooden dowel of the opposite trapeze midair. The porch looks like it needs to be completely rebuilt. But the problem is, I can't do the work due to my injuries and I cannot afford to pay someone to do the work for obvious and financial reasons. Even the busted windowpanes are in such a way as to give the front the look of eyes and the dormers over them pointy angry eyebrows.

For as rough as the house looks, there are two things that stand out: the old family graveyard and the rose bed. The moonlight highlights them both on this icy winter night. The iron fence surrounds my parents', grandparents', and great-grandparents' headstones like a lacy bodice. An old oak tree, which must be three feet around, stretches its long arms over the family plots as if to provide a roof over their heads to shield them during their eternal sleep. But there right next to the fence, all color, even in the darkest of nights, was Mom's rose garden. Ten bushes in all and a couple for tea rose bushes that wound through the lacy iron arches. Those ten bushes were Mom's pride and joy. I swear, aside from me, I think she loved them more than anything. I only barely passed them on Mom's favorite list because I reminded her of my father. She always said I look just like him.

The roof leaks in various places, another issue I cannot afford at this time. To the right as you are facing the house, you can make out the cellar steps and coal shoot where they used to deliver the coal for the old furnace. I open the hatch-style doors and drag my guest down the stairs, her feet hitting each step with a thump, thump, thump. The occasional breeze cuts all the way to the bone; it is so cold. As I disappear into the cellar, I pull her along. I take her to the room, secure her and the basement. I use a flashlight to inspect the car and give the interior a quick wipe down. A little duct tape and I have all the seats wiped of any possible hair.

At this point, I am exhausted and want nothing more than to close my eyes, only wishing it could be longer than the two to three hours I'm about to get. I sway up the stairs like a drunkard for how tired I am. I make it to my room, disrobe, and clamber into bed. I no sooner hit the pillow, then I am out.

Chapter 2

I wake up and stare at the ceiling. The paint peeled off the plaster from decades of neglect, the ceiling fan slowly whispering away saturated in dust from never being cleaned. The room is still dark as the sun has yet to crest the surrounding landscape. I lie there thinking to myself of the night before and where it all went wrong yet is so right. I must get my day started. It is my day at the pulpit to speak to the masses of the unindoctrinated, teach the ways of the promised one and how he will cleanse the world of sin, watch them as they squirm in their hard pews with that feeling that I am describing them.

"Ah, I must get up and review my notes before I confront the sinfully wicked," I say to myself out loud.

I sit up and feel my bones crack and grind against each other. The pain is overwhelming at times, but it is due to my nightly activities. I may have overdone it last night. Things did not go quite as I had planned, but when do I ever plan these things? I only follow the directions of the one inside.

I begin my daily routine of shaving and showering, awakening my physical body to the new day and the chores at hand. I adorn my clean suit that I pressed out yesterday and laid out so as not to be rushed this morning. I hate rushing. On time is late in my book; it is better to be early so that I can anticipate the unexpected.

As I venture down the stairs, the old bones of the house creak beneath my every step. No one, not even I, can sneak through this old house. I stop and straighten the picture on the wall. I must have brushed against it as I adjourned to my bed to rest after the events of the night before. The wallpaper clings to the wall like a rock climber to the face of a cliff, barely hanging on for dear life, bubbling in spots as if to explode from the plaster underneath. The railing has aged as if by a special varnish that only time can create. A century of occupants trudging up and down the stairs ate away at the fibers of the wood grain.

Through the double French doors, I see the faint light adorning the dust-covered furniture in the living room. A picture of my father in his uniform highlighted by the beam penetrates the gloom. I never knew him, but my mother was fond of his memory. He was a Marine, a full-length picture of him in his Deltas pristinely pressed with the blood strip down the seam amplified against the royal blue. There is a stern look upon his face, almost as if he is watching everything, but only his thoughts contain his opinion.

In the kitchen, I grab the cast-iron pan my mother used to make my breakfast in. I miss waking and coming down to the smell of bacon frying and permeating every nook and cranny of the house, wafting its way up the stairs to my crust-covered eyes as they spring to life with the morning sun's rays slamming against the far wall of my bedroom. A gleeful smile creeps across my solemn face, reminiscing of a time long past. Shaking the thought from my weary head, I remove the meat from the pan and start my eggs. The sizzling and crackling of the whites being smacked by the hot grease is like music to my ears.

The Beatles is playing in the background as "The Long and Winding Road" begins, again reminding me of my mother and how she would sing the lyrics softly under her breath. It truly has been a long and winding road I have traveled in my years, seeing things no other has. That is how I found my way: learning how wicked the world truly is and why I follow the path of ministry—one preaching the way toward righteousness, the other cleansing the face of humanity of the damned.

Some sit and read the paper during their morning meal; me, I prefer reflecting and preparing for my day, meticulously reviewing every line written, every "t" crossed, every "i" dotted. Why am I so precise about items no one will ever witness? That I truly cannot say; I only follow the path laid in front of me.

Before I begin my walk of daily reflection, I clean the table of my soiled dishes and stare at the door. Such a used door, stained from years of people grasping the knob and catching the solid wood before it flings open. I do as I have done more times than I can remember, a flash of chill awakening my inner soul as the musty drear assaults me. I pull the chain to the solitary naked bulb above the doorsill. The light slashes through the darkness, leaving shadows and places light may never reach. Each board creaks as if straining under my frame, thirteen times as I ascend to the bottom.

At the bottom is a concealed door made to look like heavy shelving. The rest of the cellar is dark and uninviting, a workbench with a few common tools strewn about, a stool, a solitary lamp. The hot-water heater sits in the corner next to the massive coal furnace that once warmed the house's old bones. Next to that is the oil furnace, which to look at appears to be just as old as the coal furnace, spotted with rust and makes an awful noise when it kicks on. The floor consists of half-worn brick and dirt. But there is one item that stands out from the rest, pristine and perfectly clean atop a wooden stand, shining like the full moon at night as the solitary light beams down on it. The large Kenmore chest freezer I purchased at Sears a year ago sits at the bottom of the stairs adjacent to the heavy shelf made to disguise the door and the room behind it.

I reach for the shelf, and it swings effortlessly open. The moans followed by muffled screams of profanity pierce the silence. I stare at the figure strapped to the table, acquired from the same psychiatric hospital where I retained all my other goodies. This particular table has unique features that suit my purposes perfectly. The doctors of the psychiatric hospital must have been unusually cruel and demonic as this table is more like a coroner's basin. It has raised edges and is shaped so that any bodily fluids can go through a drain in one corner. But the best feature of this particular table, and I can only imagine it was for the purpose to "study" the human anatomy, specifically the brains of supposed deranged souls, is it comes equipped with straps—thick, heavy leather straps to hold the patient in place as they performed their procedural testing to understand why they were the way they were. The whole thing is pure insanity, from the patients assigned to the hospital to the doctors working there, not to mention the nurses who drew blind eyes or the orderly that assisted in restraining the residents. How this one has any fight left in her, I'll never know. But now is not the time to worry about the fight left in her; soon, it will all dissipate. Probably the cleanest room in the house I built for this specific purpose, a surgeon would be envious of my attention to detail.

The original basement construction was nothing more than bare framework, to which I added soundproofing under the brick and mortar. Then I filled in the walls' cracks and crevices and poured the concrete floor, making everything smooth and polished. The walls I paid particular attention to using a shellac I applied many layers to fill in every porous crevice. The poured concrete I painstakingly smoothed and polished to sheen—ah, but here I made appropriate accommodations to ensure nothing could be detected. The table is secured to the concrete so that it cannot move. I incorporated a drainpipe that runs along the top of the floor into a ten-gallon collection reservoir for sanitation. The ceiling, also padded, is lined with planks and shellacked to reduce pores and ensure the cleanliness I need for my process.

The room consists of few items, just the bare necessities I require on my quest to rid the world of evil. There is a medicine cabinet mounted to the wall, modestly holding the syringes I keep in a basin of alcohol and the vials of morphine I retrieved from the psychiatric hospital when it closed. It is a good thing to know people and be a respected member of society, especially since they have no idea why I would want such things and because I am a minister, they do not ask. I acquired a stainless steel table through a restaurant that was closing in a neighboring city, upon which I have an assortment of tools I use for my process. My tools of the trade consist of a fillet knife, a butcher cleaver, a bone saw, and pliers, and I keep my old K bar down here, an old meat grinder I use to break down the bones into the tiniest fragments. I have found that bone makes for great rose-bush fertilizer. There are several containers of H_2O_2, hydrogen peroxide, as well as some cleaning materials, of which I repurposed an old metal sprayer that works perfectly in the cleaning process. I use a hose and spicket to rinse the entire area clean and dilute the remains after allowing the hydrogen peroxide to do its work, much like one might do to clean a wound. At one end of the table, I have mounted a roller of brown paper. Everything is acquired through cash to reduce a paper trail, never more than one or two items from the same location and never within a specific time frame to attract attention. I am proud of my endeavors and meticulous measures; keeping items in the room to a minimum is key to reducing time and eliminating evidence that could stop my mission.

Before I leave to address my flock, I have to silence the whore strapped to the table. It may seem unnecessary given the way I have the room soundproofed and all, but why take the chance? I have come too far and accomplished so much, so I dare not take any chances as I move to the medicine cabinet and yield a syringe with more sedative. The preferred dosage is enough to sedate her and, given the time I'll be gone, usher her into a more desirable state. This also allows me the time to handle my daily activities and return later to finish the job. Normally I would prefer to allow the blood time to drain before executing my process. But today things are not ideal since I cannot show up for service with blood on me. I slide the needle into her shoulder, releasing the pressure inside the syringe as the sedative flows into her blood stream so quickly I can hear her muffled gasp as she slumps and her muscles relax. Now she just lies there like a corpse, a premonition to what is to come.

Chapter 3

Heading to church, I am welcomed by the warmth of the sun's rays, a nice duality to the chill lingering from the winter air. The brown Chrysler Town and Country station wagon awaiting my arrival is all cleaned and shiny from the fresh wax I applied before the weekend events. The leather interior is almost as immaculate as the day I purchased it. I climb in, and the 318 comes to life as I turn the key. I've only done minor modifications to make cleaning easier and reduce identification: carpet replaced with matching vinyl, wood paneling on the exterior removed, and a whisper-quiet exhaust to not draw attention.

The drive to the church is uneventful. Not many in this sleepy town move at this hour especially on a Sunday. The side door is unlocked, signaling that the caretaker must be inside setting up for the service prior to my flocks' arrival. Jim is a good man, faithfully attending to maintenance of the building and the church's patrons. He remains every Sunday to greet the partitioners and listen to my sermon. Upon entry, I find Jim arranging the bulletins and hymnals in the pews.

"Good morning, Jim!" I say as I walk through. "Bit chilly this morning."

"Good morning, Pastor. Yes, that cold air is better than coffee for a wake-up," replies Jim.

"Would you like me to lay out the communion trays? Or leave that for the ladies?"

"I'm sure they will arrive shortly to set that up. You know how particular they can be," I reply.

I leave my notes on the pulpit and venture to my office. My office is a nice tranquil place for me to collect my thoughts. One wall with built-in books which I reference to assist in my teachings, wood paneling on the walls, my desk a modest size encapsulating my stiff leather high-backed chair, and two chairs positioned before my desk for when I am consulted. I appreciate the plainness of the room; it is not cluttered and, minus a few papers on my desk, rather organized, or at least by my standards.

I pray and meditate for a bit when I realize the time and hear parishioners moving about the sanctuary. I step out of my office and play the role. I truly love my flock and believe in the Almighty and all he stands for. But if they only knew what I do for them... I try not to think of that. I do not need those thoughts clouding my head right now. I need to warn my lambs of the wicked and how they can be accepted into the great kingdom. The organist starts the prelude, and I take my position behind the pulpit. As the service progresses, I continue to review my notes for my sermon. I want this one to really grab them; I'm fired up this morning. Something about the way that cold air smacks my skin, then the sun's rays melting the sting away.

The hymn is sung and the collection plates received.

"*I stand before you today a conflicted man. Where are we going? What lies ahead? We turn on the TV, radio, or open the paper, and it's never-ending!*" I slam my hand on the pulpit. "*People, God's lambs, are disappearing,*" I say, almost a whisper. "*Our sovereign protectors, the officers appointed to uphold the law, are searching for two young women who did not return home to their loved ones. Only one person knows where they are, and he is embracing them and protecting from further harm: God!*" I lead them to the book of Daniel as I show how God protects us, his flock, his lambs, and turns the most ferocious lions into companions.

"*So why am I conflicted? How a man of God, a leader before his lambs, is conflicted? Well, my brothers and sisters, it is hard to see, even for me, God's real plan in action. When will this stop? How can we do better? We spread the word! Prescence in society is the best deterrent.*"

(This is all true as my evil side would never jeopardize my ability to satiate its inner desires. Therefore, one of my rules is to never leave a trace no witnesses no evidence.) *"If we, as God's disciples, are out in the community witnessing of his glory, we create presence. Through this, we are doing God's will and deterring the devil!"*

Silence blankets the congregation. There was some stirring, not as much as I would have liked, but maybe that's a good thing. Maybe they didn't sin so much this week…because only the guilty squirm.

"Let us close in prayer…"

Following the benediction, I stand my post at the door leading out. Some just provide the standard thank-you for the service; others comment on how they felt it reflected something in their daily life; others just want someone to listen, and they rant on about coming over for dinner sometime or their petunias or their grandchildren being so smart. Me, I just nod and smile and say "thank you" for the invitation, but I have other plans. All the older ladies are hoping it's with a young woman to "settle down" with. They are oblivious to my reasons for staying in solitude.

"Pastor Francis, thank you for that invocation this morning," states Ms. Smith. Ms. Smith is in her '80s, a motherly figure among the congregation and, to be blunt, a bit of a busybody but sweet nonetheless.

"Thank you, Mildred, and how are you doing these days?" I reply.

"Oh, minus this cold that cuts through me like a knife, I cannot complain," she replies.

"That's good. Still meeting with the ladies for bridge on Tuesday's?" I ask.

"Oh yes! If didn't go, Edith would have the police coming to check on me to make sure I was alright… She did that once, you know…." As she retells a story I have heard possibly a dozen times, I nod in acknowledgement and the occasional "You don't say," still shaking hands and waving to those still filing out as they all recognize how I was cornered with their knowing glances. "You know, Pastor, far be it for an old woman to know anything about anything, but you should have someone to rely on too."

I must snap out of my trance as I reply, "Ms. Smith, you are probably right. But I think God has his intentions for me, and when the right lady comes along, I have no doubt he will let me know," with a smile on my face.

Mildred Smith gives me this look of semidisapproval as she remarks, "As much as I have faith in the good Lord, I have been around long enough to know there are some things in life you just cannot wait on the heavens to bring you the answer on a platter. As if the heavens will open and shine a light on you as if to wake you up." She pauses and lowers her tone just a bit, as if everyone passing by was eavesdropping. "Sometimes you have to be assertive and take the reins, Pastor." She gives me this look only a grandmother can give: stern, loving, and most eerily knowing. As her daughter ushers her away, she stops and turns. "You know, Pastor, I am making ham, mashed potatoes, and that green-bean casserole you like so much. Don't think I haven't noticed you going for seconds and thirds at the potlucks. You should come over and join us. Sarah is single now, you know." She is speaking as if I would be allowed a choice in the matter.

Sarah Smith, who was chaperoning her mother out, merely blushed in embarrassment. Sarah doesn't say much, a divorcee, leaving her abusive husband and moving in with Mildred to help take care of her as she aged. Sarah was there when my mother was sick. A nurse by profession, she has always been there when needed. Despite our connection, which goes back to our days in school, and as appealing as Sarah is on the eyes and she is, I cannot introduce outsiders into my life and risk them knowing my other side. Oh my god, the scandal that would arise if the world knew who I really was or, worse, could hear the voices in my head.

I wait while the crowd dies down. I step back inside the church and look around. Jim is cleaning up the last of the bulletins left by the congregation, placing stray hymnbooks back in their slots for the next service. The collection plates are in the back as the Sunday collection is counted by the treasurer. I head to my office; I disrobe and hang my robe and shawl neatly on a hanger, then hang it on a hook by the door. I think to myself how nice it might be if I could live an ordinary life. As much as I portray that image to the public, I have to ask myself, *Is it enough?* Realizing that I must be going home to get to the task at hand, I make sure nothing is left untidy. I grab my coat and head for the main door. Any other Sunday, I might stay and spend some time prepping for the following week. But this day, I have to get home and attend to my visitor in the cellar.

"Have a good night, Jim," I say as I head out.

"You too, Pastor. Will you be there Tuesday night?" Jim says, causing me to pause and think, *What's on Tuesday night?* Then it hits me: the weekly Bible study.

"Oh yes. I'll be there. Kind of a requirement." I chuckle.

"Well, Pastor, I don't know if it's a requirement, but we do appreciate your insight and good conversation. I'll see you then," Jim states matter-of-factly.

"Yes, you will, Jim. See you then." And I head out to my car.

But there it is again, that nagging feeling of how the people in town can see right through me and just allow my side ventures so as to not disrupt the natural cycle of things. As if to say in silence that my "other" ghastly deeds are acceptable. Is what I am giving into with this demonic presence "acceptable"? Can people see my deeds, or have I been this good at hiding the truth? So many thoughts race through my head, and I need to focus. Alive or not, waiting to handle my visitor in the cellar is not an option. I refocus as I creep through the arched drive and park in front of the house.

Chapter 4

The demon inside me has pretty much taken over at this point. He has waited all day to satisfy his own urges, of which I cannot describe or understand fully. He once told me his existence is to merely inhabit bodies in their human form and extract souls from unknowing persons so he can feed the gates of hell with fresh beings. That was how he found me. Just a brush of a hand from a half-alive corpse during my time in Vietnam and he found me. Why me? What did I ever do to deserve this "hell"? But prolonging the inevitable is futile as the longer I delay, the more insistent it becomes.

I remove all my clothing and suit up in a full-body Tyvek suit. I enter the room to find her barely coherent. The sedative from earlier is still in effect as she lies on the table like a corpse awaiting an autopsy. Odd. The way I perform my ritual is not much different than the way a coroner would break down a body to determine cause of death. But in my case, I know the cause, and I do take it a few steps further than what a coroner would do. I remove the gag over her mouth. This way, I can monitor her breathing, and the demon can relish in listening to her last breath. I take a needle attached to a rubber hose. I run the rubber hose to the drain in the corner of the table as I take the needle and insert it into the brachial artery. Though her heart rate is slowed from the sedatives, she should bleed out in about two minutes. I have found this to be the most effective location for draining my victim's blood, and it allows for the blood to drain into my collection system. Lessening the possibility of blood saturating the room provides me with two things: easier cleanup and reducing the chance of detection, should anyone make it down here. She stares up at me with her soul's distant gaze, and I can clearly identify the horror in her face in knowing what is about to happen. They say the brain remains active for a bit after death has supposedly made its mark. I assume this is what people may describe of their life flashing before their eyes as they glide toward the light. Perhaps she is a runaway, upset with Mommy and Daddy's rules and wanted to escape? Maybe she thought the big city was going to be easy and she would be able to make all her dreams come true. No matter what her circumstances for being a streetwalker, I hope she enjoys the "movie" portraying all of her bad decisions, whether it is drugs and sex or just sex for money; I do not know, nor do I care. Serves her right, spreading her legs for anyone willing to pay and transferring her diseased filth to anyone.

I turn on the radio to the local classic rock channel KGRR 97.3. I grab the chair in the corner and wait as the blood drips through the tube into the drain and down into my collection reservoir. The knife still in my hand, I reach for a sharpening stone and slowly drag the edge across, the blood on the knife acting as a lubricant like one might apply oil to the stone.

Her skin glows an eerily pale in the light, devoid of blood. This is my signal to begin my process. I unstrap her limbs as she is too weak to resist if she is still alive at all. Starting at her neck, I slide the knife down her chest perfectly placed between her sagging breasts and over the abdomen. I stop short of her pubic region, and with a slight twist of the wrist, I guide the blade to her left thigh and down her leg all the way to the top of her foot. I go back up to my initial incision and perform the same task on her right leg. With two quick slices, I open the top of her feet, enabling me to peel away the skin there later on. I reach up, and from where I started, I cut around the base of her neck, lift her head, and form a complete circle all the way around. The entire process leaves her upper torso in such a way as to resemble a jacket of her skin. I make similar incisions down each arm, starting at the centerline cut, then dragging the knife down to her wrists. By cutting around the wrist in a complete circle, I can follow through by peeling the skin away, much like I did with the feet and neck. I peel the skin to the upper torso off and too the side so that I can expose her organs. I must remove the organs inside as piercing the stomach or intestines could cause bile consequences. Doing this exposes the abdominal muscles as I peel back the skin from the muscular tissue. Very carefully I cut away the abdominal muscles, exposing the organs underneath. This part is tricky since if I cut too deep, I can puncture the stomach, the appendix (if not removed), or one of the intestines. I take the abdominal muscles after I have cut them from the body and pull out a strip of brown paper on my table. I lay the muscle on the paper and set it aside for later. I return to my specimen. I take a pair of hedge clippers and cut out the sternum. I use a spreading tool to open the rib cage, allowing me to remove the heart and liver. The lungs, stomach, kidneys, intestines, and reproductive organs I care not to keep; these are discarded into a bucket for the time being. These I will run through a grinder and provide to a friend who feeds the "slop" to his pigs. Now to be clear, to avoid detection, I include other materials to the slop as a way to mask the smell of human remains and disguise what they truly are. So far, it has been a successful endeavor as I have not been caught.

With the majority of the organs removed, I move back over to the packaging table and wrap the heart and lungs up; these need to be preserved as quickly as possible as freezing is not the ideal method for storage. I rinse them in the sink, which also drains into my collection reservoir. I take the abdominal muscles and place it into a brine I prepared earlier. Later I will smoke the meat using the old coal furnace and slice it down into strips, much like bacon from a pig. Once I have this all prepared and packaged, I return to my tasks. I roll the carcass over, removing any skin still attached to the frame, and cut the rib cages away from the spine. These I break or cut in half, producing two racks of what one might consider baby backs and the other just a nice rack of ribs times two. I pull the femur bones out of the hip sockets and remove the muscle from them, package up the meat, and roll the body over to remove the rumps from the buttocks region. Unlike using an animal for meat, a human is not engineered the same and therefore does not yield the same types of "cuts" one might get from a cow or pig. But I do my best to extract as many "select" cuts as possible and prep them for the freezer. Each cut is individually wrapped in the brown paper. I don't trim any of the fat as there is usually not a need to. I take each of the cuts, minus the heart and lungs, and place them in the freezer outside the room.

As I return to the corpse, I grab a glass jar off a shelf. The jar is filled with a solution that preserves whatever is inside, and I carefully extract her eyes and place them in the jar. I then close the jar and place it on the shelf with my collection of other eyes from previous victims. This part of the process is to satisfy the demonic soul's need to capture each soul. Now the truly burdensome part. I take the remaining bones, and using the cleaver, I remove them and break them down into smaller, more manageable portions. With a bucket positioned under the meat grinder I have on the edge of the preparation table, I crank each piece through, smashing it into tiny fragments as it collects in the bucket. Larger bones like the hips and skull, I break down using a small sledgehammer so that they will fit through the opening of the grinder. The spine is such an easy piece to run through; I save it for last as I insert the top portion of the spine into the grinder and the lower portion just barely fits through the opening. Grinding, grinding, grinding, till every piece of bone is disintegrated into tiny fragments. Amazing how breaking down the human skeleton into such tiny pieces fits so well inside a five-gallon bucket.

The last item to prepare for later is the human skin. Carefully I remove as much hair as possible, which I set aside in a metal bucket. Then I break down the skin into manageable portions. These I will turn into chicharrones, like many do with pig skin. I'll smoke the individual pieces to dry them out and then fry them for snacking later. Items like the teeth and nails are all added to the bone fragments, going through the grinder like all the other pieces.

I set the bucket aside and prepare a pan with all the tools in it, then I add hydrogen peroxide. The hydrogen peroxide should destroy any evidence of the individual cells remaining and make them less identifiable. The remaining fluid, after I wipe each tool clean and hang back on the metal strip above my preparation table, is poured over the table to wash anything remaining down the drain. Filling the spray cannister with hydrogen peroxide, I spray everything down, top to bottom. Everywhere bloody remains fizzes like a soda pop. On the wall is a special switch I added a few years back. It goes to an industrial garbage disposal grinder, like the ones people have in their kitchens. I flip this one on as I open the release valve for the collection basin. I then use the hose attached to the sink and rinse everything down the drain in the floor, watching it all mingle and wash away. Microorganisms in the septic tank will break down any evidence remaining, and when it comes time to have it extracted, everything will be so small as to not be detectable or caught in the septic-removal truck's hoses.

When everything is cleaned, at least to the visible eye, I take another sprayer and hit everything with bleach. I take care not to scrub anything. I have learned this leaves streaks seen under a black light. Another rinse with the hose and I am satisfied that the room is back to being sterile. I walk to the opening and flip on the right switch, then turn off the left. An eerie purplish glow engulfs the room. I find no bluish glows to signify blood or bodily fluid residue remaining.

With the room washed down and all my tools hanging to dry, I grab the bucket of tiny bone fragments and head to the other side of the cellar where the stairs leading out are, the very same ones I used to bring her sinful carcass to the basement last night. It's been six hours since I started; the sun has set pretty much below the tree line. I carry the bucket to the rose garden and sprinkle the remaining bone fragments over the soil. It is supposed to rain tomorrow, providing me the ability to ensure the fragments work their way down into the soil. Bone is supposed to be the best fertilizer for roses and helps give them phosphorus, and any blood remaining is what gives them such a brilliant red color in the spring and summer when they bloom.

Chapter 5

It's 8:00 a.m., March 1, 1985. I've been recently assigned to a special unit within the bureau designated with assisting sister organizations, other FBI units, local and state police forces throughout the nation, to identify unsubs or "unidentified subject." It's a quiet little bunch in the basement of the FBI building in Quantico.

Chris Bennett walks in and drops a report on my desk. "Our latest assignment."

I open the manila folder and scan the top page; it's a police report from Milwaukee's Police Department. They have had several hookers come up missing, enough so that it's drawn concern. Normally this would not warrant the attention of the FBI. I glaze over the report and turn the page. The next document is another police report from Chicago, followed by another from Detroit. Three states all with similar disappearances and same descriptions of the victims: young modestly built streetwalkers, all blonds, and by the look of them, similar facial features. No information from the reporting witnesses. All the girls were "loners," meaning they worked on their own and were less known among the other working girls. Not that they would say much to the cops anyway.

It is not uncommon for girls in that line of work to just get up and disappear. Some overdose, some move on, and some just simply disappear. It's not the best living, but sometimes it is all these girls have available to fall back on. Most of them are runaways, caught up in the wrong crowd, and/or hooked on drugs of every nature. I continue to read over the reports looking for firm connections and any possible clues. One report did have a forthcoming eyewitness report. She said she saw the victim get into a brown station wagon with out-of-state plates. But it was too dark to identify the plates, make or model of the vehicle or anything on the driver. Not a whole lot to go on, but the idea that all the victims match a profile is why it is brought to us. The timeline fits in over a ten-year period, which helps explain the lack of local forces connecting any dots.

"Chris, what do you think?" I ask after briefly reviewing the documents.

"Honestly, Nate, I don't know," Chris replies. "It could just be a coincidence. The individual cases are so spread out, and none of them show any form of pattern. You have this one"—he points to the first case in the folder—"happening on Valentine's Day and this one in Detroit three months earlier, but then you have this one in Green Bay around April of last year." He pauses as if trying to correlate all of it in his head as he speaks, "It doesn't make sense."

"The oldest one in the file dates to 1974 in Chicago, which, by the way, is the only one providing any real evidence and an actual victim, a Charlene Benito. The next one after that isn't until 1976 in Milwaukee. Are they related? Or are they just coincidence?" he continues.

"There are no such things as coincidences in this office, you know that." I sigh.

"Yeah, I know," Chris agrees. "But there is not much to go on."

We look at each other and say in unison, "Road trip."

A few years back, the FBI started a new division specifically detailed to address cases much like this. After a decade of proving our worth to crime fighting, we are still hidden away in the basement like illegitimate children. We have spent most of our time going to various parts of the country to provide training for local law enforcement in tracking, identifying, and apprehending unsubs. We also provide intimate support when called upon or when a case is found to cross state lines and becomes FBI jurisdiction. In this case, the individual local agencies are not aware of their counterparts' similar cases and therefore have not garnered the FBI's attention till now. Given the lack of evidence and eyewitnesses, we prepare to travel to the individual cities to see if we can get more information and make them aware that there is a potential for a serial killer. The current reports may not state this at this time, but the similarities are not coincidental. That is the first thing I learned when joining this unit.

* * * * *

Chris and I spend a week gathering information as best we can from every city in the Midwest. Every city we call responds with more reports of unsolved disappearances. Most don't seem to fit the profile we are after. Of those that fit the victim profile, there are three in Green Bay, two in Chicago, two in Detroit, three around St. Louis, and five in Milwaukee. That's a hell of an area to cover. This guy either moves a lot or perhaps he is centrally located and has access to all of them... But that could place him anywhere. Maybe he travels for work and these are cases of convenience? Meeting with the individual forces might give us more information to go on. Hopefully these guys are forthcoming and are willing to be open to see what we see.

During the week of compiling information, we approach the head of the department, John Murray. John reviews the information we have and grants us approval to go. This is how he started out, traveling to various areas of the country teaching and providing our services. Sometimes face-to-face and knocking on doors go further than one might realize as in-person interaction is necessary in our line of work. We purchase our tickets and make preparations for travel.

On March 15, 1985, we arrive at Dulles International with tickets to Chicago. We figure we will start there and springboard out to the neighboring cities. Also, the fact that Chicago is sort of at the center of this and shows the least amount of activity, it might be the home of the unsub. That would make things a little easier if we could be that lucky. It's a little over two hours to Chicago. We make sure we have seats next to each other, and luckily there isn't anyone else, which allows us to talk about the case quietly. Chris hates flying, so talking about the perp is a good distraction.

"I wonder if Chicago was the best choice. These cases are the oldest and fit the profile the least," Chris points out.

"I agree," I reply. "But I am looking at it this way: These could also be his first kills. He may have been just honing his skills at this point. And there is just enough resemblance that they fit.

"It could also be that he decided to not 'shit' where he eats, if you know what I mean," I continue.

Chris agrees. "Yes, that makes sense too. I just don't know. I wish we had some evidence to go off of. I mean, hell, we don't even have a body except this first case. After reading that, I have to wonder, is this guy that gruesome and demented? Or was he interrupted?"

The case in question is the oldest of all the cases and the only one that allowed for a body, which kind of excludes it from our initial inspections of the case files. However, after further review, we included it for exactly the reasons Chris mentioned above. Chris's skepticism stands to reason as every unsub follows their own distinct pattern. They learn from their mistakes and become less and less detectable, until they get to that point where they get sloppy. This particular case fits that premise. Young girl about twenty found near Buckingham Fountain under a grouping of bushes, not far from the red-light district in the city: blond, petite build, her skin partially peeled from the muscular frame underneath. It is certain details in this report that struck my eye as I read it over. It is oddly familiar in the grotesque of ways. I have seen this once before when I was in Vietnam. The mere thought has reintroduced horrific nightmares I had hoped were dismissed forever, but they have returned. The thought makes me cold, and I shudder just at the thought. But it makes me think: Is it possible? Could there be a connection between this particular case and what my platoon witnessed in Nam? I pray to God that is not the case, but the similarities are almost undeniable.

We arrive in Chicago, grab our rental car, and head to the Howard Johnson we have reservations at. Tomorrow we will meet with Chicago Police Department's Vice and Homicide squads.

Chapter 6

On March 16, 1985, Chris and I meet in the lobby of the Howard Johnson. We grab some breakfast and go over our notes to prepare for the meeting with Chicago Police Department's Homicide and Vice units. We ride over to the main headquarters on Michigan Avenue and meet with Lt. Jon Rivera.

At the reception desk, I say, "Hi, I am Special Agent Nathan Bedford, and this is Special Agent Chris Bennett. We are with the FBI's Behavioral Science Team and have a meeting with Lt. Jon Rivera."

"One moment, Special Agent," replies the sergeant sitting behind the reception area. A few moments later, Lieutenant Rivera comes around the corner with a folder in his hand.

"Special Agent Bedford?" Lieutenant Rivera asks.

"Lieutenant Rivera, I assume?" I answer back as we shake hands. "Nate and Chris is fine. Don't want to draw too much attention. Our aim is to assist and hopefully attain some knowledge ourselves."

"Feel free to call me Jon," Lieutenant Rivera answers back through a hearty handshake. "This way, gentlemen."

He leads us to a set of elevators, and we ride up to the sixth floor.

"I reserved a training classroom for all of us. Quite a bit you want to cover based on our phone conversations," Lieutenant Rivera says.

"Yes, so Detroit PD and Milwaukee PD reached out to us with very scant evidence but too closely related to be coincidental. After reviewing their case files, we talked to you and Captain Beaumont, and he agreed to have your records department send us any cases that resembled the information we already had. Specifically, *cold* cases," I explain. Even though we had already discussed most of this over the phone, I want to make sure nothing is missed in the translation.

"I see," Lieutenant Rivera acknowledges. "But from the reports I looked at, this seems like a Vice issue. What do you want with my Homicide Division?"

"Fair question," I say as we step off the elevator. "How about I try to explain that in the room?"

"Alright," Lieutenant Rivera says, a little disappointed. He probably wants to keep his team on current cases and doesn't want them tied up right now "training" on what could be just a hunch, especially not with a couple of FBI stiffs.

Lieutenant Rivera leads Chris and I down a hall to a glass room. There are shades that I request drawn closed so that there is no outside interruptions or distractions. We exchange the normal pleasantries, and I notice most of Vice is on one side and Homicide is on the other. Even within organizations, there is always some division.

Captain Beaumont enters the room. "Nate! How the hell are you?" Capt. John Beaumont and I served in the same unit during our tour in Vietnam. I chose the FBI, or basically they chose me, and John returned here to his hometown of Chicago to work his way up the chain of the police department.

"Hey, John. It's been a while, hasn't it?" I reply.

"It sure has," Captain Beaumont agrees. "So these are my teams. Both Homicide and Vice. Great group of guys and, well, gals now too, as you can see." John is referring to the two female officers on the Vice side. Things weren't always this way. Police departments around the nation are adjusting to female officers joining their ranks. Times are changing, that's for sure.

"That's great, John. Chris and I appreciate you working with us on this," I say while introducing my partner, Chris, to John.

"Unfortunately, I cannot stay, Nate. I have a meeting with the commissioner. But later maybe we can have dinner and drink," says John as he turns to head out.

THE DEMONIC SAVIOR

I have become very accustomed to reading a room especially when I am giving a presentation. Kind of goes along with the territory of being in the FBI. Both sides relax as Captain Beaumont walks back out, but I can see the uneasiness on Lieutenant Rivera's face after realizing the connection I have with his superior.

"Alright, everyone. I am Special Agent Nathan Bedford, and this is Special Agent Chris Bennett. We work in the behavioral unit for the FBI," I dive right in, not waiting for introductions. It's not customary, given that you are on someone else's turf in their house, but I have found it makes things go smoother if I set the tone early. The tone I want set is that we are here for business and we need answers.

"A few months back, we received calls from Detroit and Milwaukee about prostitutes that have gone missing. Normally this wouldn't warrant the attention of the FBI, but in the behavioral unit, we tend to find links that lead to future apprehensions." Chris turns on a projector in the middle of the room that shows each of the victims, all with blond hair and all slight of build.

"Now you may notice that each of these women share similar features and likeness: blond, slight of build, and they are all prostitutes or work in the sex trade." I continue on, "Each of these women were brought to our attention by Detroit PD and Milwaukee PD. Therefore, you are probably wondering why we are here talking to you in Chicago. Well…" Chris changes the slide to two women matching the descriptions of the other victims, and each of them have *Chicago PD* lettering along the bottom. "We think all these cases are related." I pause and let that information sink in, as well as the pictures on the screen. I find this helps to bring the purpose to home and act as an attention-grabber.

In the back, a detective raises his hand. "Detective Anthony Hempfield, Homicide. If these ladies are all prostitutes, why are we [meaning Homicide] here? Isn't this a Vice issue?"

"Detective Hempfield, I don't disagree with you," I say, and upon saying it, half of Homicide reaches to grab their jackets as if to leave. "*But,*" I say loud but not shout, "according to reports, none of these women have surfaced, leading us to believe that they are all dead."

Detective Hempfield, again, says, "What evidence is there suggesting these hookers are dead and not just shacked up somewhere high as a kite?"

"Because in each of the reports, there is paperwork showing that the local hospitals and morgues have not received these women through their doors, *ever*," I emphasized.

That caught the Homicide's attention. Vice was still laid-back as if enjoying the show.

"We have a suspicion that there could be an unsub serial killer floating from city to city. Given that the last case here in Chicago was in the mid-'70s, we have reason to believe either the unsub lives here and doesn't want to attract attention in his hometown or something about Chicago holds a place in this guy's heart," I announce to the room.

Several in attendance shift in their seats, a little uneasy. No one likes the prospect of being a targeted area for a serial killer. They create panic and can be extremely hard to apprehend, especially in cases like this where there is so little evidence and information to go on. Chris and I spend the next hour going through the case files showing what steered us in this direction and things we use to pick out "trends." By the time we finish, it is close to lunch.

I turn to Lieutenant Rivera. "Lieutenant, I was wondering if it would be okay if we broke for lunch and picked back up in an hour or so," I ask.

"That sounds like a good plan. Just curious how much more time do you think you guys need?" he asks.

"Honestly, I can't answer that. What we'd like to do when we return is work with your team and formulate a plan on how we might be able to get more information or even catch this guy," I say.

Lieutenant Rivera nods in agreement and understanding, and we break for lunch. "Just a reminder, ladies and gentlemen. None of these cases are to be discussed outside this room. Not even in the building," Lieutenant Rivera reminds everyone.

The detectives and officers all head out. I wait for Chris, who is talking to Lieutenant Rivera. As the three of us leave the room, I'm caught by John Beaumont.

"Nate! Join me for lunch so we can catch up," John says. I look at Chris like "You okay with this?"

"Yeah, Nate, go with John, and I'll have lunch with Lieutenant Rivera." Chris approves.

"Okay, John, I guess I am all yours." I raise my hands in a lead-the-way motion.

John takes me to this little deli where oddly enough not one uniform or suit from the police headquarters is having lunch. Something tells me this is more than just "lunch."

"How ya been, Nate?" John starts. "Last I saw you was Nam, and you were one gung ho son of a bitch. Now you're with the FBI's Behavioral Science Team? Far cry from 'I was made to be a Marine!'"

I laugh a good hearty laugh. "Yeah, I was pretty high-strung as a kid back in those days."

"And look at you now, a G-man," John says mockingly. "Tell me, you ever run into the old platoon? Did you keep up with any of them?" John is rattling off questions like the inquisition.

"You know, minus a few guys that were not in our group but must have been in our unit, because I recognize them and all, you know...not one, minus you, of course," I tell him. "You know, I take that back. I got a call from Francis many years back now. He was hiking the Appalachian Trail. I met him around the Delaware Water Gap, and we did lunch. But that was a long time ago now. After I was released, I applied for the academy, and they accepted me. Weird, I thought Marine boot was tough, nothing like what the FBI training program puts you through."

I continue, "Anyways, I was, you know, doing FBI things, and I decided to take a few psych courses at the local college. This guy I never met approaches me and hands me a folder. The case file inside is completely wild and devoid of a whole lot of detail. He says to me, 'Read this over and let me know what you think.' He hands me his card and walks away. Anyway, I read over the case file that night, and the next day I give him a call. He says, 'Come on over to my office.' He gives me the building and room number, and I head over there. I hand him back the file, and he asks me what I think. I say, 'Look, I'm just an analytical field agent. I'm not the profiling type.' He says, 'Really? Okay, you're still going to tell me what you think. Because according to Special Agent Mills [who was my supervisor at the time], you have "profiled" a few perps and he tells me you are taking psych courses at the college.' At this point, I'm thinking, *Shit, this guy has me pegged.* So I sit down and tell him what I saw in the report. Next thing I know, I am being transferred to the Behavioral Science Team at Quantico."

"Holy shit, man," John says with a smile and chuckle. "So this case, you think this guy is a Chicago native and all these cases are related somehow?"

"From what Chris and I see, and I know it's far-fetched, but yes," I reply. "Minus one thing: I don't think he is from here. Maybe he lives here, maybe he has an affection for the Windy City. Maybe he hates this town. I don't know. But all these disappearances, I believe, are related, and despite his inactivity here in this town, I think he will strike here again. I just cannot tell you when."

John sits back in the booth we are sitting in and sets down his sandwich. "Well, I'll be damned. You got all that just by reading those reports." More of a statement of fact than a question.

"I mean, let me be truthful here, John. I could be wrong, yeah, I could be. We are scheduled to do the same exact training with Milwaukee, Detroit, and St. Louis. Hell, we even reached out to Kansas City and Green Bay, where we found similar cold cases. For all I know, this guy could be a traveling salesman, and we may never catch him. But we should. I know there isn't a lot of evidence or eyewitnesses—this guy is good, really good, a hit-and-forget kind of guy—but my gut says it's the same guy and these are all related. Beyond that, I think he's going to hit soon, and I have this suspicion that Chicago is top of his list of targets." When I finish, I look up at John, who is staring back at me with a look of admiration.

"Crazy, man. Absolutely crazy. On the one hand, I hope you're wrong. On the other, I hope you're right because I want to see this guy caught. I just don't know if I want it to be here in Chicago."

John finishes his sandwich, as do I, and we head back to the police headquarters.

John escorts me back to the room, and Chris has already started the afternoon session.

"What we are looking for, ladies and gentlemen, is any information, maybe a CI [confidential informant] that dropped a hint. Maybe a witness or a habitual pickup you have that may have seen something. Just because there hasn't been a report like this here in Chicago doesn't mean he hasn't been here," Chris is telling the "class" as I walk in.

A hand is raised in the back. "What happens or what should we do if we come up with nothing?" a young female officer on the Vice side of the room asks.

With a tinge of shock and surprise on Chris and mine's faces, we look at the young female officer and then at each other. She fits the MO (modus operandi) perfectly: blond, young, petite, and could even be called wirily. "Well, Officer..." Chris starts.

"Sutton," she cuts in. "Officer Patricia Sutton."

"Well, Officer Sutton, that was our next topic. We, Nate and I, believe that the unsub is going to strike again soon. So our recommendation is that we...I mean, *you* place an undercover out on the street to try and identify the subject. Worst case scenario is *you* are able to book some johns and hopefully reduce your prostitution population here in Chicago." Laughter erupts at the thought of reducing the prostitution in Chicago. As much as that is the aim of the Vice Division in any police department, the fact is, prostitution has been around since biblical times, and though reduction is feasible, reality has to set in. Prostitution in any major city is a "way of life" that cannot be completely eliminated. It's just a fact of life.

Silence captures the room after the laughter dies down. "That sums up our part of the meeting. Any questions?" I ask. A few members raise their hands and ask things like "When did you want to start?" or "What role will Homicide play in this?"—mostly questions Chris and I cannot entertain as they are more suited for Lieutenant Rivera and/or Captain Beaumont. Our involvement at this point would be seen as FBI interference. We entertain as many questions as we can without overstepping as we collect our things and conclude the training.

As the room begins to clear out, Chris and I are talking with Lieutenant Rivera on details involving the sting, things like how many officers to assign, best candidates, what to look for, etc. As Officer Sutton is headed for the door, Lieutenant Rivera calls out, "Officer Sutton, could you join us please?"

"Yes, sir." Office Sutton walks over to us. She is an absolutely perfect fit for the modus operandi of this operation.

"Officer Sutton, we have been discussing how closely you fit the description of the victims in this case," Lieutenant Rivera states. "I could order you to be our undercover, but I would rather like to know if you would volunteer. If this guy is as savvy as these agents believe, this is not going to be an easy task."

An enthusiastic smile creeps across Officer Sutton's face, "Yes! Yes, sir! I would greatly appreciate this opportunity. This is exactly why I wanted to get into police work."

"Great!" Lt. Rivera exclaims. "Then that's settled. We will fill you in on details after I put together the team. In the meantime, I would like you to get as intimately familiar with all the cold cases as possible. Thank you. Dismissed."

"Yes, sir. Thank *you*." Her enthusiasm toned down a bit knowing she has a lot of work in front of her. She heads out of the room with what appears to be a little pep in her step.

"She is a good officer. I specifically requested based on her merit. She might look small, but her motivation and personality are huge. Her father was a beat cop for Chicago PD years ago," Lieutenant Rivera tells us.

"*Was?*" I ask.

"Yeah, cold case there too. He was found shot in an alley while on duty one night. They never found the shooter, or the gun, and ballistics has not been able to match the bullet. Strange case that one. He radioed in that he was following a suspicious person, and then nothing. He never reported in after that, and he didn't check in at the end of his shift. They found him, after an extensive search, about a day later half covered in a pile of trash about five blocks from his last check-in. Three holes in the chest, perfect marksmanship," Lieutenant Rivera tells us.

"No one reported the shots?" Chris asks.

"Not in that part of town. Most officers avoid that section. Even during the day, it can be that bad. But George was a 'big boy' and feared nothing. He built a repertoire with the business owners in the area, and when he walked the beat, most of the gangs in the area let him pass. He actually had their respect, I think," Lieutenant Rivera explains.

Chapter 7

The demon assaults my thoughts. Never has it been so loud and obnoxious. Usually, I can subdue it for a time through prayer or reading the Good Book, but today it seems agitated even as I look at the well-worn cover. I don't know what to do. The only thing to satiate its desires is a kill. But if I kill too soon, I could draw attention to myself. It leads to mistakes and mistakes lead to revelation and revelation can lead to being caught. I cannot be caught. There is one thing I might be able to do that might calm it; yes, I will give that a try as I have no other options.

Despite the cold, I grab the keys for the station wagon and drive to Maquoketa Caves State Park; being in nature can sometimes calm the mind-numbing dribble of the voice. The scenic forty-minute drive is uneventful as I enter the state park and find a place to park my vehicle. I grab my hiking stick out of the back of the station wagon, the same one I used while hiking the Appalachian Trail. That was an experience, 2,200 miles over five months. The thought of my time on the trail brings back memories; some good, some bad. I have come here numerous times over the years as a way to escape and reflect, especially when I get stuck on what to say in one of my sermons. But today is especially unique as I need to clear my mind of the demon's voice that keeps taunting me. Looking over the park's map of trails, I choose the longest one in hopes it draws me away from other visitors. Firebreak Trail, a nice, easy two-plus-mile jaunt through Mother Nature's seclusion. The early morning brings a few birds chirping despite the chill. Occasionally a squirrel passes my gaze as I saunter along. Realizing I am out of view and earshot of anyone else, I confront the demon inside me and try to calm him.

"What is it that you want?" I whisper to myself.

"You already know," the voice replies.

"I cannot follow through with another kill right now. Too many killings this close together could result in me getting caught. If I get caught, you don't get what you want," I explain.

"That is not my concern. You are the one who chose to kill vile whores, not me. I didn't give you specifics to kill. I only want you to fulfill my destiny, and since I cannot do this alone, I have to rely on your weak fleshy body to do it for me," responds the beast within.

"You have to give me time," I plead.

"I have waited centuries. I have nothing but time, you fool. Time is not the issue. Fulfilling my demands is all you need to be concerned with," the demon commands.

I recite the Lord's Prayer over and over as a way to quiet the voice, "Our Father who art in heaven, hallowed be thy name. Thy kingdom come, thy will be done on earth as it is in heaven. Give us this day our daily bread. And forgive us our trespasses, as we forgive those who trespass against us. And lead us not into temptation but deliver us from evil. For thine is the kingdom and the power and the glory forever and ever. Amen." Over and over, I recite the words, the demon screaming at me to stop.

"He cannot help or save you. Nothing earthly nor heavenly can save you. Your soul is MINE! And I will be obeyed," screeches the demon trying to be heard as I continue to recite the prayer.

I continue for the entire two-mile hike through the woods. Finally, I stop, and there is silence. Then there's crippling pain as the demon centers his attack on the shrapnel in my back. I crumple in agony, nauseated by the pain as it shoots up and down my spine. This entity is relentless in its pursuit. I've tried to understand why or what could have possibly created it in hopes that I can combat it. But everything I have tried has failed, and when he takes over, I am subconsciously disabled to stop it until it is satisfied. As the pain subsides, I struggle to stand using my hiking stick as a crutch.

Another hiker passes. "Are you okay?" they ask.

"Yes, I'll be fine. Just an old war injury. Must have turned wrong and set it off," I say.

"Are you sure? You look like you are in a lot of pain," the other hiker states.

"No. No, I'll be fine, just need to rest a bit. My vehicle is not far. I have some aspirin I can take, and I'll be on my way right as rain!" I say with a half-smile on my face.

"Okay. Well, you have a good day," they begrudgingly state, still with earnest concern.

"You too. God bless." I start toward my vehicle.

"They would have been perfect," comes the demon from within.

"Not here. Not NOW!" I say in my head.

"Why do you defy me? Do I need to hurt you again?" the demon retorts.

"No, let me get back home, and I'll plan the next outing." I must have whispered a little loudly as a group that was gathered look my way. I wave, place my hiking stick in the back, and climb in.

"Why, me Lord?" I exclaim out loud as I grasp the steering wheel tightly, turning my knuckles white. I lean over to the glove box and pull the aspirin bottle out. Popping two in my mouth, I chew them to powder, and despite my mouth being dry, I choke down the painkiller.

The entire drive home, I contemplate the repercussions of finding a new victim so soon. I also wonder how long I can delay the demon inside me before I truly am forced to meet his desires. Upon returning to the house, I go in and head to my office. It's a quaint room lined with bookshelves filled with books I use for writing my sermons. There I sit at my desk cluttered with papers of past teachings and books I used for this Sunday's sermon. A daily devotional is opened, and the title is "Serving One Master" and on the other page is "Broken Spirit." *How fitting*, I thought. It is almost as if my own religious tombs are talking to me and coincidentally know what is wrong with my life. Normally most would see this as a sign from God. I wish my problem is that easy and I could turn to him and he could make it all go away: this demon, the pain, the reclusiveness, the loneliness. I turn to faith as a way to deter the inevitable truths I know to be real and to provide myself some solace to my inevitable future. But nothing has worked for me to date; nothing has shown me any form of salvation as I stare at the "mess" before me. Why? Why do I bother to pretend to be something I am not? Because I am not that man. I am more than that. I didn't chose this path; it was thrust on me.

"You're delaying. Get to work and find me another soul to steal," the voice returns.

"Go the hell away!" is my only answer.

"In due time, I will. When you find the one to succeed you. You've been a good servant for me to carry out my plans. Very obedient. Your God will reward you for the hell I have put you through. He will forgive you," says the demon.

"God does not forgive those that kill. 'Thou shall NOT kill,'" I exclaim.

"He is all knowing and knows you do not do these things willingly. That you do these at my bidding."

"As true as that may be, you are a part of me. Why? I do not know. But if God truly is watching over me and understands, then WHY? Won't he expel you from me? So that I may live a more peaceful and meaningful life?" At this point, I am sobbing. The inner fight is draining my physical being to a point where I am truly and utterly exhausted.

"You pathetic waste of a man," states the demon with candid distaste. "God will not help you. He will continue to test your very fiber as I consume your spiritual soul. There is nothing after this. Just you on your knees pleading to St. Peter to allow you into your Father's kingdom. OH, he will let you pass… You will have the reward that he denies me: entrance into the land beyond this world that he expelled me from."

It was at this point that I start to think I may actually be possessed by the devil himself.

> How you have fallen from heaven, O Day Star, son of Dawn! How you are cut down to the ground, you who laid the nations low! You said

> in your heart, "I will ascend to heaven; above the stars of God, I will set my throne on high; I will sit on the mount of assembly in the far reaches of the north; I will ascend above the heights of the clouds; I will make myself like the Most High." But you are brought down to Sheol, to the far reaches of the pit. (Isaiah 14:12–15)

It truly is something I never considered all these years. Surely the prince of hell, once God's right hand cast out for thinking he could overtake the heavens, would walk in a much different form than a wispy soul that survives by transferring from one human flesh to another. However, it kind of makes sense, as if he were to take on the flesh in his own way. How would he age? How would he deceive all those around him and not divulge his true identity? The idea is truly intriguing, and I would love to get the real answer, but I hear nothing except this tormented soul that embodies everything evil in this world and controls me to do the unthinkable.

I delay no longer as further delay only invites the beast back into my head. I close the devotional and place books back on the shelf as I grab the map nearby and a pad of paper. The last victim came from Milwaukee. Where do I go next? St. Louis? Green Bay? Detroit? No, none of those seem to fit. Glancing over the map, the word stares at me as if a lit-up sign on a dark street. I have avoided it as much as I have; I cannot avoid it much more: Chicago. It's the place where this all sort of began and where I found my current identity. It'll be interesting as I have not even visited in over a decade, not since that night.

"Yes! Yes, Chicago! It's perfect. Ah, how I remember that night so well. That night you finally succumbed to me and followed my direction. Yes! Chicago it is." The demon is dancing around in my head like a gleeful cherub.

Chapter 8

With the city chosen for this next kill, I make preparations of the vehicle and lay out the date to be executed. Going back to Chicago is a huge risk for me. First, it is so soon after the last kill even if it was in another city, then the emotional connection to Chicago. I had started to have feelings for Charlene before she sealed her fate. Not to mention this is where I went to seminary. The demon is right; that night is the night I gave over myself to him and his way of doing things. There are factors I have to be wary of since if I follow his methods, I would surely be caught and sentenced. No one would ever believe I was possessed.

I ensure the car is immaculate, minus the necessary tools I need to accomplish the night's misgivings. Bible, check. Cash, check. Gas, check. Sedative? That I need to prepare prior to my departure. I check downstairs in the room for my forearm apparatus and ensure it is cleaned with alcohol. Odd as it may seem, I believe in ensuring my equipment is as sanitary as possible between victims. The drive to Chicago is only 180 miles. Ideally I can make the trip on one tank easily, but I will most likely top off once I am in town prior to attaining my victim. *Now, what night is best to follow through with this plan?* I ask myself. Given that it is Tuesday now, I suppose tomorrow would work. I verify my appointment book to ensure I have no pending commitments for the church or the community.

The following night right after the sun set, I head out for Chicago. The drive into the city is uneventful; all the normal commuter traffic is heading out, making my venture in relatively smooth. I make my way down to the red-light district, where I first met Charlene. Memories of our first meeting come flooding back: A moderately young man I was then, completely lost as I was trying to find a place to eat. This young woman approached me and helped by pointing me back in the right direction.

I must have picked a good night as there are a lot of groups milling around, bouncing from one establishment to another. I sit back, assessing the situation, making sure no one is paying me any mind. Then I see her. She looks almost exactly like Charlene: short skirt, blond hair, fishnet stockings; the resemblance is uncanny. I give another cursory look around and see nothing too suspicious. So I turn on to the drag and slowly glide down as if I am just another john.

I roll down the window. "Hi," I say to the lady of choice.

"Hi," she replies. "Are you looking for a good time?"

"I could be," I reply.

Patricia eyes the Bible on the front seat. "Padre, you should move along," she says.

"*Padre*?" I realize she saw the Bible. "Oh, that. No, I guess I just forgot to take it out of the car Sunday after church," I say.

"You are in the wrong neighborhood if you are a good Christian boy," Patricia replies.

"You could be right," I say. "But I can explain if you are willing to listen."

Patricia looks up from the window of the car, not sure what to do. During the briefing, they said they had no idea who the serial killer was. Could this be him?

I call from inside the car, "Look, you're right. But you got me all wrong. I make it a point to come down here and offer a young lady dinner and some cash to give her a break for the night. It's my way of trying to minister to those that need it."

Patricia looks at him like he is nuts. She really doesn't believe him, but this could also be the way this guy operates. Something about him doesn't seem right.

"Okay," she says as she opens the door. "I have a confession, Padre."

As she reaches into her bag to pull something out, I drive the needle into her arm, instantly injecting the sedative. She immediately slumps over in the passenger seat, and I pull away nice and easy.

Four hours later as we are nearing the house, she is starting to come to. I stop at an empty rest area and tie up her hands and legs, laying her down in the back of the station wagon. I hear her moving about in the back.

* * * * *

"Hey!" Patricia yells. "I'm a cop. Where the hell are we, and what the hell did you give me?"

The realization hits me. Then again she could have been just pulling my chain. I pull into the drive and up to the dark house. I park, get out, and open the back door of the car.

"How do I know you aren't lying?" I ask her.

"Check my bag, moron," she replies.

I walk around to the passenger door and grab her small handbag that was on the floor. I open it, and inside is a Chicago Police Department badge. *Fuck*! I think to myself, but I maintain my composure as I walk back around to the back of the car.

"Well, I have good news and I have bad news," I say. "The good news is, I might not kill you. The bad news is, we are no longer in Chicago."

Patricia is obviously pissed but maintains her composure. "I'll make you a deal," she says. "I won't scream or try to run away if you release me."

"That is not an option," I say. "But if you promise to cooperate, I will agree to let you be comfortable."

"Okay," she agrees. She knows it won't be long before they start to look for her. She knows they will eventually figure out who this bozo is and this place will be swarming with cops. She wonders where she is. But in order for her to get answers, she has to remain civil and keep his mindset calm. She is afraid that if he gets upset, he might kill her and dispose of her before help arrives. Whenever that might be.

I take Patricia in the house and set her on the metal chair in the basement.

"Mind untying me?" she asks.

"For now, I do," I reply.

"So where are we?" she asks.

"Iowa," I say.

Patricia realizes that the chances of them finding her or coming to her rescue just decreased. Although the FBI behavioral unit alerted them to this case, no one in the division thought it was true. This guy had left no witnesses or evidence. He is basically a ghost. She swallows hard at the realization of her situation.

"Are you going to kill me?" she asks.

"I have not decided," I reply.

"Is there anything you *do* know?" She presses him to see how far she can go before he shows agitation.

I remain calm, cool, and collected. But the ideas are racing through my head. I took an undercover cop. I know there is little time, but at the same time, I know this might be the opportunity I have been needing to get out of this mess.

"I'll be back," I say. "Can I get you anything?"

"Yeah, out of these bindings."

I send her a glare that says NO but is still caring and heartfelt. I understand the situation but cannot let her go. Not yet.

"Water, please," she says finally.

Moments later, I return with a metal chair and some glasses. Both glasses are empty.

"Bourbon?" I offer.

"Yeah, that sounds better than water," Patricia replies.

I pour two drinks. I set down my glass. I look at her tied up and just set hers on the dissection table.

"It is bad enough you have left me tied up, and then to pour me a drink and leave it sitting there in front of me is just absolutely the definition of cruel and unusual punishment. Last I checked, you are the perpetrator, and I am the good guy," Patricia points out.

"You know nothing about me," I say. "I know this is the end for me. I can accept that fact. In fact, I actually appreciate that I can be done with this burden that has befell me. But I do not know how far I can trust you at this point."

"If you know this is the end, then why not make it easier and just let me go? I can go call the police, and they can come arrest you," Patricia offers.

"Because that is not how the story ends. *My* story. It will make me out to be a monster, and I am *not* a monster. None of this is my fault," I try to explain.

"I don't know your name. I just realized that. What is your name? Will you tell me?" Patricia asks.

"Francis. Francis Isaiah Fleming," I respond.

"Francis, I am Patricia," she says. "Why not tell me what caused you to start killing women?" Patricia says, more as a statement than a question. Something she had picked up in her own therapy sessions.

"Even if I told you, you wouldn't believe me," I say. Now I am asking myself why I didn't or still don't just kill her. Caught is caught; nothing at this point matters.

"Oh, I don't know. I may understand," Patricia says, thinking of her own demonic experiences.

"If you really want to know, I will tell you," I say. Realizing I had not given her the bourbon, I grab the glass and place it to her lips, tipping it back enough for her to get a sip.

"It all began after I finished college for engineering and joined the Marines after receiving a draft notice…"

Chapter 9

The heat is atrocious as I sit there with my back against a tree. My body is soaked to the bone, half perspiration and half from the rain pelting me and my platoon. The Seventh Marine Regiment, where I have been assigned, has been ordered into the mountain ranges around Quang Nam province. Our objective is to disrupt the supply lines of the People's Army of Vietnam, which, according to Intelligence reports, the "Front 4 Headquarters" is supposedly using to supply the Vietcong. Our platoon leader approaches as the time nears for our patrol. We are going to "inspect" a local village that is suspected of harboring Vietcong. As the platoon's assigned engineer, my job is to disarm any booby traps and inspect suspected "holes" where the enemy could be hiding. Being that this is a village patrol, I doubt I will be needed much, except to support my team.

"Load 'em up," the lieutenant states. Three squads, approximately twenty-seven Devil Dogs, moan and groan as they grab their gear and stand up. We have been here for about two weeks and have encountered nothing. Everyone back home is enraged with us even being here. I wonder the same thing. But it was better than the alternative.

In January 1969, I graduated from the University of Iowa, with a degree in mechanical engineering; the next day, the draft notice arrived in the mail from the Army. Knowing that I didn't want to join the Army, I went directly to the Marine recruiter. Now that might not make sense to many, but for me, if I was going to have to serve, I felt it best to follow the family tradition; so like my father,

THE DEMONIC SAVIOR

I joined the Marines. Typically, a college graduate would join the officer ranks, but in my case, I was short on time after receiving the draft notice and took whatever the Marines had to offer. In my case, given my mechanical-engineering background, they assigned me to the engineering corps. after boot…not exactly what I went to college for. Engineers in the Marines provide mobility, counter mobility, survivability, and limited general engineering support to the First Marine Division. Basically, we disarm explosives, set our own traps, and have been affectionately deemed "tunnel rats" because if a "hole" is found on patrol, I must go ensure it is cleaned out and then make it unusable. It could be deemed one of the most dangerous jobs in the platoon, but oddly I enjoy it.

As we grab our gear and "form up," it's more like a gaggle despite all those formation runs and training we were made to do in boot. Joe is on point, the lead in the squad, followed by Johnny and Big John. Johnny and Big John are always together as Big John carries the .50 cal and Johnny supports him by feeding the heavy gun its favorite meal, .50-caliber bullets that can saw apart anything in its path. Next is Tommy; he hails from California and is the farthest from being a Marine than any of us: laid-back and not a care in the world.

Tommy says, "Where to, Lieutenant? The beach so I can catch some rays and maybe a nice wave?"

"Shut the hell up, Tommy, and get in line," says a voice from behind: Sergeant Head, quietly referred to as Dickhead by the platoon. Now Sergeant Head is a hard-ass. I think this is his third tour in Nam. Rumors say he was a part of the original force that was with General Westmoreland back in '65, but none of us know for sure. He should be of a higher rank, but he has a thing with "finishing" bar fights. But despite his rough exterior, and with good reason, Sergeant Head would do anything for us, but he holds that stare like my father shows in his picture, cold and relentless.

"Copy that." And Tommy falls in line.

I follow Tommy. I must be near the front in case I see something that warrants further inspection. Next to me is Mike. Mike is probably the closest being I call a "friend" here. Like me, he comes from a single family home in the Midwest, raised in church, and just goes with the flow. His path was a bit different; he received the dreaded draft card after high school and went straight to the Navy, where he became a Navy corpsman, or "Doc."

"Francis?" comes a cracking squeaky voice behind Mike and I. Nathan Bedford Jr., aka Junior, a slim kid from New Jersey who thinks he knows everything and is God's gift to the Marine Corps, is all of 110 pounds, soaking wet, stands about 5'11", and fits the Napolean complex to a tee. He is the most annoying member of the platoon, and for some reason, he has it stuck in his head that Mike and I need him as a friend. We don't. But we tolerate him to a point.

"What, Junior?" I say as I whisper *Shit!* in my head.

"Do you think we are going to see any action? I can't wait to kill me a VC," says Junior enthusiastically.

"Junior, what does it matter? With our luck, if we did see anything, they would hit all of us and miss you!" Mike says unempathetically.

"Aw, you don't mean that, Mike. And don't you worry, I'll cover for you guys. I was born for this!" exclaims Junior as the thoughts of seeing action seem to heighten his excitement.

"Jesus, Junior, the last thing I want to think about is that my life might rest in your incapable hands," I respond. "Now form up, before Sergeant Dickhead hears you rambling on and you get us all in trouble."

"Too late," a raspy voice remarks. "All of you, shut the hell up and move out, NOW."

"Yes, Sergeant."

The platoon moves forward, mostly in single formation. The single formation allows for a few things: It ensures whoever on point is the first target, should we encounter the enemy, and if we are followed, it makes it harder to know how many are in the movement. In this rain, I can't see where any of it would matter as you can't see but a few feet in front and, within minutes, our tracks are washed away.

A few clicks away, which felt like an eternity in this rain, we enter this small village of Vietnamese who, according to Intelligence reports, are harboring or assisting the Vietcong. Sergeant Head speaks to the elders in the village and tells them to gather everyone in the center. We break down into teams of two and search the huts these people call homes.

Sergeant Head says in Vietnamese, "Đưa mọi người ra khỏi đây. (Get everyone out here.)"

The village mayor responds, "Nhưng trời đang mưa. Không có gì ở đây bạn đã ở đây ngày hôm qua, và ngày hôm trước. Tại sao bạn không thể để chúng tôi yên? (But it is raining. There is nothing here. You were here yesterday and the day before. Why can't you leave us alone?)"

Sergeant Head says, "Tôi không quan tâm tất cả mọi người ở đây bây giờ hoặc chúng tôi giết tất cả mọi người và đốt cháy nơi này. (I don't care. Everyone out here now, or we kill everyone and burn this place down.)"

The village mayor complies. Crying ensues as villagers carry children into the courtyard-like area. The town is made up mostly of women and old men. The Vietcong took all the males of fighting age. An entire generation will be wiped out over this. But you can tell the enemy has been here as these women carry babies drenched in the monsoon-like rain blanketing the village. In the din of the turmoil, you hear things like "Quỷ Mỹ" ("American devil"), "Về nhà GI" ("Go home, GI"), and other phrases said through the sobbing. After being here for a while, you pick up a few things, but for the most part, we have no idea what's being said, except the sergeant, who, at this point, is fluent.

"You guys get started. Check all these huts for contraband and stowaways," Sergeant Head commands.

We start by each taking a hut. I am paired with Junior as we grab a hut for inspection. We flip their bedding and tables, poke at the woven baskets, and beat on the floorboards for openings or voids. There's nothing here. There probably never has been. Intelligence reports the same information daily as if we need something to do. But we keep the pace as nothing is worse than trying to argue with the sergeant. You can still hear the sobbing outside, women and babies screaming about being cold and wet. They try to calm the babies, I know they do, but it is no use. The moans, cries, and screams are relentless; it is enough to drive a man insane.

I have other things to worry about as I have Junior with me.

"I know these gooks are hiding something. Intelligence wouldn't send us if they weren't," says Junior.

"You're an idiot. Intelligence has no idea better than we do if something is here or not. Just keep searching so we can move on," I respond.

"Com'on, Francis. Why would they keep sending us in here if these people weren't hiding something?" Junior goes on. "They are Intelligence for a reason. And Command knows it would be a waste of our time to send us if these gooks"—he hollers out the door—"weren't aiding the enemy."

"Junior, military intelligence is the biggest oxymoron known to man," I explain. "Whether these people are aiding the Vietcong or not is irrelevant as they know we will be around to inspect. So if there is anything here, it is well hidden, and we won't find shit. So hurry up and get it done so we can move on!"

Over the patter of the rain and the crying, I hear a shout. "Sergeant! You should come take a look at this!" Johnny yells from one of the huts.

"Be right there!" Sergeant Head yells back. The look on the villagers tells all as there is a grim look of shock and worry.

Sergeant Head notices, and the anger creeps across his face. "Có gì trong đó? (What's in there?)" The villager starts speaking frantically; none of it is understood, not even by Sergeant Head. "Ở lại đây. Không ai nhúc nhích. (Stay here. No one moves.)" He says this with a deathlike gaze, and he heads toward the hut where Johnny called out.

As he approaches, he catches a whiff of something rancid, like roadkill in the middle of summer just baking away before the vultures can pick it clean. As he enters the hut, there before him is a man, he thinks, skinned with only the flesh exposed. The stench is enough to make one gag, but Sergeant Head is not affected. The man is like none other; nothing seems to bother him.

He leaves the hut, walks over to the leader, and grabs him. "Cái quái gì thế này? (What the hell is this?)" He drags the man across the courtyard and up the steps into the hut. The man is shaking and cowering, barely able to stand, and he avoids looking at the carcass. The carcass gasps as if having its final breath and trying to answer Sergeant Head's question. The realization that this figure strung up before them was still alive amazes them all, and the shock followed by dread is expressed on everyone's faces. Realizing that there is nothing they can do to save the poor soul, Sergeant Head gives the order to cut it down. At this point, the rest of us have finished our searches of the other huts and are gathered outside to see what all the commotion is about.

Johnny and Big John carry out the corpse, and as it passes through the group, its fleshy hand reaches out to me as if still animated with life. A weird feeling comes over me as I see this poor soul's life flash before my eyes. But it's odd as I see things that are not of this world: ghastly things, things that no man should ever see or encounter. Johnny, Big John, Tommy, and Junior take the body away from the village, dig a hole, say some words of peace, and fill it in. As they finish, we hear Sergeant Head say, "Alright, let's go." We load up, form up, and move on. Interrogation of the villagers at this point is pointless as we all know what happened. The Vietcong comes into the villages at night, raids their supplies of rice and other rations, then leaves. In this case, they also tortured and killed this man for information and left him moments before we arrived. It's a sad situation as the villagers know as little as we do and are torn as both factions disrupt their lives and destroy their homes. It's no wonder why they don't want us there as much as they need us there.

Chapter 10

We head out of the village and move toward our next objective. This three-day patrol has already been eventful enough. I can't say I want to see much more of this country. But this is becoming almost routine, and after a while, you become comfortably numb to the carnage of war. At least the rain stopped; now the incessant heat in the soaked ground evaporates into the air, creating a virtual steam bath for us and everyone inhabiting the earth. About five clicks out, point stops us again and calls for me. This can only mean one thing: a possible hole for me to inspect. I head to the front of the formation. Point and Sergeant Head are there talking softly.

"Right there, Sergeant." Joe points to what appears to be a crude hole cover. Maybe this means I will get lucky and this one will be abandoned—quick easy inspection and we can move on.

"Alright, Corporal Fleming, you're up. Check it out and let's get on," Sergeant Head says to me.

"Aye aye," I reply in compliance.

I suit up, nothing much if anything. I strip down so that my uniform doesn't get caught on anything. Just pants and my jungle boots. They tie off a rope to me, a way to pull out my carcass should things go wrong. I inspect the cover of the hole, and yes, it is a makeshift tunnel. These Vietcong love these things to hide, live, and plan their guerilla tactics on us. As if we are the invaders. No traps at the entrance, that's a good sign. I flip on my 90-degree flashlight and slide in. I barely fit; most of these Vietcong are tiny little guys, maybe 5'5" and only about ninety pounds. Me, I am around 6', but thanks to training and the constant sauna this country provides, my weight is the lowest of my adult life, so I can slip into these tunnels with ease.

I shimmy in about twenty feet and find myself in a rather large opening almost like a natural cave. It's odd I never met anything like this before; usually the rooms the Vietcong create are smaller and barely big enough to crouch and sit in. I heard stories of the first Marines encountering massive networks with rooms big enough to hold full-sized desks and chairs. This is not like that. I shine my light around and see no booby traps. Things are eerily quiet and empty. I stand up; that's how big this cavity is. I can actually stand unhindered. Weird…the feeling actually makes me nervous and uneasy. There is a smell of what I think is stale decaying flesh. I heard stories of the Vietcong using unusually cruel interrogation techniques, where they skin the captor but keep them alive to gain information. It's a slow, painful process, but I can only imagine its effectiveness. I also smell an extinguished fire, which is also a rarity in these holes as the smoke can give away your position, and the enemy is very good at concealing themselves.

I scan the room slowly so as to not miss any potential wires that would signify a possible booby trap. I dare not move as there may be something concealed in the dirt floor. As I scan, my light falls on what appears to be…oh my god. I gag into my mouth. A man, maybe 5'2", is suspended from the ceiling of this cavern. I move my light as I try to control myself from vomiting, and there is another, and another. Three of them are in various stages of what appears to be a torture chamber of epic proportions. The bodies are in various stages of being defleshed. The fire pit in the middle of the room has a slight whisp of smoke trailing off into a natural vent in the ceiling somewhere. Two stakes hold a skewer draped across the fire with remnants of half-cooked flesh clinking to the stake. I barely get out the words "What the fuck?" as the room starts to spin, then I double over as if I was hit in the stomach by the worst punch to the gut ever and expel all the contents of my stomach onto the ground.

As I come to, after the heaving, I scan the room again. I can hear Sergeant Head calling from outside, "Francis, you okay?" He never calls anyone by their first name. I'm shocked he even knows mine.

I call back, "Yeah, Sergeant, you might want to come see this." I few minutes later, Sergeant Head enters the room. As we scan the room with our flashlights, I tell him what I've found.

"Holy mother of God" is all Sergeant Head can utter.

"What do you want to do, Sergeant?"

"The right thing to do is cut them down and give them a proper burial," Sergeant Head replies. "What kind of person can do this?"

"I have no idea" is all I can get out through the nasty stale bile taste in my mouth.

"This explains the body we found in the village," Sergeant Head explains. "I wonder if the Vietcong happened upon this and thought it was the villagers. Then they took one of their own as a message or way to extract information?"

"That makes some sense, I suppose. But even that seems extreme for them," I reply.

"At this point, Francis, after everything I have seen in this godforsaken country over the past few years, nothing surprises me anymore."

We grab our K bars. Sergeant Head goes to cut down the one on the right, and I go for the one on the left. As soon as Sergeant Head's knife hits the rope suspending the body, the fleshy mass suspended from it explodes. Sergeant Head immediately disintegrates into a mixture of him and the victim. I become deafened by the sound and then the pain. It feels like tiny, hot knife points are picking at my back, arms, and legs. The guys outside hear the blast and start to come into the hole. Apparently the blast was enough to make the opening bigger. The rest of the platoon drags me out. All I remember is Joe hovering over me with Mike.

"Don't worry, buddy, we are going to get you out of here," I hear Joe say as I feel Mike pulling shards of shrapnel out of my body. Mike is silent as he works covering the open wounds with each extraction.

"I can't get this one," Mike identifies. "We have to get him out of here and back to base camp."

THE DEMONIC SAVIOR

That is all I heard as I succumb to the pain and pass out.

* * * *

Patricia is listening intently. A lot of this story is not believable as the thought of finding a man skinned and hanging in a hut in a village in Vietnam is preposterous despite some of the other stories told about servicemen's experiences over there.

"Do you have the shrapnel in your back now?" she asks.

"Yes," I respond.

"I have to admit that is a traumatic story, but it doesn't say why you kill people now," she says.

"My ability to become who I am today took some time to build," I tell her.

"Sounds to me like you enjoy it," she remarks.

"I can assure you killing others is not how I envisioned my life," I say.

"So what happens after you are taken out for your injuries?" she asks finally. "I can only assume there is more to this than you just waking up one day and deciding to be a serial killer."

"There is more…"

Chapter 11

I fall in and out of consciousness as I am transported to the medical unit. I barely remember the helicopter ride or being carried out. I wake lying on my stomach and feel someone touching me and then this excruciating sting.

"Ow! What the hell?" I try to move.

"Stay still. I am almost done," a female voice remarks as I am pressed back down into the mattress.

"Well, it hurts. Who the hell are you, and where the hell am I?" I exclaim.

"You are on the hospital ship USS *Sanctuary*," she responds.

"Why am I here? Where is my platoon? What happened?" As I was asking all this, it starts to return to me: the bodies, the explosion, the pain… "Damn! That hurts. What is that?"

"Peroxide to clean your wounds. You had a lot of shrapnel removed from you," the nurse responds. "You're very lucky, you know."

"I don't know how lucky I am." I drift back off as she finishes the assault, but not before seeing the most beautiful woman I have ever seen. Blond hair golden and glistening. Hazel eyes, gray with a touch of these emerald streaks. Slight build, not much to her by most standards, but absolute perfection in my eyes. I dream of her soft facial features with a look of unyielding strength that silhouettes her like an aura. As I drift off, I feel her lean down and whisper, "Sleep now. I'll be back." Not sure if it was a dream or reality as I disintegrate into thoughts of her behind my closed eyes.

THE DEMONIC SAVIOR

After what seemed like minutes but could have been hours, I wake from a groggy fog of sedated slumber. Standing next to my bed is the stunning creature from my dreams. Now I don't know if I am dreaming or awake. "I see you're awake again. The doctor wants to speak with you. I'll go get him," I hear her say in this mellow tone; it reminds me of my mother's voice, so soft and saturated with caring.

"Please don't go," I respond. I sound desperate; how pathetic am I? But she was already away. Moments later, a stringy fellow in a white doctor's jacket walks up and sits next to the head of my bed.

"I am Dr. Hauk. I understand you had quite an ordeal."

"I don't remember anything, Doc. Or not much, anyway," I state.

"That's probably the morphine. Good stuff that is. Kills everything and I hear you sleep like a baby," he says with a cheerful tone.

I am not amused; my sense of humor is diminished as I am still half out of it. "So what's the prognosis, Doc? How bad is it?"

"Well, to give it to you straight, you had numerous pieces of shrapnel removed from you. Whoever was in the field, a Corpsman Nolan, did a nice job patching you up. But unfortunately, he was not able to get everything, which is why you are here." Doctor Hauk provides the diagnosis. "You had over thirty pieces of metal and other fragments in you. We removed 99 percent of them."

"Only 99 percent? Why not all?" I ask.

"There is one piece that is lying right next to your spine that I feel is inoperable. The risk of removing could leave you paralyzed," he says grimly.

"So what does that mean, Doc? Can I move? Walk? Anything?" I ask.

"Oh, I think you will have full mobility after some RNR and physical therapy." He explains, "But in time, that last piece in your back will start to cause you much pain as I am sure you can understand. There is one other thing: A piece of bone must have hit one of your testicles. I had to remove it."

"Wait, WHAT? You removed one of my testicles?" I exclaim.

"Yes, I am afraid it had to go. But don't worry, everything is still functional," he assures me.

He must be freaking crazy. A piece of metal in my spine that could leave me crippled and I am short a "nut." This guy is off his rocker.

"Great. Thanks, Doc," I say sarcastically. "Can I roll over and get something to eat? I'm starving."

"I think we can arrange that. I saw a cart with Jell-O at the end of the bay. I'll have Nurse Engel come assist you," he says as he gets up and leaves.

Engel, Nurse Engel, so that's her name. If I am not mistaken, that is *Angel* in German. How fitting, as she glowed like an angel when I first awoke. But what would I be to her? Nothing. I am half a man. She probably gets hit on by all these jarheads in here. I doubt she even finds me attractive; I am just another Marine. Ah, well, it's probably for the best. Having only one testicle doesn't make me suitable for any female anyway. To hell with this war. We shouldn't be here anyway.

Nurse Engel comes by and helps me roll over. I can feel the piece they left near my spine shift as I sit back in the bed.

"Your wounds should be able to breathe. Covering them like this just to sit up is not going to help you recover," she says to me with stern lips but a glint in her eye. Could I be wrong?

"Nurse Engel. Right?" I ask. "That's what the doctor said your name was."

"Yes, but you can call me Clara," she tells me.

"Clara Engel. Your parents must have known what they were doing when they gave you that name," I say.

"Why do you say that?" she asks.

"In German, it means 'Savior Angel,' which is fitting for you, if you don't mind me saying," I explain.

"No, I don't mind." She smiles. "But I won't let you stay like this. I'll bring you some Jell-O, and in a bit, you lay back down. I have to check your dressings in a few hours."

The bay is full of Marines in various forms of recovery. It is at this point that I realize the room is rocking and swaying. Looking at my fellow brethren, I realize they are worse off than me. But I can't shake the self-remorse of my situation. Taking or losing one's testicle is a massive blow to one's masculine ego. Wait. JELL-O! Why Jell-O? Maybe I can ask her for a steak when she returns.

"Here is your Jell-O." She hands me a cup with little green squares of gelatin.

"What's a guy got to do to get a steak around here, medium rare, please," I quip as flirtatious as I can be. Heads nearby turn in anticipation of her response, and I think I saw a few lick their lips.

She gives me a devilish smile, leans forward, and says, "Maybe when your strength is up, I'll show you."

I sheepishly grin in return as she leans back upright and says much louder this time, "Jell-O, to keep your fluids up." Those watching frown in response to her answer and return to what they were doing.

A week goes by. At this point, I have begun my physical therapy. It's arduous "relearning" to walk and wincing through the pain. The first trip felt like every wound reopened as the stitches pulled at the cells of my skin. But as time passed, my strength returned; not sure if it was the Jell-O squares or Nurse Engel that was the greatest motivator. Either way, I did as I was told, wondering if I would return to my unit or be shipped home. Then one day, a staff sergeant in Charlies (the Marines' version of semidress) waltzes in like he owns the ward.

"Corporal Fleming?" he barks.

"Yes, Staff Sergeant, here," I answer.

He briskly walks over to my rack, says "Orders," then he moves on to the next Marine.

> From: 1st Engineer Battalion Commanding Officer
> To: Cpl Francis I. Fleming (Last 4 5202)
> Orders: You are to be Honorably Discharged (Medical) from service of the United States Marine Corps. Effective 1 Jan. 1971.

The rest is just normal correspondence jargon about where to report and my flight back to headquarters in San Diego before getting my ticket home, probably on a bus. *Well, that's that*, I think to myself. Mom will be happy to see me return. She hated that I had to go in the first place, but when she saw the initial draft notice, she knew what it meant. She originally pleaded for me to go to Canada, then rescinded as she knew the blood that coursed through my veins.

* * * * *

"So you fell in love," Patricia interrupts.
"Yes," I say.
"Where is she? Did you kill her too?" she asks almost tauntingly.
"No, but if you would like to hear, I will get there," I offer.
"Lead the way," Patricia states.

Her agitation for still being bound is taking a toll on her sense of humor. But she is willing to listen to this psychopath's story. Her hope is he eventually lets his guard down and she gets free.

Chapter 12

On January 5, 1971, I stand before the long drive surrounded by trees. My seabag is full on my back and a small attaché case I purchased for any items I needed quick access to is in my left hand and I'm in my Deltas (Marine full-dress uniform). The trip took an extra day as I had to wait for Command to get my paperwork straight. Nothing in the military, regardless of branch, is easily accomplished, and there is nothing routine. One foot in front of the other, I'm a little stiff from the travel as I step out from the wooded opening and into the small clearing where our house rests. Brightly painted a beautiful bluish gray with darker but accommodating trim, the porch railing a brilliant white, the whole house glows in the January sunlight beaming on the facade like a spotlight. Off to the right stands the massive oak tree that overlooks the family plots like a sentry swaying in an uncanny warm breeze given the time of year. Right next to it is Mother's rose garden. Currently the bushes are not in bloom, but my goodness, when they are, they are vibrant and full of the deepest red. Each petal is velvety to the touch and soft like a newborn's skin.

Out the front door flies my mother, arms wide and tears streaming down her face. She engulfs me in a grasp only a mother can provide to her offspring. It feels like an eternity. When she releases me, she clasps my face and pulls me down as she gives me a kiss on my forehead.

"Thank God you're home, Francis." Tears are still flowing as she sobs for joy.

"Yes, Mother. I am home" is all I can muster in reply.

She puts her arm in mine, and we finish the walk up the porch steps and in the front door.

"I have your favorite meal prepared, Francis. But you must be exhausted. What would you like?" She is always accommodating.

I won't say that she waited on me hand and foot, no. I was raised to pull my weight growing up. But as long as I did my part (and I usually did), she made sure I had everything else I needed to be a happy boy. My grandfather had left my grandmother a substantial amount of money when he passed; that was around 1948, when I was around three years old. I vaguely remember him, burly guy about 6'5" and must have weighed in around 275 pounds, mostly muscle, but he did have a squishy belly, I remember that. My grandmother was a slight woman around 4'11" and barely ninety pounds, always with a joyful smile on her face and a hard candy in her pocket. Despite her stature, she had a mountainous personality, and everyone she interacted with in town paid her respect; of course that could have been because of my grandfather. They owned a hardware store in town and were well respected in the community. My mother is a teacher, but when Grandmother passed in 1965, she left the store and the house to my mother to assist raising me. Mother sold the store and all the inventory to Mr. Clark, who had worked for my grandparents for years. She used the money from the sale to allow me to go to school for engineering before the war. Mr. Clark still helps out around the house occasionally, knowing I was away and Mom is by herself. The people at church all treat us like family and pitch in where they can. My father was well loved by the townsfolk prior to leaving to serve as a Marine in WWII. He died on June 6, 1944, five days before I was born. Poor Mom gave birth to me and a week later received the letter that my father was killed storming the beaches of France.

"Steak, Mother," I answer her. "I haven't had a good steak in, well, I don't know how long." I chuckle.

"Of course, Francis. I happen to have two steaks in the fridge. I can bake up some potatoes and green beans too. If you like?" She plans the meal out in her head.

"That sounds wonderful, Mother. Thank you," I reply graciously.

"Your room is as you left it. You can go put your things away and wash up. I'll have supper ready in a bit." She is beaming at me through her swollen eyes. "I placed your mail on your dresser. Not to be nosy, but who is Clara Engel?"

"She is a nurse who cared for me when they transported me to the USS *Sanctuary* after I received my injuries," I say, allowing my emotions of being home to be stifled as I fondly think of Clara.

"Well, given the scent of that envelope, you'd think she used an entire bottle of perfume. I guess she wanted your attention."

I half chuckle and say, "Yes, Mother, most likely. When the ship returned me to Sasebo, Clara and I spent some time together."

"Oh?" she says, giving me a knowing look. "Maybe you'll have to tell me about her later."

"Perhaps, Mother. We shall see" is all I can muster. I want to get upstairs before the emotions of being home overtook me, and I don't want to break down in front of Mother.

Mother goes to the kitchen and starts preparing the meal. I head upstairs and drop off my gear. Everything is just as I left it, just like she said. I can even tell she came in and dusted the furnishings. I shake my head and chuckle as I know not much will ever change her. Having me and my father passing left her not much time for herself. She teaches at the school and raised me; that was pretty much it. If there had ever been a suitor who came calling, I was unaware. Mother was not a bad-looking woman; she just loved my father so much she had no inclination in finding anyone else.

I turn, and in the full-length mirror that sits in the corner stands a man I no longer recognize: standing straight, shoulders back, fresh shave, freshly pressed full-dress uniformed man with a solemn, weary gaze upon his face. My eyes well up a bit, and I wipe them quickly. Being home after everything is a bit overwhelming. I decide unpacking at this point is not in me as I undress, taking each item and hanging it on a bare hanger in the closet. I open my dresser drawer and find an old white T-shirt I don and grab a pair of slacks hanging in the closet. By my bed is the pair of shoes I wore before the war. I slide them on and tie them; they fit like a glove, a little stiff from resting for so long. I head for the door to go downstairs, and as I pass that mirror, I see me and I still have that weary look on my face. That look tells everything about me. It's not from the war or what I experienced. It's a look of "What the hell do I do now?" I went to school for engineering, but I cannot say that is what I want anymore. I look one more time in that mirror, and I see a lost soul trying to find a way out of the gloom. The longer I stare, the more I see this darkened halo surround that individual staring back at me, and it frightens me. I walk out closing the door and down the stairs I head. The distinctive smell of bovine flesh searing in a cast-iron pan emanates through the house.

"Smells good, Mom." I kiss her on the cheek as I enter the kitchen.

"You have a seat, Francis. The meal will be ready soon," she states, not missing a beat as she tends to the meal.

I sit in silence as she finishes the preparations. Moments later, she brings me a plate with a perfectly cooked sirloin, a baked potato, and some green beans. She sets her portion at her spot across from me, and we say grace.

"Father, thank you for bringing home my boy safely. We bless this food in your name. Amen," she says, her eyes closed and hands folded neatly on the edge of the kitchen table.

I do the same so as not to upset her, but my eyes remain open as closing them may induce tears I dare not show her. We sit in relative silence. I dig in, and half of my meal has disappeared from my plate.

"Francis, you should slow down and taste it. I'd ask how it was, but I'm not sure you can answer me," Mother says frankly. I look down and realize that I'm almost finished as she hasn't made it through but a few bits.

I give a light chuckle. "I am sorry, Mom. I guess I am used to hurrying up and to get moving that I didn't realize how fast I was eating."

"Well, we will have to work on those bad habits you picked up," she remarks.

"How's teaching this year? Are the kids being polite?" I ask.

"Oh, they get more and more ornery every year, or I am just starting to show my age," she says with a sigh. "I saw Sarah yesterday. Her and Henry Jones are getting married."

"Oh! Good for them," I answer.

Sarah and I dated for a bit in high school. Now that I am home, she is hoping I might settle down and marry myself. But I don't know. The idea is semi-appealing, but my heart lies with another. Clara and I did have a few dates before I was shipped back to the States. When the ship returned to Sasebo, Japan, to off-load those of us it carried, we spent a day out on the town. My heart is hers if she will have it. She knows of my condition and did not seem to mind. But there is no indication at this time as to when she will be finished with her service. We agreed to write and stay in touch, so I guess we shall see.

After we finish eating, I clear the plates and do the dishes. Mother makes some tea for us both and sips hers at the table while I wrap up. We head to the living room lighted by the various lamps throughout as the sun has descended and the moon has graced the early night with its brilliant glow. Mother grabs up her knitting, and I start a book I picked up on my travel home. We remain there for the remaining hours of the night till we both decide around 10:00 p.m. it is time to call it a night.

Chapter 13

That night, I have vicious nightmares of the bodies hanging and, in one dream, reaching for me as if to pull me in and make me one of them. I wake in a cold sweat drenched head to toe, the sheets of my bed saturated. I don't sleep the rest of the night. I just lay there looking out the window, watching the oak tree over the family plot sway its barren branches in the breeze. A storm is coming. The shrapnel in my back aches, telling me it is probably going to be a rough snowstorm. As I watch, I can see the first flakes start to fall around 4:00 a.m., then the precipitation picks up with the wind and it pounds the house, saturating the ground to a glistening white. I wasn't sure it would stick at first, given how warm the day was when I came home. But apparently the temperature dropped 30 degrees and the ground seized its warmth to the blanketing of snow now covering it.

More and more descend from the heavens as I watch. Normally I would find this very peaceful, but as I stare out the window, a figure appears over my shoulder. "The time has come, Francis," the figure says. I continue to stare out the window, watching the storm pick up and the flakes of snow accumulate.

"The time has come for you to meet my needs," the reflection continues. I continue to stare.

"I need a soul, and you will get it for me," the figure continues as plainly and matter-of-factly, as if being told to get up and start my day.

"How do you propose I do that?" I finally state in acknowledgement.

"Oh, it will come to you, Francis. Soon enough, it will come to you. Because if you do not obey and fulfill my needs, I can make your life a true living hell. What you experienced during the war is nothing compared to what I can do to you."

As the reflection speaks, the piece of metal in my back starts to throb, and then the pain changes from a dull ache to severe sharp stabbing. I cry out and slump to the floor. Mother knocks and enters the room, finding me in a pile next to the window.

"Francis! Are you okay?" Mother asks in a worried and scared tone.

"Yes, Mother. I'll be fine. It's just the weather affecting the wound I received that I told you about."

She holds me and helps me up.

"Well, they have cancelled school today." She must have been listening to the radio for the announcement. I didn't even hear it in the silence. "How would you like some breakfast?"

"Yes, that would be nice. Thank you," I reply.

The Beatles' "Here Comes the Sun" is now audible in the background. How fitting given the weather outside, the irony.

"I'll be down in a bit. Let me stretch out my back, and I'll be down," I tell her so I can have a minute to collect my thoughts. If she knew the truth… No, I cannot tell her. I do not want her to worry. I have to find a way to deal with this on my own. She quietly leaves with a simple "okay." Looking back as she passes through the doorway, closing the door partially but not completely, I sit on the bed and release a great sigh. As much as I love my mother, I yearn for Clara, her soft but firm lips, her bright eyes, her hand in mine.

Downstairs, Mother is in the kitchen and making Cream of Wheat of all things. I chuckle in my head as I had not had Cream of Wheat in I don't know how long, probably last I was home. Either way, Mother makes it good half water and half milk and a good dosage of butter, making it extra rich and creamy. She tends to sprinkle sugar on hers, while I eat mine with a dash of salt and normally plain or with some fruit.

"Francis, are you okay?" Mother asks with concern.

"Yes" is all I can muster.

"I know the news exaggerates things a bit or only tells half the story. I can't imagine what being there was like, and I won't press you about it either." She continues, "I want you to relax and try to forget everything. When you are ready, maybe we can discuss what is next for you."

"I've actually given that some thought, Mother. Honestly, I cannot come up with a good answer," I provide. What I really want is to get back to Clara and start a life with her, but she is still on the *Sanctuary* and won't be finished with her time for a while. For now, we write to stay in touch and talk about what could be.

"If you need something to do while you figure it out, Mr. Clark would probably appreciate the assistance at the hardware store," Mother suggests.

"You know, that's not a half-bad idea, Mother. I think I'll visit him tomorrow. At the very least, I can say hello," I respond cheerfully. I truly do like the idea. Mr. Clark was always good to me when I was growing up. He would find things for me to build and put together while waiting for Mother to finish at school and take me home or ride back with her with Grandmother.

The day tarries on, and I mostly sit in Grandfather's old high-backed chair in the living room reading. After some lunch, I head upstairs to my room. I unpack finally, and in doing so, I find a note from Clara in my seabag.

My dearest Francis,

I am so happy we met. I only wish it had been under better circumstances. You truly have captured my eye and my heart. I pray you have had safe travels, and I can't wait to see you again. I think of the life we can have together. How I miss your curly red hair and your green eyes. Be well, my dearest Francis. We will be together soon.

Clara

After putting everything of importance away, I leave my old uniforms in the seabag and take them to the attic. Memories I would much rather forget. War is hell, and not to sound sorry for me but… Well, let's just say I saw enough shit to last a lifetime.

"Just wait, Francis. With your curly red hair and green eyes, you haven't seen what I have in store for you yet," the voice projects in my head. A glass-framed photo shows the embodied head of the demon lingering over my shoulder in the pale light of the attic.

"You again," I remark. "I deny your existence. So you might as well move along."

"Oh, well, since you feel that way, Francis, maybe I'll just inhabit your dear mother?" says the demon sardonically.

"No!" I exclaim out loud.

"Francis?" Mother calls from below. "Was that you? Did you need something?"

"No. I mean, yes, Mother. I am fine! I just knocked into something up here in the attic, and it startled me is all!" I yell down.

"Okay. It's cold up there. Don't keep it open too long," she replies, and I can hear her walking back to whatever she was doing.

"Yes. That does sound appealing. I haven't been with a woman in a long, long time. Besides, you are dull, Francis. Maybe your mother will be more to my liking and willing to meet my needs," the demon says.

"You leave her out of this, whatever this is," I state with vehemence. "Whatever it is you expect of me, I'll do," I say as I think of ways to be rid of this evil entity.

"Good. That's better," the Demon states in a more satisfied tone. "But in due time. I have not completely decided just how useful you can be for me, not yet anyway."

"Take your time," I mutter under my breath. Odd. This thing is inside of me and clearly reads my thoughts. Why speaking softly or even at all would matter, I have no idea.

I close up the attic and adjourn to my room. I sit at my old desk where I once did homework, and I write a letter to Clara.

My lovely Clara, my angel,

To say I miss you would be an understatement. The trip home was uneventful, minus being long and arduous. Mother clearly missed me. I have no idea what I am going to do now. My back reminds me of changes in the weather. Speaking of which, it is snowing here. The yard and the surrounding woods glisten like twinkling lights at Christmas. It is so beautiful. But not as beautiful as you and your eyes that I cannot wait to lose myself in. Ah, to hold you and feel your soft skin against mine. We truly made a connection in such a short period of time. But I feel like I've known you forever and know you even more for the rest of my life. I look forward to the time we can be together forever. Be safe as I dream of you every night.

Yours sincerely,
Francis

I lay down and rest. I must have slept the afternoon away as I woke to the smell of dinner. I go down and see Mother.

"Just in time," she says with a smile. "I made your favorite meal, liver and fried onions with mashed potatoes."

"Sounds wonderful, Mother," I reply thankfully.

Dinner is just perfect. I cannot say why I appreciate liver and onions, but the way my mother makes it is so delicate and absolutely delicious. It is like none other. The rest of the evening goes as the one before. The snow has finally stopped, and the landscape is like a thick white pristine blanket, Perfectly laid like a nice comforter on a freshly made bed, not even tracks from any wildlife. Around 10:00 p.m., we adjourn for the night, same as the night before. It's nice to be back into a calming routine.

I cannot say that I had a restful sleep. Something about the "witching" hours of midnight to 2:00 a.m. is like an alarm clock for devilish spirits like the one inhabiting my mind. I wake again in a drenched sweat from a hellish nightmare. Except this time, it involves Clara; all I can remember after waking is her hand outstretched to me as she falls into some abyss and, as she falls, whispering that she loves me. Despite the attraction we share and the fiery whimsicalness of our romance, we have yet to speak those eternal words of "love" to each other.

I climb out of bed and stand looking out the window over the back lawn, the old oak standing still and sentry-like over the family resting plots. The iron fencing casts its shadow over the blanket of white like it is reaching for a way to escape its duty of enclosing or marking the grave site.

"Forget her" comes that raspy, ghastly voice from inside my head. "She doesn't really love you. It was just a fling, and you're lucky it was even that, given your station in life. You're barely a man."

The voice taunts me at my very fiber of existence as a way to control me. I do well to subdue his comments, but it doesn't last, and eventually his gnawing will eat at my soul, my confidence, and my stature. But for now, I am still able to keep it at bay.

"What do you know? You're not even real," I retort back.

"Not real? Hmmm, shall I remind you just how real I am?" the inward beast roars.

"No. You don't need to tout yourself to me. Whether you are a figment of my imagination based on the ordeals I have had to witness or whether you are reality is irrelevant," I conclude.

The demon screams, infuriated at my indifference to his existence. But we both know I am right. Whether it is real or just a creation of events I have suffered is irrelevant at this time. Oh, sure, the time may come where he shows his true teeth and devours me. But that time is not now. Like a hair festering under one's skin creating that painful boil, the demon has to have time to grow and nurture its own occupancy inside me. Human willpower is not as forthcoming to evil as some might believe. No, it has to be nurtured just as love has to be nurtured. Ying versus yang. Good versus evil. War versus peace. Yet now that he has made his presence known, I know it is only a matter of time before he becomes so strong that I cannot control him. All I can do at this time is try to keep it at bay until I can find a way to extract or exterminate it.

* * * * *

"So you are claiming to be possessed? Is that your angle?" Patricia taunts. If this guy really is possessed, then she knows she has to confront the demon inside. Clearly he is suppressing it, provided it even exists.

"I can assure you it is not an angle," I say. "The demon is real. I have an idea of what you are trying to do, and I beg you, if you want the whole story, you cannot force him out. Yes, I am suppressing him right now. Because if I do not, he will surely use me to kill you like all the others."

"How many, Francis? How many women have you killed?" she asks.

"Enough that I have lost count. But if I was to guess, I would say twenty-five to thirty," I say, my eyes welling with tears as I look down and away. The thought of all these people I have killed or allowed the demon to kill over the years sickens me to the core.

"Jesus Christ..." Patricia says under her breath but still audible.

"Please don't. I know this sounds crazy, but I assure you it is all true," I say. "In time, I will tell you how even God has been unable to save me from this affliction, and believe me, I have tried."

"Francis, so far, this is the most insane story I have ever heard. To think that it gets even more strange, I have a hard time believing it. But I am curious. How did you become a pastor? I also would like to know when the killing started." Patricia is showing interest in the rest of the story.

"My path to becoming a pastor goes back to after I returned home from Vietnam," I start. "After returning, I was lost and had no real direction to follow. So I turned to an old friend."

Chapter 14

The day breaks over the tree line, and I have already dressed for the mile walk into town. Mother has not risen yet; I leave her a note letting her know I am venturing in to see Mr. Clark at the hardware store. It'll be nice to get some fresh air and exercise. Adorning my heavy wool lined denim jacket, I exit the front door, closing it as softly as I can so as not to wake Mother. I grab the broom on the porch and sweep off the steps just in case she decides to venture out later. The snowfall reaches to just past my ankles as I trudge down the covered driveway, through the archway of trees that have mingled overhead like interwoven fingers of hands springing from Mother Earth—one on the left, the other on the right. The underbrush is thick even in the winter. I may have to address that when things start to warm up.

As I get to the main road, I see the county crews had worked through the night to clear the asphalt of snow. I get out where it is clear and with my hands in my pockets tarry into town. As I walk down the main street, I base a few houses on the outskirts. But as I venture on, it takes on this serene setting much like a Norman Rockwell painting. There is the local shoe peddler, the town butcher, a bakery that makes my mouth water with the smells of fresh donuts and baked breads. The town theatre is dark at this early hour, but I can see *Diamonds Are Forever,* the latest James Bond film, is playing on the marque. There is a tailor shop, a five-and-ten, and the local pharmacy; all line the street that normally is bustling with activity even at this hour as the stores are usually opening. But the weather has most people sleeping in or avoiding the cold. At the end of main, watching over all that passed through town was the Baptist church, its steeple, the highest point in town, erect like a beacon of faith topped with the cross, so there is no doubt that God watches over this town. There, about two doors down from the two banks that stand like sentries in the center of this one light town, is Mr. Clark's hardware store. The simple sign over the front facade just says "Hardware"; underneath on the windows is painted "Tools, Paint, Camping Gear, Fasteners, Electrical, etc." and a little slogan on the other window, "If you need it, we probably have it!" It's true. I cannot think of any item the store did not have or could not acquire over the past two decades I had been in there working. As I look through the windows reminiscing of days when I played and later worked in the store, I see Mr. Clark checking inventory down some of the aisles. I stand there for a bit, remembering a time when I would watch my grandfather do the same thing and Grandmother standing behind the counter talking to customers. There are some stools off to the side out of the way of business for friends and family to sit and talk. The nice thing about little stores like this is that everyone is family and everyone is welcome. Not one person is ever turned away, and everyone feels at home. Small-town living is unlike any other. When I was in San Diego before shipping out for Okinawa and then Vietnam, it was different. Oh, sure, people said hello and smiled…but it was more impersonable. Here, everyone knows you, and because it is a small town, you best remember, especially as a kid, everybody knows you. The thought crosses my brain and makes me chuckle.

 As I come out of my little daydream, there through the window is Mr. Clark beaming at me. I can hear his boisterous voice through the window, "Francis! Come inside." I smile and nod, shift to the left, step up, and open the door. I am barely through the threshold, and Mr. Clark lays his monstrous hands on my shoulders and says, "My god. Francis. How are you? It's been so long. I am glad you are home safe."

 It is quite a different feeling here in my hometown than it was when I first arrived back in San Diego. In San Diego, there were protests and "hippies" all lounging about with peace signs and groups playing instruments and singing about peace. Now don't get me wrong, I am all for peace. I also know, especially after being there, that we are not wanted over there. But the overall atmosphere is just different here at home. Maybe it is because everyone knows me, or perhaps it's the fact that this is small-town America and therefore secluded from the societal changes that directly affect larger towns and cities.

"Mr. Clark." I smile. "It's good to be home."

"When did you get in? How was it? Oh, wait, I'm sorry if you don't want to talk about it," Mr. Clark says inquisitively.

"I got in the other day. The trip wasn't too bad, long and confining, but otherwise not bad," I reply.

Mr. Clark is an instrumental piece in how I was raised. He is the same age as my father and mother, but when the draft was inducted for World War II, he was denied entry into service for a heart condition, which I always found odd, given the fact that he has a heart of gold and treats everyone with kindness and respect.

"You know, Francis, war is hell. Granted, I was not able to go like your father and therefore have not experienced it. But I knew your dad. He wouldn't agree with everything going on in today's world, but he would have been proud of you for your choice and he would have supported you. I know he was watching out for you while you were over there."

The thought of my father watching over is a duality, given the facts of what I experienced and that I never knew him. I reflect on what Mr. Clark said as I take a seat on one of the stools.

"Is there anything I can do to help you?" I ask.

"No, no. Francis, you just sit there. Your company and conversation alone is enough for me today. With this weather being what it is, I doubt there will be many stopping in. I almost didn't open today, but if I didn't, I know someone would miss out on a shovel that they would need," explains Mr. Clark.

"Well, I have to be honest. Since I was handed orders by Command releasing me from duty, I…" I trail off. "I'm not sure what I want to do anymore."

Mr. Clark stops and looks at me. "Francis, I've known you your whole life. I remember when you decided to go get an engineering degree. I remember the day you got your draft card and immediately went to the Marine Corps Recruiting Office. I'll admit, I've never known you to be indecisive." Mr. Clark pauses. "But I understand."

I sigh a deep long sigh, and my entire body deflates. "I've never felt 'lost' like this, you know."

"I do," Mr. Clark says as he lays a hand on my shoulder and looks at me, the way a father consoles his son. "I was there once myself."

"You were? I thought you had worked for my grandparents since I was born," I say, surprised.

"For the most part, I did. But when I was rejected by the Marines because of my heart, I met this guy who told me about this trail. The Appalachian Trail. It runs from Georgia to Maine and is 2,200 miles long," he tells me.

"Wait, why go hike a trail that's 2,200 miles long after being told you have a bad heart?" I question.

"To prove that I could and that I didn't have a bad heart," Mr. Clark explains. As it turns out, Mr. Clark actually did not have a bad heart; there was a mistake made in his physical. By the time he found this out, World War II was over and life's course had changed for him and he never looked back at the military again. One might even say that his employment with my grandparents and perhaps an affection for my mother or his loyalty to my father convinced him that his real purpose in life was watching over me. Looking back as I tell this story, that is the only thing that makes sense to me.

"Okay," I say. "So what happened? Did you hike the whole thing? Did Mother Nature talk to you?"

"In a way, it did." He sits down to tell the story. "I went, and I took a bus or hitched or walked all the way down to Georgia. I didn't have a clue what I was doing or what to expect. I didn't pack per se. I think I had maybe two to three changes of clothes and no food." He sighs and looks at me. "I was young and dumb, but I learned quick and met some good people that looked after me." He smiles. "Anyway, I walked the whole thing Georgia to Maine. I earned a few bucks along the way helping out people I met. Sometimes they would just feed me a fresh meal. I learned what was edible and what was not. Let me tell you, the edible is more desirable than the inedible." He grabs his gut. "In it all, I learned the best lesson. Humility. I learned not just how to care of myself but that I was valuable to those I met and that were around me. I found out who I am and the man you see before you today."

I think about it for a minute, letting Mr. Clark's story sink in a bit. "Do you think that is what I should do? Hike the Appalachian Trail to figure out who I am?" I ask.

"Francis, only you can decide that. I am merely telling you what worked for me and letting you know that you are not alone," he responds.

"Everyone's path through life is different," he goes on. "What works for one may not work for another. But only you can decide the path you take. God gives us choices as long as he is in our hearts and we believe. But he doesn't decide for us. He leaves us to make our own decisions."

We sit there for a bit in silence. "Here, come give me a hand please," he finally says, knowing his message hit home. He leads me to a rack of tools and asks me to straighten up the aisle. Then he goes to the register to help out a customer that came in to buy a shovel. By the end of the day, I am exhausted; my back is killing me from bending over and arranging things. He was right; it was a slow day with only five customers. But each person that came in knew me and said hello and welcomed me home and said they were glad I was safe. I couldn't help but feel warmth inside from the attention but empty all at the same time.

Chapter 15

The walk home is much the same as the walk into town. The sun has started to set, and by the time I arrive back at the house, the trees over the drive are like a deep dark tunnel with a faint light at the end, signifying Mother has turned on the porch light. She had called the store at one point. I know because Mr. Clark merely said, "Yes, things are well. You have nothing to worry about." He didn't have to identify the caller. I knew it was her making sure I was okay.

As I walk in the front door, Mother is sitting in the living room knitting away, and the radio is playing Elvis on the station. We don't have a TV; Mother never believed in them and felt they weren't worth the money to spend. So she spends her time knitting when not grading papers.

"I left you some dinner on the stove. Did you have a nice time at the store with Mr. Clark?" she asks as I take off my jacket and hang it by the door.

"Yes, Mother. It was a good day, I feel. But I am sore, all that moving around. Guess I've been away too long and forgot what it's like to tend that store," I say with a half-hearted laugh.

"The school called. They will be open tomorrow. If you don't mind taking me into town, you can use the car for the day, and I can walk to the store in the end," she says.

"I would be honored to drive you to school in the morning." I give her a kiss on the forehead and head back to fix myself a plate.

Mother drove an old Chrysler Saratoga that my grandparents left her when they passed. They would drive the old panel truck into town that was used for delivery of orders when they owned the hardware store. But when Mother sold the hardware store to Mr. Clark, the panel truck was included. They kept the Saratoga for family trips, which were not taken often, and daily needs around town like getting groceries.

I was so exhausted from helping out at the hardware store that after I ate the meal prepared by Mother and cleaned up the kitchen, I adjourn to my room after a nice hot bath. For the first time in a while, I slept the entire night. The next morning, I wake early and make the coffee for Mother as she prepares for classes. We exchange the normal morning pleasantries, and I take her into town and deliver her to school. I then venture over to the hardware store to assist Mr. Clark.

"Francis, oh, good, I am glad you are here. Mr. Thomas over on Union Street called me and placed an order. Would you mind taking it over to him and delivering it, please." Mr. Clark hands me a brown paper bag with some paint and materials. "The other items are already loaded in the truck out back. Let me know if there are any issues."

"Not a problem, Mr. Clark. I'll be back shortly," I say. "Happy I can be of assistance."

Off I go and deliver the materials. Mrs. Thomas greets me when I knock on the door and invites me in.

"I appreciate it, Mrs. Thomas, but I cannot stay long," I accept.

"Don't be silly, Francis. Mr. Clark won't be surprised if you're a minute long on the run. Especially when you give him these." She hands me a plate of freshly baked cookies. That woman makes the absolute best oatmeal raisin cookies, unlike any I have ever had.

"Yes, ma'am." I smile.

With the delivery complete and cookies in hand, I head back to the store. Thinking of what Mr. Clark suggested yesterday about the Appalachian Trail has left me thinking it may not be such a bad idea after all. A chance for me to get out into nature, let the fresh air clear my head. Maybe even provide me a way to relinquish this devil that has taken hold of me. Back at the store, I back the old truck in next to the Saratoga.

"Francis, how did everything go?" Mr. Clark requests.

"All went well, and Mrs. Thomas asked me to deliver this to you." I hand over the plate of oatmeal cookies.

"God bless that woman. It's a wonder I am not bigger around the waist than I am. I could eat this entire plate," he states.

"Mr. Clark?" I say inquisitively. "I've given some thought to what you were talking about yesterday with the trail and all."

"Oh?" he acknowledges.

"What would you recommend I take on such a trip? I mean, I have some idea, but if I am to plan such a thing, I don't want to go all willy-nilly," I say.

"No, Francis, my first and strongest advice is to not try that adventure like I did." He laughs. "Here, follow me." He grabs another cookie and heads to the basement stairs.

Down in the basement is where some of the sporting and camping gear is kept. Kind of an offshoot to the hardware supplies available on the main floor.

"First, I would take one of these." He hands me a backpack. "And this." Then a sleeping bag. "Oh, and…well, you know what, I'll let you decide. It is your trip and all." He looks back at me as I stand there, a bit overwhelmed. "You were in Scouts, right?"

"Yes, sir. I was in Scouts for a few years," I reply.

"Well, use your knowledge of what they taught you and what you learned in the Marines, and I have no doubt you will know what you will need," he says. "Just let me know what you grab so I can adjust the inventory."

I look over all the supplies, and I grab a cooking set. I leave the sleeping bag as I feel it's a bit bulky and cumbersome. Besides, I'm used to sleeping under the stars with little more than a blanket and the clothes on my back. I do grab an oiled canvas poncho as I discarded the one I was issued in the Marines. Aside from that, I grab some flint and a first-aid kit. After I gave some thought on what I probably need, I figure I have some stuff at home in my seabag. I feel a bit foolish asking, knowing that hiking this trail will not be much different than the patrols we went on. A flashback of being on patrol hit me, but I shook it off.

Back upstairs, I walk over to the counter where Mr. Clark is working on another cookie and say, "These are the things I grabbed. What do I owe you, Mr. Clark?" I ask, feeling much better about this idea.

"Nothing, Francis." He looks at me. "You have helped me out so much over the years. It's yours."

"Oh, Mr. Clark, I couldn't. I mean, I am thankful for sure but…" He raises his hand to me to stop me. I smile. "Thank you. You've meant a lot to me over the years too, and I'll never forget it."

"I made chili last night," Mr. Clark says, changing the subject. "Would you like some? Before I eat this entire plate of cookies…" He laughs.

"That sounds good. Yes, I would like some. Thank you." I look back as I take the backpack and items out to the car, and I think, *Life is good.*

After lunch, we do some odds and ends around the store, and at 2:30 p.m., Mother walks in the store.

"Mary! How are you?" Mr. Clark exclaims.

"Hello, Clark. I am fine. How are you?" she answers. "Keeping him busy, I see." She motions toward me.

"Mary, he is a fine boy and has been a great help," Mr. Clark replies.

She gazes at me with a loving look only given by a mother. I wrap up what I am doing and smile, looking over at her.

"Mr. Clark, is there anything else you need from me?"

"No, Francis, you truly have been a great assistance for me. You take your mother home, and I'll see you tomorrow. Yes?"

"Yes, bright and early. Well, as soon as I drop Mother off at school, that is," I state.

Mother and I climb into the old Saratoga and pull out onto the main road.

"Francis? What is in the back?" Mother says quizzically.

"Oh, remember how you said I should come up here and assist Mr. Clark at the store until I could figure out what I should do now?" I state.

"Yes?" Mother replies.

"Well, Mr. Clark told me about a time where he was in a similar predicament and hitched down to Georgia to hike the Appalachian Trail," I tell her. "He said it was a good period in his life for reflection and recentering himself and understanding his goals in life. I have given it some thought and figured it may serve to do the same for me."

"It is a thought, I suppose," she answers as she stares out at the town passing by.

"You okay?" I ask.

"Yes, it's just…and I don't want to seem selfish. But you just returned home. Don't you think there is a better way to 'find' yourself without leaving again?" she states with concern, just not sure if it was a concern for me or herself.

"*If* I do this, and at this point it is an *if*, I would not head out till it warms up a bit more." I try to sooth her concerns.

"I see" is all she remarks and remains silent the rest of the ride to the house.

The following weeks establish a decent routine for me. Wake, take Mother to school during the week, and help at the store. Every day I ask Mr. Clark questions about his hike and gain knowledge of what to expect and what I should plan for. I think he spends more time laughing at me and my questions than anything. But he does give me some great advice. Letters between Clara and I are sent sporadically. It is hard to know where the ship is or when she might receive my letters. Then there is the time she may have to be able to write back to me, all things I understand. I tell her I am helping out at the hardware store and that I was planning on hiking the Appalachian Trail. She lets me know that she likes both ideas and she hopes that the hike allows me to find a better direction, given my circumstances.

I research bus schedules and acquire a map of the trail for Georgia to start. Mr. Clark does let me know that the trail is well marked with white markers that are steady throughout. He said there would be days where I would see people for miles, other "thru" hikers (those hiking from Georgia to Maine or vice versa), day hikers (just people out for a day hike), and short timers (people who hike short portions of the trail at a time like in pieces). I intend to leave or head out in late March. I figure out how much I should be able to maintain mileage-wise every day and a rough guess of when I should be in Maine. Beginning of March, I tell Mother.

"I have made my decision, Mother," I announce.

"Oh, and what decision is that?" she asks.

"I intend to leave at the end of the month for Georgia to hike the Appalachian Trail," I say with confidence.

"I see" is all she says at first. "Francis, I would be remiss to say that I like this idea of you hiking this trail. But I, too, have been giving it some thought. I cannot imagine anything you have dealt with or anything you may still be dealing with. I have heard you scream out in the middle of the night, I have heard you sobbing, and I know you do not sleep through the night most of the time. I am worried about you. But I also talked to Mr. Clark about this, at first to tell him my disappointment in filling your head with this idea. But… well, I have known Clark for a long time, and after listening to his side of it, I get it. I may not like it, but I understand." She takes a deep breath, and I can see a tear welling up in her eye.

I stand up from Grandfather's old high-back and walk over to her. I give her a hug and kiss her forehead. "Thank you for understanding, Mother" is all I say in response.

* * * * *

Patricia doesn't interrupt this time. She allows me to continue as to this point, I have not killed anyone. She wants to know when I start the actual killing. Despite what I've told her so far, she still has doubts that I'm possessed by a demonic spirit.

Chapter 16

On March 21, 1972, I board a train headed for Chicago, Illinois, where I will change trains and head South to Atlanta, Georgia. From there, I will take a bus to Springer Mountain where the trail starts/ends in Georgia. The trip there is set to take about three to four days. Mother agrees to take me to the train station for the trip to Chicago. She gives me a hug and wishes me safe travels. I hate leaving her so soon after getting home, but I cannot stay. I am afraid of what may transpire if I stay.

On March 27, 1972, I begin my adventure on the Appalachian Trail, as I stand looking up at the stone archway that marks the start—or end, depending on which direction you are headed—to a path that is to lead me on a five-to-six-months excursion. I breathe a deep sigh—one of exasperation, knowing what lies ahead, and one of ease and contentment—as I make that first step up the winding path.

Arriving a few days ago, I took some time to ensure I had all the provisions I might need and maps for the Southern states to begin. In the ranger station, I verified a few last-minute questions I had and, in doing so, was informed of a book they had started where individuals embarking on the "walk of a lifetime" could sign and place their mark on Appalachian Trail history.

I take that first step, just me and about fifty pounds on my back. The beginning is not too bad as I truck along. The elevation begins slowly at first with a few spots where rocks are arranged like steps. I mosey along a creek and come to crossroads of sorts. Ensuring I have the correct path, I venture on till I finally get to the top of this ridge.

THE DEMONIC SAVIOR

The sight looking out when available, of course, is absolutely breathtaking. One item I do not have and feel is a good idea to attain while on this adventure is a hiking stick. As I walk near Justus Creek, I happen upon a healthy shagbark hickory tree. My time in Boy Scouts growing up and the research I conducted before embarking on this adventure has me feeling confident that this would make a good sturdy walking stick. I look around the base of the tree and the general vicinity, and no luck; I cannot find a suitable branch already on the ground. Looking up just outside my reach is the perfect branch, nice and straight, not too many branches coming off of it. I grab a half-hewn log nearby to allow me to climb up and break or cut down the branch. As I grab the branch of choice, I find its diameter fits my hand perfectly; it's like an omen telling me that this is a good decision and that all will work out. Just as the thought crossed my brain, the half-hewn log rolls out from under me. The branch and I fall to the ground with a resounding thud. Luckily no one is around to watch this happen as I would have been a bit embarrassed. Minus being a bit sore from falling on my arse, I pick myself up, brush myself off, and see the branch I desire lying next to me. What luck! I measure out the length I felt fit me best, cut off the remainder, trim the branches of what I intend to use, and strap the stick to my pack.

I get moving onward toward my first overnight stop. About fifteen miles later, I reach the Gooch Mountain Shelter, not much of a shelter, more like a lean two that is half falling over. I make camp for the night as I am used to sleeping under the stars, and though a bit brisk in this early spring, I make do. There are several stumps arranged around the shelter, albeit from various hikers that made camp there over the years. I see a useable firepit and various other odds and ends resting inside the shelter on ledges. I fix myself something to eat and establish bedding, some pine needles and leaves I gather up, then roll out my wool blanket and settle down on a stump. I grab my newly acquired hiking stick and my K bar. My K bar is the one cherished item I was issued during my service. I fell in love with its blackened finish, the grooved leather hilt, and the only identifying feature to signify my service is the *USMC* letters and Marine Corps emblem on the sheathing. I proceed to trim the tips of the branch into uniform ends beveling the edges to help keep the wood from splintering during use. I trim off some bark at the location I want to create a comfortable hold. Knowing I brought along some parachute line, I make a notch around the top edge. I then secure the para line inside the notch and create a looped strap that allows me to rest my wrist as I walk or gives me a way to hang my walking stick when not in use. The last thing I do for the night is notch my initials on the top of the stick. My back is killing me from the hike, the fall, the pack, and the shrapnel I carry with me everywhere as a constant reminder of that fateful day.

The next morning, I set out early. I prefer the early morning air to the warmer afternoons as the heat can cause extra irritation that I care to avoid. Early departure also allows me to maintain the daily goal I have for myself of attempting to average fifteen miles daily. Some may find those goals lofty, but I figure given that I am hiking this alone and can set my own pace, this would be realistic and achievable. Besides, during my time in the Marines, we would hike/run fifteen/twenty miles a day through uncharted (at times) territory loaded with gear. I fail to see where this excursion would be much different, minus twenty-plus pounds of tools and weaponry.

Today is an easier day as I make for Blood Mountain Shelter. About 13.6 miles of average terrain should make for a good day, and I would like time to research and explore the surrounding area as there was once a battle between the Cherokee and Creek Indians fought there, thus the namesake of Blood Mountain. The day passes relatively smoothly. I see very few people, and even if I do, I keep to myself with a nod and friendly hello but constantly moving. Blood Mountain is the highest peak along the trail in Georgia and makes for a hell of a hike. I persevere and reach the summit. The view allows you to see out over the various ridges of mountains. I cannot fathom a more serene connection with nature and Mother Earth than this undertaking I have embarked. After a bit of absorbing the peace, I venture to find the shelter before it gets dark. I make my camp and start a small campfire. I eat my meal and review my maps for the next part of the journey. Before long, a few hikers alight for the night and follow their own routine. We exchange pleasantries and tell each other where we are from. I keep my answers brief as I prefer the solitude, thus excusing myself early for the night and heading to bed.

My early to bed after such a long first day allows me to fall asleep quickly and easily. I drift off into what starts as a nice dream sequence of Clara and Mother sitting at the table back home having a nice conversation and getting along splendidly. Then the scene turns dark as in the door looms a shadowy figure resembling the demon. It floats through the door as if it was not even there, and the women stop what they are conversing about with fear streaked across their faces. The demon grabs Clara by her hair, pulls her head back, and, with its finger, slashes across her throat. Mother moves across the kitchen for a knife out of the knife block to attack or defend herself, and the demon just stares at her and laughs.

"Mortal weapons cannot harm me," it taunts as she slashes at the demon, laying a blow across its abdomen that would slow any man. She speaks not a word, but the expression on her face shows anger and horror as it reaches for her, releasing Clara, whose head slumps forward.

Mother swings again with the knife, this time catching the demon's forearm, and it grabs her knife-wielding hand. It turns its arm to show the cut she just inflicted, and it seals back up as it stares directly at her with the evilest of grins. The demon's grip tightens on her forearm, and she drops the knife as the demon reaches and extracts her eyes as she stands there screaming. I see myself standing in the doorway of the kitchen area, paralyzed and unable to assist my mother and my love. The demon turns toward me and says, "See, Francis, nothing you do will stop me. I am forever and never-ending. I have spent centuries walking this forsaken ground feeding souls to my father."

"They were good people that would never be sent to your hellish kingdom!" I scream back in frustration.

"Oh, but they will, Francis. They will," the demon replies as it pulls the eyes out of Clara, and there holding the eyes in its hands, it rattles of a chant in a language I have never heard before, then places them in a pouch. "You see, the minute I extract their eyes, I steal their souls, and they no longer fall under the same rules as everyone else.

They go where I send them, and their passage to your God's heaven is vanquished. Father will appreciate the extra company in the fiery depths. One day you will join them, once I am through with you."

I wake to drops of water on my head. The start of a light rain. I can hear another hiker staying in the shelter move. I can only assume I may have screamed out and awoken them. Things have been so quiet I have almost forgotten about the demon. I guess the spirits surrounding this mountain that was fought over by the Native Americans must have awoken it from its hiding spot. Or perhaps the demon's proclamation to never go away is revealing itself to me, telling me that I have nowhere to find sanctuary. Regardless of the reason behind the demon's awakening, I realize I cannot stay too close to people. From now on, I will find less-obvious locations to make camp and only use the shelters as markers for which to plan out my travels. It is too early to begin my day as there is hardly any light, so I lay there trying to calm myself and eventually doze back off to sleep—this time, with no thoughts or dreams.

Chapter 17

As unfortunate as the night's events may seem, it brings about something unexpected. There by my bedding as I open my eyes, barely protruding from the ground, is what appears to be a sharp-edged rock. I extrude it from the soil's firm grip, and yes, yes, it is an arrowhead. I learned a bit about this growing up: The Cherokee, who were indigenous to this region, would use deer antler and a stone hammer to chip the flint, creating the arrowhead I now hold in my palm. Feeling proud of my find, I take my souvenir and place it in a pouch on my backpack. I load up the rest of my gear and head out. As I venture on to my next destination, Low Gap Shelter, I stray off the path to experience the battlefield. I cannot let the demon win; I must keep going through life as if it only exists in my dreams. To allow for anything more would... I shudder at the thought of what allowing the demon to take a firm hold of could produce.

The battlefield proves to not be anything of real relevance. Someone had installed a placard to denote the location and significance of the events that transpired. According to history, the Cherokee held Blood Mountain as a resting place or home of the immortals, a race of Spirit People that resided in the highlands the Cherokee called home. Reading the posted sign makes me think of the Greeks and Mount Olympus where Greek mythology has written it as home to their gods. Odd how different cultures thousands of miles apart share similar ideals and folklore. It is almost as if we are all connected in one way or another. There was nothing to denote the reason that the Creek Tribe entered into a bloody battle with the

Cherokee over this land. But it could have stemmed from the same reasons any separate factions wage war over anything. The human race is very territorial, and nothing will ever change that, I am afraid.

I tarry on to Low Gap and make my camp about a half mile past the shelter. Next stop is around Steel Trap Gap and just past Plum Orchard Gap Shelter, thereafter a place called AS Knob on the map. By the first of April, I cross the state line of Georgia into North Carolina. I take refuge at Standing Indian Shelter this night and luckily end up being the only hiker there. The next day, I stray off the main trail about a quarter mile and make camp along a little stream called Long Branch. Now here, I place myself in a very strange predicament as I stumble onto a distillery. It is clearly not in service as this would have been the wrong time of the year for moonshiners to be practicing their craft. However, the site is not empty. A very stringy, gangly older man steps out from behind a tree with shotgun in hand.

"You best clear outta here," the moonshiner states with the click of the firing pin being pulled back on the double barrel.

I raise my hands. "Ah…I'm sorry, sir. I was just hiking the trail and followed this trail alongside this creek. The still looked abandoned, so I made camp figuring this was a relatively safe spot," I say.

"Well, it ain't safe, and I'm gonna give you to the count of 3 to move on or be holier than Jesus himself," the old moonshiner counters.

"I must say that sounds like a pretty fair choice. I'll just be on my way then," I answer.

At that moment, the demon starts.

"His gun is not loaded, and the safety is on," the demon says. "He is just an old man. You can easily take him."

As I start packing things up, I ask the man, "You live out here alone?"

"That's not your concern," he replies.

I continue to pack and test the man's fortitude, believing what the demon said.

"Well, I agree it is not. But if you are alone, I know how lonely that can be and was thinking we might be able to help each other out," I say, still loading things in my backpack, stalling for time.

"What help could you give me? I don't need anything," the old moonshiner replies.

"How about some company? I just returned from Nam, and I know what it's like to be alone. Sometimes it's nice to have someone to talk to," I say.

The old moonshiner lowers his shotgun to his hip but has it still trained on me. At this point, I know if the demon is wrong and that gun is loaded, there is no way this old man can hit me before the kick of that gun knocks him on his arse.

"You know, I haven't talked to anyone but myself for a few months…" He pauses. "Do you have any peaches?"

The question throws me off so much I have to think.

"Well, do ya?" he asks again, the shotgun in his hands starting to go back up.

"Yes, I think I do have a can of peaches," I finally reply.

"I got a rabbit I just finished skinning. I'll share some of the rabbit with ya, and you can give me that can of peaches," he states flatly.

Now things like a can of peaches are a commodity on the trail. It's an easy bargaining tool should you need something of importance. But it is heavy to lug around, and seeing as how this man aims to shoot me, I think it is a fair time to bargain. "Sounds like a fair deal to me," I say.

He leads the way through the woods in a way that amazes me since there is no discernable trail, and he walks so softly you don't hear a sound. He stealthily misses every stick on the ground and not one leaf rustles. Not more than fifty yards from the stream is this little shack nestled against the hillside. There's moss on the roof, and the age of the wood helps camouflage it into the surroundings. One could have stood right on top of it and never know it's there. It is just big enough for this old-timer and a few provisions.

"Lived here most of my adult life," he says. "The only visitors I get are my brother or nephew who bring me things I may need. But I don't need much."

"I appreciate you letting me join you," I say.

"You were right. I don't talk to too many people, and after you said you just returned from Nam and out hiking the trail, I figured you were safe. Besides, the gun's not even loaded. I used my last shell shooting that rabbit," he tells me.

I don't know if I should feel sorry for him or praise him. I hadn't had meat in some time, nor anything actually cooked. Here I see he has the rabbit spit over a campfire that is nearly undetectable as the trees overhead disperse any smoke. I would say I am not the cleanest of guests since I haven't showered in almost a week, but given the way this guy looked, I'd say that won't be a concern. He is pretty crusty and looks rather unkept.

"So where are you from?" he asks.

"Iowa," I reply. "Little town outside Dubuque."

"I've only known two places: just down the hill there where I grew up and France," he tells me.

"France? That's a hell of trip for a gentleman of your stature." I try not to be disrespectful.

"World War II. I was drafted by the Army, and they felt I was small enough to ride in the tanks. D-Day we rode in on one of the last landings. The beach was just littered with bodies. I felt bad because there wasn't anywhere for us to drive the tank except over the dead. It felt disrespectful. But it was that or drown in that steel coffin," he tells me the story of his time in service.

"My father died at Saipan. He was a Marine," I tell him.

"Gruesome thing war is," he says. "You said you just returned from Vietnam?"

"Yeah, I was a 'tunnel rat' attached to the Seventh Marine Battalion. Got hurt and ended up being sent home early," I explain.

"I have something for ya." He disappears into the shack. Afraid he might return with a loaded gun this time, I brace for the worst. Instead, he has an old mason jar.

"To your service, young man." He takes a deep swig and hands me the open jar.

I give it a quick sniff; it smells of peaches. I take a swig, and to my surprise, it tastes just like peach cobbler, just with a kick. "Phew! That's good stuff. Thanks," I say in that half-winded tone only derived from a swig of good moonshine.

"That's my grandpappy's recipe. Guaranteed to grow some hair on ya, that's fo' sure," he says as he takes another long draw, damn near finishing off the jar. "That rabbit is about ready. You said you had peaches?"

For an old guy, he doesn't miss a beat. I reach into my bag and produce the can of peaches I have. He grins from ear to ear; never seen a man so happy over a can of peaches.

"These were 'gold' during the war. After we landed on the beaches for D-Day, unit was assigned to the back. Somehow they forgot about us, and we never got called up to the front. After the Army sent me home, I found my grandpappy's recipe, and my brother and I went into business together. I stay up here away from people, and he brings me what I need to make more shine. One day we might teach his son, my nephew, but we aren't ready to give up the family business just yet." He goes on, telling me his life story, and I sit there listening while eating the rabbit he prepared.

"Ever thought of going legit?" I ask.

"Too strong for Uncle Sam and his damn regulations. Besides, screw those bastards in Washington, always taking our money to throw it away. They've taken enough from me. I'm not giving them anything else." Clearly, his views on politics are shining through. At that, I let it go. Best not overstay my welcome.

The night passes, and we talk half of it away. I fall asleep by the fire, my back resting against a tree. Reminds me of my time in Nam.

The demon hits me again in the middle of the night. "Francis, OH, Francis," he chimes in a taunting tone. "Why haven't you killed him yet, Francis?" Now he's more demanding.

"I can't," I reply. "He was nice to me. He is just an old man," I reply.

"Oh, Francis, when will you learn?" And the demon stops. He doesn't say another word the rest of the night.

In the morning, I wake up, and I grab my things. I knock on the shack, but there is no answer. Poor guy is probably passed out from all the shine we drank last night. I head out and up to the trail to resume my journey.

Chapter 18

I make my way to Licklog Gap; the next day, I make camp along the Nantahala River. Here I decide to spend an extra day relaxing, and I bath in the cool waters. It is on the second day that I see her. As I am lounging in the cooling waters and trying to relax the ache in my back and feet, I see this beautiful blond hiking past. She has flowing glowing locks with strands of red that make her hair look like they are on fire. She just stares and smiles. I am so taken by her that I don't even see her companion standing next to her giggling as she stares and smiles. Then reality hits me, and I realize why her friend is giggling like a schoolgirl. I am naked in the water, and my clothes are hanging to air out on a nearby tree. The water is so clear and cold, and yep, not my most modest moment. I immediately cover myself with my hand and say, "I'm sorry. I hadn't seen anyone in so long I didn't think I would."

She just replies, "You're fine. It's a nice day for a swim."

"Looks to me like the water is a little chilly," her friend states.

"Yeah, it is a bit cold but refreshing," I say as I blush but try to maintain my composure.

I step out of the stream while they stand there watching, and I dry off as best as I can with my back turned to them and get dressed.

The beautiful blond semigasps and asks, "What happened to you?"

I don't think of what she is referring to and ask, "What do you mean?"

"You're covered in scars," she remarks with concern.

"Oh, yeah, I was injured in Vietnam," I explain. By this point, her friend has controlled herself and calmed down. I've dressed and realize they have walked down toward my campsite.

"I'm Melody," the blond says, extending her hand. "And this is Judy." She points to her friend.

"Francis" is all I can muster as she is more beautiful the closer she came. She is wearing a pair of khaki shorts and a half-buttoned plaid flannel shirt with what appears to be a white tank top underneath and clearly no bra. Her eyes glisten from the sun's reflection off the water and just setting her emerald green eyes ablaze.

"Which way are you headed, Francis? I assume you are hiking the trail like us," Melody says.

"I am," I reply. I can barely speak. It is like I have a ball of dough stuck in my throat keeping words from escaping. "I am headed to Maine."

"Ah, so a northbound thru-hiker like us," Melody exclaims with a tinge of excitement.

"Uh…" I stumble. "I guess so."

"Would you like to join us?" she asks as Judy mutters, "Melody, no," under her breath.

"It'll be fine, Judy, hush," remarks Melody, not caring if I heard or not.

"I don't want to be a burden. I kind of have a planned-out trek," I start.

"Oh, you won't burden us," Melody says without missing a beat. "If anything, we might be holding you up, unless you don't mind?"

"You know what," I say after thinking for a bit, "a little company wouldn't be such a bad thing."

"Then it's settled," Melody says with a huge smile across her ruby lips.

"Great," half-hearted Judy replies.

"Well, after watching you in the water, I'm half tempted to freshen up a bit myself," says Melody as she swings out of her backpack and starts to undress.

"Really, Melody?" says Judy.

"Don't be uptight, Judy," replies Melody, who is clearly the more carefree of the two.

Melody runs off stark naked into the river. I grab a piece of fruit I picked off an apple tree I stumbled across on the trail and sit. Judy sighs, removes her pack, and sits a little bit from me.

"She is impossible," Judy says after a bit.

I just sit in silence. I can clearly tell Judy is not happy with my presence or that Melody asked for me to join them.

"We take the semester off from the University of Georgia to do this. I was hoping it would mellow her out a bit, but I guess I was wrong," Judy tells me.

"University of Georgia, huh. Good school," I say. "What year and majors are you?"

"I'm a junior majoring in psychology. Melody is a sophomore and still undecided. I talked her into this trip to help pull her head out of the clouds and hopefully help center her. Lotta good it's doing," Judy explains.

"You got time. The trail is still young," I say with hope.

"We are together, you know," Judy states bluntly.

"You're what?" I ask, half choking on the bite of apple I had in my mouth.

"Together. Like in a relationship. Melody and I are a couple," Judy explains.

"Oh, I see. Okay," I say with little care.

"I just thought you should know that there is no chance of anything 'happening' here," she states.

"Never crossed my mind," I reply.

Judy gives me this side-eye that I felt burn through me. But despite the attraction I have for Melody, my heart is still with Clara. I have other problems I need to address. Involving two women that have nothing to do with my issues is not my plan.

"Maybe I should get going then and let you two have your space," I offer.

"Oh god. No. If you leave now, Melody would just blame me, and I'd have to listen to her accusations for the next five miles," Judy says half pleadingly. "This conversation never happened, and it would be in your best interest to not mention anything of it to Melody."

I drop it and lay back.

"Come join me!" Melody calls up from the river to Judy. Judy undresses. "Do you mind watching our things?" she asks.

"Nope. Your things are safe with me," I answer. Off down the hill Judy heads to join her partner.

Judy is not that bad on the eyes either as I watch her saunter down to the river. Dark hair, little portly but not fat. She has a decently rounded backside though as I watch it bounce back and forth with each step. I lay back against my pack, cross my fingers across my chest, and watch them "play" in the river. A few hikers pass by and pause, but I just glance their way and they move on.

Time passes when I hear "Hey, sleepyhead, time to wake up." It's Melody standing over me, nudging me with her foot still naked and dripping wet. Judy is drying off and getting dressed.

"Sorry, must have dozed off," I say, shaking the sleep off. We decide to make camp as moving on from here would put us at the next shelter after dark. The girls set up a tent that they split parts of between them. After creating a meal from our provisions, we spend the night getting to know each other and sharing stories long after the sun sets.

In the morning, I rise ahead of them and am tempted to just take off. But as I am about to do just that, Judy pokes her head out of their tent.

"Good morning," she says in a much better mood than she was yesterday.

"Morning," I reply. "I'm making some coffee if you are interested."

"Coffee? We haven't had coffee since we hit the trail," Judy says. She finishes getting out of their tent and stretching while the coffee I hastily threw together is finishing.

"It's hot, careful," I say as I hand her the pot.

"This is good. Where'd you get the pot?" she asks. About this time, we hear movement inside the tent, and Melody emerges.

"An old friend of mine that suggested this trip to me lent me his. At first, I felt it would be too much to lug around, but I found a good way to pack everything and it doesn't take up too much room," I explain.

"I noticed you don't have a tent," Judy states.

"Yeah, chalk that up to my time in Nam on patrol. I learned to live without a lot of luxuries," I reply.

"Is that coffee?" Melody asks as she wakes up.

"It sure is. Francis has a coffeepot," Judy states with some admiration in her voice. Guess she is warming up to the idea of having me around. They both smile at me like I'm some form of savior. I give in and figure having company isn't such a bad thing. I kind of missed human contact.

We pack up the camp and get ready to head out.

"Usually try to get about fifteen miles in a day," I say to the girls. "Brown Fork Gap Shelter is about that. I thought we could make that our next overnight spot."

"I think that is reasonable," Judy says, a bit to my surprise. "Melody?"

"That's a long way. I don't know," Melody says.

"We will go at your pace. Right, Francis?" says Judy to reassure Melody.

"Yeah. We have plenty of time to make it," I say as reassuringly as possible.

I am starting to see the dynamic between these two. Clearly Judy is the stronger-willed one and more up for this adventure. While Melody is more of a flirtatious party type and is only doing it because Judy sort of talked her into it.

"I think we can make Cheoah Bald Summit by lunch, and from there, it should be mostly downhill to the shelter," I say to give Melody a bit of encouragement.

"Okay, off we go!" says Melody, full of excitement as she slings her green pack with the initials *MJ* embroidered on the flap on her back. Must have been the coffee kicking in.

We move along and head for Cheoah Bald Summit. Along the trail, we make the usual stops for bathroom breaks and to rest after especially steep, rough areas. The girls sing at various times. We decide Melody should lead and I would take up the rear, kind of like an anchor of sorts for our little group. A little after twelve, we crest the summit. Not quite the pace I was keeping on my own as it takes us five hours to get up here, but if the rest is mostly downhill and less rugged, we can camp by sundown. We eat a quick lunch. One thing I have learned about being on the trail is, plan your meals out in small quick portions. It's easier to eat small and quick than to prep a larger, more "normal" meal. Luckily the girls have learned this too, and aside from enjoying the view, we are on our way again. Fifteen minutes later and we are on our way. This is doable, and I start to relax some in my new arrangement. Just as planned, we reach the shelter with thirty minutes to spare before the sun dips below the trees too much, and combining our available supplies, we work together to make a decent meal. Only one other camper enters the area for the night, and we all share the shelter as there is plenty of room. In the morning, I make coffee again for all to enjoy, and we discuss the day's plan.

"It looks like we are about twelve miles or so from the Fontana Dam," I say.

"That sounds more reasonable," Melody remarks. Clearly by her tone, the coffee hasn't kicked in yet.

Judy and I share a gaze and chuckle. Off we go, and today is not much different from yesterday. We pause for nature's call, the girls sing, and I take up the rear as we trudge along. When we get close to Fontana Dam, another hiker tells of a little motel off Route 129 that is accommodating to hikers and that there is a little country store not too far off to collect supplies. The girls light up as we all would like a nice hot shower and each of us are low on supplies.

We find the hotel, and they have two rooms available. The girls go off to theirs, and I take mine. They offer for me to share their room, but I decline. I need a break of my own. The motel has a small diner next to it, and we meet for dinner. A nice hot cooked meal is a great way to fill the belly and relax a bit. After the past few weeks on the trail, I take a nice long hot shower and settle into my bed. I review the maps of the trail and figure out what would be more feasible for the girls given that they hold a slower pace than I do. I then settle down to read a book I keep in my gear as a way to relax and pass time. It doesn't take long before I fall into a deep, sound sleep. The bed at the motel isn't the best I have slept on, but it sure beats the ground.

I preset Mother to send me some "care packages" with needed supplies. In the morning, I grab my much-needed-to-be-cleaned laundry and head toward the post office nearby. The manager at the motel mentioned there to be a laundromat next to it. I start a load of laundry and venture into the post office. I give them my name, and they retrieve my care package. By this point, my load is ready to be shifted over to the dryer, and I notice a pay phone out front. I figured I would call home to Mother and let her know I received the package and give her updates on how things are going.

"You have a collect call from…Francis," the operator says when my mother answers the phone back home. "Will you accept?"

"Yes," she responds. "Francis?"

"Hello, Mother," I speak. "I received the care package. Thank you."

"Oh, good," she says. "Are you okay?"

"Yes, Mother. Things are going well," I reply.

"I am a bit worried. There was a news report of a man found murdered at the beginning of the month. It was a place called 'Long Branch,' I think. They said whoever did it took the man's eyes," she says.

At this point, I myself become alarmed. But I do not want to show Mother my own concern.

"No, Mother, I am fine. I met this group of young women a couple of days ago, and we agreed to travel together," I tell her, trying to change the subject and reduce her concern.

"Oh, good," she says. "I am glad you've made some friends and are not traveling alone. Are they cute?"

"Mother!" I exclaim. "We are just friends. Besides, they seem to be a couple."

"Oh." I can hear the disappointment in her voice. But I do my best to ignore it and move the conversation along.

"The next time I call will a bit from now as I probably won't get a chance before I hit Hot Springs, North Carolina, in about ten days. So please send the next package a day or two before that in case I make good time," I tell her.

"I will, Francis. I miss you. Please be safe. Mr. Clark was asking about you too," she says.

"Tell Mr. Clark I am doing well. Please do not worry about me, Mother. I am very capable, I assure you," I say reassuringly. "I don't want to run up your phone bill. I am going to let you go, and I will call from Hot Springs, I promise."

"Okay. Francis. I love you. I'll talk to you in a few days," she says as she hangs up.

A murdered man in the same area I was just in a few days ago. It cannot be related. I go and grab my care package and laundry when it finishes. I head back to the room to see how the girls are making out.

Back at the motel, I find both of them sitting outside their room drinking what appears to be iced tea.

"There is a post office and laundromat about a mile down the road," I tell them. "There is also a pay phone at the laundromat if you have anyone you need to call."

"Thank God. My clothes reek. I can't wait to get them fresh again," Melody remarks.

Judy lets out a half-hearted laugh. "Welcome to life on the trail, my dear." It's the first time I have heard either say anything endearing to the other.

"I am going to put my things away. Maybe we can get some lunch afterward?" I offer.

"I think we are going to head down to do some laundry," replies Judy. "We can catch you for dinner, if that's okay."

"Sure," I say. And I head into my room.

I fold all my garments back in the best space-saving way I know. As I am cleaning out the other items in my pack and releasing all the accumulated pine needles, leaves, and dirt, I reach the bottom to find a small mason jar with a set of eyes inside. Fear, shock, and disbelief strike my face, and if someone was watching me, they would see all the blood drain from me. I run to the bathroom and vomit in the toilet. The man, the moonshiner I met, I killed him. No. No, I didn't kill him. I couldn't have. I do not remember anything from that night after we passed out… That's it! I blacked out. "Oh, shit!" I say out loud. The demon used me to kill a man. The realization hits me like a ton of bricks. I sit on the edge of the bed, and reality takes over. I sit there and weep with my face in my hands.

Chapter 19

After I pull myself together, I realize that I have to remove myself from people in general. I decide that dinner tonight will be the last time I see the girls. I won't say anything to them. I'll just leave early tomorrow, with no explanation. I go to the general store a half mile away, gather some provisions I did not anticipate, and head back to the room to finish packing. I also stop in the motel office and settle my bill so that I can just head out in the morning after dropping my key.

The girls return a few hours later, and I clean myself up so as to not reveal anything. We partake in dinner together and have a few beers before we call it a night. The next morning, I wake up very early around 4:00 a.m., and I head out. They say it is always darkest before the dawn; there is a lot of truth to that as it is pitch-black out here. By the time I find the trail again, the sun has started its ascent, and I can see well enough so as to not break an ankle.

I easily get back into my old pace, and with walking stick in hand, I add some haste to my steps. Before long, I am well out of range of Fontana. I push myself to Rocky Top just between the Spence Field Shelter and Thunderhead Mountain. Interesting fact is that today as I pass Doe Knob, I am now straddling two states. To my right is North Carolina and to my left is Tennessee, but the trail does not distinguish state lines per se as hikers normally cross over and usually don't even realize the difference. Eighteen miles in one day puts a toll on my back especially with a now very full pack. But I want to ensure the girls could not catch up to me. I feel bad not leaving even a note, but I see no other option. If I stay with them, I have no idea what could happen to them because of me or what the demon might make me do. No, this is the best way.

No one else is camping near me, and I am far enough away from any shelters that I feel more at ease. I dig deep into my pack and retrieve the jar. I go away, off the trail, dig a deep hole the depth of my trench shovel, and bury the jar. Hopefully, it is far enough down that no scavengers will dig it up and no passersby will find it. The next morning, I head back out, putting what has happened behind me, or so I hope.

Tomorrow I will reach Clingman's Dome, the highest point along the trail and, according to this map, the highest elevation in the state of Tennessee at 6,643 feet above sea level. I intend to push just a bit past that to Collins Gap as I want to increase my distance. An uneventful night should allow me to rise nice and early and maintain my lead, thus enabling me to pick my campsite and avoid other hikers. The last thing I want is to give this demon any hold on me.

However, the night is not peaceful.

"Why did you do it, Francis?" speaks the demon without me being asleep for a change.

"Excuse me?" I say as if I am talking to myself now, but I know this voice all too well. "What did I do?"

"You buried his eyes, Francis" says the demon with a vengeful tone.

"I cannot get caught with those," I reply frankly. "If I get caught with those, I go to jail, and you do not get what you want." I say this as if it will save me from his torment.

"If you get caught, Francis, I'll just find another weak body to inhabit and continue my mission. When will you realize that you cannot stop me?" the demon inquires.

"As much as I realize I may not be able to stop you completely, which is painfully obvious in what you did while I was unconscious, it doesn't prevent me from doing all I can to slow you down," I reply.

"You! Hahaha!" The demon is laughing at me. "You of all people think you can stop me, do you?"

I sigh long and deep. "As futile as the idea may seem, I have to try," I speak softly, trying to maintain my composure. I am hoping by keeping levelheaded or as level as I possibly can, I can deter the demon until I can find a good solution. So far, that seems to be working. If nothing else, it seems to sound good at this point. I can only pray that the Lord will save me from this evil.

The voice of the demon finally stops, and I am able to get a small bite to eat before falling off to sleep. Luckily for me, my sleep is restful enough that I wake early and feel ready to take on the day. Maybe by pushing myself, I am able to be too weary for the demon to interact or disrupt my sleep. That may be a good tactic for the future. I will see how that works. For now, I have another long day ahead of me. I break camp and head for Clingman's Dome.

Five days later, I walk into Hot Springs, North Carolina. I am completely exhausted and realize I cannot keep this up. The only good thing is, the demon has not said one word since Collins Gap where I buried the eyes of the man I killed. I find a quiet motel and check in. The hot shower is invigorating, and I feel alive again. I pass out in my room after a hot meal and sleep the soundest sleep I think I have ever slept, and for once, I had the best dream since leaving home. I dream of Clara and I holding each other in a natural hot spring. Such a nice peaceful dream, one that I could not wait till I could make it a reality.

After getting breakfast, I head to the post office. The post office is not open. I realize that it is Sunday and I am a day early. After pushing so hard, I figure the extra day of rest would be good. I continue the same routine I followed back at Fontana Lake: laundry, reading, provision acquisition. The next day, Monday, I go back to the post office, and to my relief, my package is there. Given the time, I would have to wait till later to call Mother as she would be in school at this hour. I take the opportunity to explore the town a bit and read some more. That evening after dinner, I call Mother from my motel room.

"You have a collect call from…Francis," the operator says when my mother answers the phone back home. "Will you accept?"

"Yes," she responds. "Francis?"

"Hello, Mother," I speak. "How have you been?"

"I am good. Things are not much different," she tells me. "Mr. Clark stopped to check on me yesterday after church. He asked about you."

"Please tell him this has been the best thing for me so far. That things are going well and the fresh air is doing me a lot of good," I respond. "Excuse me, Mother." I set the phone down as I hear the sound of female voices bickering outside my room. I peek out, and it's them, Melody and Judy. How the hell did they get here so fast? I know I outdistanced them.

"Sorry about that," I say as I pick up the receiver and speak softer.

"Is everything alright?" she asks.

"Oh yes, everything is fine. Just some teenagers outside my room carrying on is all." Not a complete lie, but not the truth either.

"Did the package arrive?" she asks.

"Yes, it did. Thank you," I say. "I intend to be in Hampton, Tennessee, which is my next stop in about eight days, so you can plan for the next care package. It's getting late, and I have an early start again tomorrow, Mother, so I am going to let you go."

"Okay, Francis. Be safe, and I love you."

"I will, Mother. I love you too."

I hang up and peek out the window. They're gone, which is a relief. I guess the extra day worked against me. Another hard push and I should be able to fix that. Early the next morning, I head out again, fully refreshed and ready to hit it hard.

Eight days later, I arrive in Hampton, Tennessee. The care package arrives, and I get to call home to Mother. Damascus, Virginia, to follow, which is a long forty-day excursion to Harpers Ferry, the halfway point of the Appalachian Trail. About ten days in, I reach the iconic McAfee Knob Trailhead, a beautiful granite rock jutting out over the scenic valley. This is the type of place a person can feel closest to the heavens without actually going. You can see for miles all the majestic ridges and valleys. I force myself to push through the Shenandoah Valley. I pause only for care packages, but nothing like in the past. Just an overnight here and there to refresh and get back on the trail. In Harpers Ferry, I intend to spend an extra day seeing the historical aspects, as well as check in at the AT Headquarters and then back at it. After attaining my motel room, I settle in for the night. The next morning, I head to the post office to receive the care package. This is a special package as I set aside some cash that is coming in this one, and given how low on cash I'm running, it will be much appreciated.

With laundry complete, some sightseeing accomplished, and a full belly, I get back to the room to go through the care package and call Mother. I open the package, and sitting right on top is a letter from Clara. Mother must have slid it in before sending it. My heart leaps a bit as I have not spoken or written to Clara in so long.

My dearest Francis,

I hope this finds you well. I have some fortunate and unfortunate news to tell you. I will be released from my service obligations in the next month. After which I will be going to live in Hawaii with my new husband. We met just a few weeks ago. He is a doctor that was assigned here and, well, things have been such a whirlwind. I truly don't know what to say. As much as I have left space for you in my heart, I have love for him too. I know this may come as a huge shock. I am sorry. I wish you the best, my dear Francis. I know somewhere out there is your true love.

Clara

My heart sinks so far, it feels like I have a massive pit in my gut. Tears start to roll down my cheeks as I realize the one woman I thought actually understood me is now gone. I feel lost and destroyed. I spend the next hour sobbing.

"Stop your sobbing, you big baby. I told you she didn't love you. I told you nobody will EVER love you," the demon remarks.

"Fuck you!" I say through sobs. "Why don't you go to hell, where you belong?"

"Been there, done that. Been kicked out till I fill my duty," the demon says mockingly. "That's where you come in, Francis. ONLY YOU can send me back to hell. Help me fulfill my destiny, and I can leave you. You can live in peace. Just let me be free."

This last part makes me realize I have been keeping the demon at bay. But if that is so and the rest of what he says is true…maybe *if* I let go and let him have his way, he will finally leave me in peace.

Chapter 20

I assess my supply situation and pull myself together. I make the decision to call an old buddy from the unit. I still have to call Mother too. First, I call Mother. I think it's a Saturday... I have no idea anymore.

The operator comes back, "I'm sorry, sir, there is no answer. You'll have to try again another time."

"Okay, thank you," I say. "Umm...quick question, what day is it?" I ask.

"Thursday, sir," the operator replies.

"That explains it. Thank you. Have a nice day," I respond.

"You too." And the line goes dead.

I cannot call my buddy collect. So I swing into the motel's front office.

"Is it possible to make a long-distance call from my room?" I ask the tenant.

"Which room?" he replies.

"Room 108," I say.

"Yeah, it'll be attached to your bill though. Just dial *9*, wait for the tone, then the number," the tenant replies.

"That's fine. Thank you." I leave and head back to my room.

I press *9*, then punch *1-709-555-9867* into the phone.

"Hello," a voice says on the other side.

"Hi. This is Francis Fleming. I am looking for Mr. Nate—" I start to say but am cut off.

"Francis! How the hell are you?" Nate says on the other line.

"Hi, Nate. I've been better, and I've been worse," I say. "You still live in New Jersey? Sorry, guess I didn't think that through." I realized that if Nate wasn't in New Jersey, he wouldn't have answered his own phone number.

"All good. So what have you been up to?" Nate asks.

"To be honest, I am hiking the Appalachian Trail. Currently I am in Harpers Ferry about halfway through," I tell him. "What about you?"

"I applied for Princeton. I start in the fall," he says.

"Princeton! Really? I never took you for being that smart. What are you planning to study?" I ask.

"I was thinking about law," he says.

"Holy crap! That's great, man. I'm happy for you. Look, there was another reason I called. It so happens I'll be passing through the Delaware Water Gap in about two weeks. I remember you talking about it, and I was wondering if you might like to catch up?" I ask him.

"Two weeks, yeah, I can do that. I know a place where we can have a bite to eat near there. How does that sound?" Nate suggests.

"Sounds good to me," I say. "I'll let you go for now, and we can catch up over a meal in two weeks."

"See you then. Be safe." Nate hangs up, and I check the clock. At least another hour before Mother will be home for me to call. I lay down to take a nap and try to forget the events of the day and think about meeting up with Nate in two weeks.

Sleep came, and I wake up three hours later. Crazy. Luckily, it is still early enough to call Mother, so I just dial; no collect this time.

"Hello." Her voice sounds a bit weak on the line.

"Hi, Mother," I reply.

"Francis! You didn't call collect?" she asks.

"No, I'm having it charged to the room, so I don't want to be too long," I tell her. "Wanted to let you know I received the care package."

"Oh, good. Did you see the letter from Clara?" she asks.

"Yes, I read it," I tell her, trying to hold back the contents.

"I feel like you are not telling me something," Mother states.

"It wasn't a good letter. If you don't mind, I'd like to leave it at that," I say.

"I see. Okay, Francis," she says in an understanding tone.

"How are things with you?" I ask to change the topic.

"Things are normal. Nothing too exciting, really. Looking forward to the school year to be over. I can't tell if these kids are just getting ornerier or if I am just getting old," she says it in a way as to lighten the mood.

"Probably a little of both, Mother," I say to make her feel a little better and to not say she is getting old.

"Yes, I suppose you are right, Francis," she agrees. "I don't want to run up your bill. I'm going to let you go, and I will talk to you in a few weeks, right?"

"Yes, I should reach the Delaware Water Gap in about fifteen days," I confirm.

"You get some rest. I know you are making good progress. I'll talk to you then."

"Yes, Mother. Talk to you then. Love you. Goodbye."

"Goodbye, dear." And she hangs up.

The pangs of hunger attack me, and I go find some food. I go to a bar that I hear serves good burgers down the road. After today, a burger and beer or two sound just about right. Off I go and find this little hole in the wall pub that serves burgers and fries. I sit down at the bar, and the bartender slides over.

"What can I get ya?" he says.

"What's the best burger in the house and the coldest beer?"

"Well, all the beer is ice-cold, and for a burger, I suggest the bacon and cheeseburger," the bartender replies.

"Sounds great. Thank you," I answer and run my hands over my face to wipe away any semblance of exhaustion.

The bartender brings me an ice-cold beer and says, "That good, huh?"

"Ah, I'm just tired, I guess," I say to talk but not talk. "Been hiking the trail and received a letter from a girl…" Before I could finish, the bartender cuts me off.

"No need to explain. I think we have all been there. Listen, I truly am sorry. That one's on the house." He points to the beer he set in front of me.

"Really? Gee. Thanks," I answer with a smile and raise the glass. Damn did that beer taste good passing my lips. It's strange how a trip that's supposed to provide me answers and keep me away from the crazy in this world has done nothing but create new problems and bring me closer to the world.

The burger is just as good as the beer. Though I have stopped several times along the way, this particular meal and libations are especially good. I think that when people experience disheartening news or unfortunate events in life, the little things, like this burger and this beer, taste better. Like your senses are heightened in a way that makes things seem more enjoyable.

After finishing, I head back to my room at the motel and fall right asleep. Tomorrow I embark on the last half of this excursion, driven more than ever to not only finish but to find the answer I need to relieve myself of my inner demon.

* * * * *

"Wait," Patricia says. "You know Nathan Bedford?" Patricia is finally putting two and two together.

"Yes, the same Nathan Bedford I served with in Vietnam and the one I called and arranged to meet while I was hiking the trail," I confirm.

"When did you last talk to Nathan?" she asks.

"Well, that's the next part when I meet up with him when I was around the Delaware Water Gap," I say. "Can't say I've spoken to him since. Why do you ask?"

"Because I have met Nathan Bedford. He is now Special Agent Nathan Bedford, if it is the same guy. But I have a feeling it is. If I am right, he already knows about you, and I suspect they will figure out where you are soon enough," she says now more confidently.

"Until he shows up, would you care to hear the rest of the story?" I ask.

"Why not? The end for you is near anyway," she says.

Chapter 21

The next morning, I set out. The air is light and crisp despite being the height of summer. I move along at a good pace as I have a plan to make the Delaware Water Gap in fourteen days. My trek goes smoothly, and a day out in a place called Wind Gap, Pennsylvania, I find a place to stay the night, knock out some laundry, and call Nate to confirm our plans for tomorrow.

"Nate? It's Francis. I made it to Wind Gap, Pennsylvania, and just wanted to confirm our plans for tomorrow. Unfortunately, I am calling from a pay phone, but I expect to be in around noon. If you're still on, I'll look for you in the parking lot," I say to a machine as Nate isn't home.

The next day, I start out and things go just as planned. I reach the Gap around noon just as I had intended. I venture to the main parking lot, and there standing next to a beautiful 1972 Mustang Mach 1 is Nate Bedford smoking a Marlboro Red and looking just as cool as a cucumber. Not surprising he would drive such a car; always a little bit of a show-off.

"Nate!" I call out. "Look at you all grown up."

"Francis, you sum bitch. You look like hell warmed over." He laughs at me.

Despite how annoying Nate may have seemed at the time to Mike and I, he truly is a good guy. That day in the cave, he was there before Mike, and he didn't freak out. The entire walk to the helo, Nate was there. As I was about to be lifted out, I remember him saying, "Don't you worry, Francis. They'll get you patched up. You look me up any time, buddy." It's odd how things manage to work out. At the time, I don't think I had any intention of looking him up. But luckily I remembered to bring his number with me, and well...right now, I need a friend.

"Let me tell ya, Nate, that trail is no f———n joke. Ups and downs, rock after rock, I'd almost say it's worse than that damn jungle in Nam," I tell him.

He just laughs at me. "When's the last time you had a good meal and beer?"

"The day I called you," I reply.

"Damn, man, you're overdue." He reaches into the trunk of the 'Stang and hands me an ice-cold Budweiser. "Here you go."

I don't even have my pack off yet. I crack the top and chug that beer down like it's water. It brings back some fine memories, and some not so fine.

"Okay, you have to tell me. What the hell made you want to hike the Appalachian Trail?" he asks, lighting another smoke.

"Nate, it's not an easy story to tell, to be honest," I start. "But here it goes..." I tell him what I felt when the body in that village brushed against me. I tell him about what really happened in that cave. I tell him about the nightmares I had recently. I tell him about Clara and the letter. The only thing I don't tell him is about the old moonshiner on the trail and that I keep the demon possession to a minimum. "And since getting back, I haven't a clue what to do with my life. I have a degree in engineering, and after Nam, I can't say I want to do that anymore. I don't want to work the hardware store the rest of my life. I...I don't know, I just feel lost. So I was hoping by walking the trail, I might find some clarity."

"And halfway through, you still felt lost and figured you call your buddy Nate." It's the same way he would talk when we were together in Nam, semi-conceded.

I chuckle this time. "You know, Nate, I know Mike and I gave you plenty of shit back there. And you deserved a lot of what we dished out to you." I pause. "But I remember what you did that day. I remember you were the first one by my side. I remember you carrying me to the chopper. I know you are a good man, Nathan Bedford."

"Don't kid yourself. I was young and stupid back then. Way too much energy," he tells me. "After you left and with Sergeant Head dead, well, things just weren't the same. We saw some shit like you wouldn't believe. Trust me, you left at the right time. You want to go get something to eat?"

"Hell yes."

We climb into the Mustang, and he fires up the 351 HO 4bbl V8; she roars to life. Now I can't say I am a huge Ford or Mustang fan, but just the sound of her breathing gave me goose bumps. There really is a thrill to be had in driving an American Muscle car. He pulls out of the parking spot and heads to the main road. With no other cars to be seen, he hits the gas; as we pull out, I can hear the rear tires chirp as he sends her through the gears. We launch down the road a streak of red and black blur as he guides her through the turns. Phew, what a ride. He brings her back down to a dull purr and eases up a bit as we see other vehicles ahead of us.

"What do you think?" Nate asks.

"Man, this is a hell of a car," I say. "I may be a bit envious."

"Eh, it's just a car. She is fun to drive though," he replies.

We get to the restaurant and are shown a table. The waitress brings us menus, and we both order burgers, fries, and beers.

"So law school? What made you go that route?" I ask.

"Well, my family is full of lawyers, and after I returned, my uncle approached me and asked what my plan was. He convinced me to apply to Princeton, which was his alma mater. No doubt he probably called in a few favors, but either way, that's the plan for now," Nate says nonchalantly.

"At least I know who to call should I find myself in a pickle here in New Jersey," I say jokingly. "How were things after I left?"

"With the platoon? Brother, it all went to shit after you left, with Sergeant Head dead and all. About a week later, this guy shows up. We all assume he was CIA. He wanted to go on our next patrol and be taken to that village. We comply. Orders are orders, right? When we get to the village, he has us identify the village leader, you know, the guy Sergeant Head was talking to. Then he takes this guy into the hut where the guy was strung up. Next thing we know, he pokes his head out and tells us to continue with our patrol and he would find his way back to camp. So we left him there. About three days later, I see him strolling around camp, and he heads into the Command tent. After that, he disappears. Really freaking weird. Anyways, you know me. I get curious. So I talk to Bob, the radio operator, and I ask him what the hell was going on. He tells me the guy interrogated the village leader for two days. Apparently the half-dead corpse we pulled out of that hut was one of our own."

"No shit!" I say.

"It gets better." Nate says, "According to the village leader, the guy strung up was brought in by the Vietcong in the middle of the night just before we got there. They are the ones who skinned him and left him to die just before we arrived."

"That explains a lot. The Vietcong are some vicious motherfuckers," I say.

"It gets better still. From the interrogation, the reason the Vietcong skinned this guy was to make a statement. They found him in that cave where you got hurt and Sergeant Head bit the bullet. The guy we pulled out of that hut was skinning Vietcong and eating them like a cannibal," Nate tells me.

"No freaking way," I exclaim.

"It's all legit. I swear. Anyway. You know how we all thought Sergeant Head was a 'dickhead.' He was a pussy cat compared to his replacement. Luckily I got a gut wound that wasn't that bad and was medically discharged like you," Nate finishes.

"What was his name?" I ask.

"Who?" Nate replies.

"The guy who replaced Sergeant Head?" I clarify.

"I don't remember. Some douchebag from HQ," Nate says.

We enjoy the meal, tell a few more funnier "war" stories, and finish our beers. Nathan takes me back to the parking lot of the Delaware Water Gap to drop me back off.

"So where are you off to now?" he asks.

"Well, I figure I'll make camp here for the night and tomorrow head out for the New York border," I say.

"How much more do you have to go?" he asks.

"According to the maps and the pace I have been keeping, I should finish in about two months. Beginning of September hopefully." I show a crossed-finger sign.

"I wish you luck. In time, what you are destined to do on this earth will be revealed. Just have faith and keep an open mind," he tells me. Then we shake hands, and I head off to the trail again. I probably should have called Mother, but that opportunity has passed. It was nice to catch up with Nathan. He truly has matured since the last I saw him. A lawyer, I couldn't imagine Nathan as a lawyer two years ago. But come to think of it, I guess I can see it. I look back and wave as I hear that Mustang roar to life and he coasts out of view.

I pass the big sightseer attraction, Lookout Point, and hike another mile or so before I stop to make camp. Tomorrow is a new day as I sit there and think about what I am to do when I return to Iowa. I lay there looking up at the dark sky filled with all those lights and ask myself, *If you can see the stars and moon and night, is there a heaven?* The thoughts just run through my head as I drift off to sleep.

I head out, knowing in a few days I have to be in a town near Prospect Park for my next care package. I spend the night in the area, gather my things, and off to the next overnight spot. I recalculate my travels a bit and figure I can make Katahdin in Maine in approximately fifty-five days. That should put me back in Iowa just in time for Labor Day.

Chapter 22

Things seem to be going rather well as I trek along. I make my way to the New Jersey–New York border and then up through the Catskills. I kind of like it up here; it is as if the range is older than the Southern parts. Not sure if that is true, but it feels that way. One day on the trail, I'm taking a break while hiking along Canopus Lake, my now very worn boots taken off and soaking my sore feet in the cool water.

A man approaches me and says, "Beautiful morning view, isn't it?"

"It is," I reply, slightly taken aback and looking at the morning mist rise off the cool lake.

"I come out here and walk every chance I get. It helps clear my head," he keeps going.

"I can relate. I suppose," I reply, and almost as soon as the words leave my mouth, I regret them. Oh, sure, I stop briefly to talk to people here and there. But I do my best and actually have gone out of my way to avoid other hikers and people while on the trail. So for this older gentleman to just walk up and start talking to me is a bit unsettling. But I remain polite and cordial. We all need to talk to someone at some point in our lives.

"Oh, how is that, young man?" he asks. The gentleman takes off his shoes and socks like me and then proceeds to sit right next to me as if I opened the invitation for him. I shake it off and reply.

"Well, for starters, my name is Francis." I hold out my hand. At this point, I figure he isn't leaving right away and for me to just up and go might be rude. Besides, he seems to be a well-meaning individual.

He takes and shakes my hand. "Reverend John Luke."

"You're kidding, right? That sounds kind of redundant," I remark.

"How so?" he replies, half chuckling as if I am not the first to realize the irony.

"Well, you are a pastor with a name consisting of the names of two of the most notable disciples of Jesus, albeit a debatable coincidence, or you intended it," I note.

He laughs out loud and stronger than before. "No, it was not intended. Possibly a cruel joke or intuition by my folks when I was born, but it really is my name."

"That's downright interesting," I say. "Anyways, as I was about to say, I started out hiking the Appalachian Trail all the way down in Georgia back in March. I've made it this far and figured I'd finish what I have started. When you mentioned you walk along here to clear your mind, I said that it was similar to my situation as my initial purpose in hiking this trail was to 'clear' my mind."

"Is it working?" he asks.

"No," I say with a tinge of frustration.

He smiles a knowing grin. "Francis… It is okay if I call you Francis?"

"Yes, sir," I reply.

"I have spent my whole life wondering if I am following the path I am supposed to be on," he tells me.

"But you're a pastor. Doesn't God give you a sign and tell you this is the path he deems for you?" I say, trying not to be mocking.

"For some, I believe that might be true. But these last few years, I have asked if maybe there was something else I was destined to be. I pray and pray. But I never seem to get an answer," he continues.

"Perhaps that is because there is no answer," I say, slightly dissatisfied.

"Oh, I think there is a path we are all destined to take and is all part of the plan he has for us. But I also believe he has a tendency to get a kick out of watching us wander a bit, like Moses through the dessert," Reverend Luke says.

I reflect on that notion for a bit.

"I've killed people, Reverend," I blurt out.

"I had a feeling. The boots and fatigues kind of give it away. I figured you had been in Vietnam. Am I correct?" he asks.

"Yes," I reply, not wanting to give away too much.

"Awful thing that war. Excuse me, they call it a conflict, not a war. What they have done to your generation is simply not the right way," he says. "When I returned from Korea, I was in a similar situation as you. I felt lost and couldn't find my direction. So I turned to the Lord in hopes of finding answers and 'peace.' It worked for a bit. I met a nice woman, whom I later married, became a minister, and now I walk here asking the same questions I did twenty-plus years ago."

"At least you found someone," I tell him. "I lost the only woman I knew to love outside my mother."

He smiles. "I am sorry to hear that, Francis. But I can assure you that she is not the only one out there, and if it was truly meant to be, then it would be. God has no plans when it comes to our soulmates. No, that is left to a different being." He pauses while I reflect on the words he just shared with me. "For every bump in the road of life that we encounter, there is a joy to be had at his discretion. If nothing else, I feel you should embrace that notion."

His words hit like a brick wall. There are things that he does not know about me, and I cannot tell him. But it has made me start to wonder. Despite what I have inside of me, is God really watching over me? Is he looking out for my best interest? Is this just a test of my will and that it will soon pass? Then I think of what the demon last said to me: "Only you can send me back to hell. Help me fulfill my destiny, and I can leave you… Just let me be free."

"Are you okay, Francis?" Reverend Luke asks.

"Yes, sir. Why?" I respond.

"Well, you seemed to have gone off into another place and you were speaking but no words were uttered," he explains.

"I'm sorry. I guess I drifted off thinking about what you just said," I tell him.

"If you don't find the answers you are looking for, Francis, and I will pray for you that you do, give me call. Anytime," he says as he hands me a card with his number on it. "Sometimes we cannot force the answers. We have to allow them to come to us. It takes time. I will pray God leads you to the right path, Francis." He starts to get up, after putting his socks and shoes back on.

I stand as he does. "Thank you, sir. Your words were more helpful than you may realize. I greatly appreciate you stopping and talking with me. Usually, I avoid people, but this seems to have helped. Thank you." I extend my hand again as he brushes himself off and takes my hand in his.

He smiles and says, "No matter what may have happened or is to happen, *he* knows the truth and will be there in your greatest time of need. Just have faith."

With that, the reverend turns and starts to walk on his way. I blink for just a second, and he's gone, just like that. Like a mist filtering through the trees. I blink again and wonder if I dreamt the whole thing. Was it real or just my mind playing tricks on me? I look down at the embankment, and there where he sat is an impression of someone sitting next to me but there are no shoe prints. The ground is too moist for there to not be shoe prints, especially when I can clearly see where the man sat. *Weird* is the only thing I can think of on what just transpired.

Chapter 23

I gather up my belongings, and I keep moving along. It has been about six days since I saw Nathan. I finally hike into Connecticut and then Massachusetts. Vermont and New Hampshire are next. As I start the last state, the last leg of the Appalachian Trail, I realize, and to this day I am still not sure how I managed this on the trail, but I had not crossed paths with any dangerous wildlife, like bears or wolves. Maybe I am loud hiker and I have kept all the wildlife at bay this entire time. But as my luck would have it, I encounter my first bear on the second day in Maine somewhere around Sawyer Mountain. A typical black bear is more afraid of you than you are of it. It's foraging on some berries near the trail, and as soon as it hears my clunky boots on the path, it moves on. I swear it turns back and grunts as I pass and watch it saunter off into the woods.

Now I am no expert on what berries are safe to eat or what to forage for. But I figured if it's safe for a bear to eat, then it would be safe for me. It also just so happens I know a few berries that are safe from my time in the Scouts. This bear is picking away at some elderberries, which I know to be "healthy" for you. Before I move along the path, I grab an empty bag I keep for cases just like this and pick as many as I can hold. Looking around, I don't see the bear anymore. I wonder how he feels about sharing his lunch with me. Maine encompasses approximately 265 miles of the trail from Mount Carlo to Katahdin.

I get back out on the trail and keep moving. This section is supposed to be one of the most beautiful untouched sections of the entire journey. But the reason it remains so beautiful is the fact that it remains so remote and desolate. Day 2 brings a moose across my path. I was told they can be docile, but at the same time, they prefer their privacy. In my case, I turn a bend and stare one right in the face. He takes one look at me and snorts. I freeze, then I remember what I read and had been told: Find a tree and get out of view. So I did. I shift to my left where a big pine was and hide behind it. About five minutes or so later, when I guess the moose has decided I wasn't there anymore, he moves on, and I could hear him trotting back into the woods. I peek out from behind the tree, and he isn't there anymore so I continue on.

The next day or two ends up being a blur. Now this is 100 percent my fault. God and I both know I should have known better than to do the things I did next. That night as I plan to make camp, I find a nice stream, Orberton Stream, I believe. It's quiet, and I enjoy sleeping next to a bubbling stream; the sound soothes my soul, and I rest easier. But after making camp, I get some water from the stream that I make sure I purify accordingly and prepare my meal. After finishing my meal, I decide that the elderberries I had picked would make a good dessert, and while reading my book and listening to the stream bubble nearby, I eat them. I give in to my drooping eyes and fall into a deep slumber.

Late in the night, I wake to a roaring in my gut and the feeling of nausea coming on. The next forty-eight hours are a living hell as I cannot control the nausea and diarrhea. I remember thinking to myself, *This is the end for me*, and I pray to God to make it stop.

"You FOOL!" the voice of the demon returns. "You are supposed to cook the elderberry before you eat them. Now you have killed us both and I'll be stuck in this purgatory forever."

Through fits of my body expelling the poisonous raw berries and periods of consciousness, I reply, "Good, then we both die and I will be rid of you finally."

Laughing at me, the demon replies, "I won't die. I'll just be stuck here till another poor soul comes along for me to inhabit. Then I will live on to complete my destiny through them. You, you will just degrade away as the saying goes: 'ashes to ashes and dust to dust.'"

"Fuck you!" I scream at nothingness through gasps of air between bouts of anguish.

Then out of the mindless fog surrounding me, there's a voice, a female voice, one I recognize.

"Francis? Francis! You don't look too good..."

I drift back out of consciousness.

"Sit up, Francis. Drink this..."

I hear the voice like a dream say as the water in my eyes blur everything around me, the sweat dripping from me like a monsoon. I think back to my time in Vietnam where there was endless rain.

I cannot tell how long I have slept for or what transpired. But my eyes open, and it's barely light out. There by a campfire sits a female figure.

"Welcome back," I hear her say.

All I can do is moan. My entire body feels like a knot of twisted insides and outsides. As my eyes adjust, I see the face of Judy through the fog of my vision.

"Judy?" I say weakly.

"Hello again, Francis," Judy replies.

"Where am I? What happened?" I ask.

"Best I can tell is, you ate some raw elderberries based on the bag I found and you became violently ill," she tells me. "I have no idea how long ago or how long it was before I found you, but had I not found you, you might be dead."

"Really?" I'm still semi-incoherent to the situation or what's going on. All I know is, I have a god-awful taste in my mouth, my arse feels like it's inside out, and my stomach feels like someone is using it for a punching bag. "Thank you. I'm sorry."

"Sorry? Sorry for ditching us back in Virginia, or sorry that I had to nurse you back to health?" she asks with a touch of disdain.

"Both, I guess," I say as I try to sit up. "I am sorry you found me like this, and I appreciate you helping me out," I say finally. "As far as Virginia goes...I can explain."

"It's okay. You don't have to explain. In all honesty, it was for the best," she tells me with a sigh.

"Oh?" I say with a bit of surprise. "Why is that?"

"Well, after you ditched us, Melody and I spent the next few days in a massive fight," she tells me. "She left me in Hot Springs. I had planned to finish the trail, and therefore I hadn't signed up for classes this fall, so I was left with little options and figured I'd finish. Besides, where was I to go? I had just spent the last year devoting everything I had into Melody, and, well, things just didn't work out. That's life, I suppose."

"I really am sorry. I could tell you loved her when we met," I say as consoling as I could.

"Yeah." She nods. "Too bad it wasn't reciprocated."

"How did you nurse me back to health?" I ask.

"I keep mint in my supply because I like to use it to make tea most evenings. Mint is good to help settle a stomach and flush out toxins," she says. "What the hell possessed you to eat raw elderberry? Don't you know those will kill you?"

"I do now," I say as another pang of nausea crosses through my midregion. "What time is it?" I ask. "And what day?"

"Well, it's about 6:00 p.m., and today is Tuesday," she says with confidence.

"How long was I out for?" is my next question.

"I've been here watching over you for two days. By the looks of you and surrounding area, I'd say you had been sick for almost a day and half before I found you," she tells me.

"Holy shit..." I say, trying to put it all together. "Thank you for helping me," I finally say to her.

"You're welcome. Now my suggestion is, you get some more fluids to get your strength up. I made some more mint tea. If you're feeling better in the morning, we can assess moving on or getting you to a town and a doctor," she says.

I thank her again as I take the tea and sip on it. Soon after, I fall back asleep. Late in the night, the demon visits my dreams. "You can kill her now," it claims.

"I can't do that. She saved me and nursed me back to health," I say.

"All the more reason to kill her. We are not far from The Wilderness, and back there, no one will ever find her." The demon is relentless.

"I cannot. It's not right. Besides, I have already killed once for you, and that should have been enough," I respond.

"Enough is when I say it is enough. You will soon learn, Francis Fleming, you are not in control of this," the demon proclaims as it drifts back into the depths of my head where it rests.

In the morning, I wake up and make coffee enough for two. Judy wakes to the smell of the coffee.

"Good morning," she says as she emerges from the tent. "You seem to be feeling better, I see."

I hand her a cup of coffee. "I cannot say I am 100 percent yet, but I figured I would try to repay your hospitality. For nursing me back to health," I reply.

"Do you feel good enough to keep hiking?" she asks.

"I think so. At the least we need to get away from this place," I state.

We gather up our belongings and prepare to head out.

"You sure you want to finish this with me?" I'm giving her the out as I fear the demon might resurface and make me do something in my subconscious state.

"I'm okay with this arrangement if you are. Besides, I have to ensure you don't eat any more poisonous berries," she says bluntly.

"Gee, thanks," I reply. "Make one mistake on the trail and you never live it down."

"A mistake that almost killed you had I not come along," she says. We share looks and leave it at that.

Judy is good people. I don't have any issues with her. Despite how territorial she was during our first meeting, she has been an interesting person to talk to. She seems to be quite intelligent and knows quite a bit about the world. We trek on for the first part of day in relative silence. We stop at the summit of Spaulding Mountain and enjoy our lunch with a view.

"There is something that's inwardly peaceful about this trail," I remark as a way to break the silence.

"It is. I agree," Judy says. "How are you feeling?"

"A little slower than I normally would be hiking, but as the day moves on, I feel my strength and endurance returning," I reply.

"You lost a ton of fluids, Francis. It may be a few days before your body recoups from all that," she says.

"Yeah, how about you?" I ask. "How are you feeling?"

"If you are up for it, I feel we should pick up the pace just a bit," Judy starts. "We still have a lot of ground to cover before The Wilderness, and then the finish line at Katahdin."

With our lunch complete, I say, "I guess we better get going. You lead and set the pace you want. If I fall off, I'll let you know."

"Sounds good."

And just like that, she is headed down the mountainside. For a woman of her stature, she keeps a hell of a pace. I can see how she ended up catching me on the trail all this time.

"So what is your plan when you return to the University of Georgia?" I ask.

"I am not sure I intend to return," she says.

"Really? I thought you were planning on being a psychiatrist," I say quizzically.

"I am. But I am not sure I want to continue at the University of Georgia. I really do not want to cross paths with Melody again," she tells me.

"I see. It is a big campus. What is the likelihood of your paths crossing?" I ask. "Isn't she a liberal arts major?"

"We run in the same crowds to a point. As much time as I spend studying, we would see each other when I do venture out," she explains.

"I understand. But I also feel like you shouldn't have to worry about that, given the difference in majors and the fact that I got this vibe from her that she might continue. I don't know, it was just a feeling," I say to try and soothe her thoughts.

"Currently I missed fall signups. I will have to wait till the spring semester. I figure in the meantime, I can go back to my parents and take up my old job at the grocery store until then," she tells me. "I am sure my parents will give me a hard time about the situation, since they weren't keen on this idea of me hiking the Appalachian Trail in the first place."

"I see," I say. "Where is 'home'?" I ask.

"Augusta, Georgia. Home of the Masters. Nice town that turns to hell once a year," she replies.

"I can imagine. We don't have anything like that back in Dubuque, where I am from," I say.

"Not surprised. Who the hell would want to visit Dubuque?" she says sardonically.

"Hey!" I exclaim. And we both share a laugh. It is good that she is lightening up a bit. I feel bad for her with Melody leaving her halfway through and all.

Chapter 24

We hike along and camp around Crocker Mountain. As we pull out supplies for dinner, I find a can of peaches that was deep in my pack. Thoughts of the old moonshiner and his hospitality flood my mind. Then a new thought shines through: me standing over his sleeping body, his hands folded across his chest, the gentle rise and fall, my K bar in my hand as I raise it. His eyes open just as I swiftly slam the K bar down into his chest and watch as his eyes go from surprise to lifeless as the blood pours from his body, soaking his clothes and bedding. I see my hand with the knife gouge out his eyes and place them in the jar from my bag. There's a feeling of relief from the demonic soul as it absorbs the old man's very being…

"Francis… Francis…" Judy's voice calls from what seems like a hundred yards away. "You okay?" She lays a hand on my shoulder.

I jump, and she leaps back, nearly tripping over a rock. I shake my head. "Yeah, sorry. Guess I got lost in my thoughts. I didn't mean to startle you," I say.

"It's okay," she replies. "Are those peaches for us?" She stares at the can with want.

"Oh, yeah, they can be… I was saving them for a special occasion. I guess this suits that." I hand the can over to her outstretched hand.

"Great! I haven't had peaches since Georgia," she remarks excitedly. "Nothing beats a good Georgia peach, sweet and juicy right off the tree. The fuzz against your lips and that first bite as the nectar fills your mouth."

"You still talking about peaches?" I say sardonically this time.

She shoots me a glare and then laughs. "Well…" she trails off. "I guess it could be implied as other things." We both laugh at this thought and open the can, each taking a peach until the can is nothing but juice.

"Here, you can drink the juice." I hand her the can. "It can remind you of times before."

"Thanks…" she says, shooting me another glare, and we both laugh at the inuendo.

She slams the juice from the can into her mouth and holds it there for a minute, savoring the sweet thick nectar. Then she lets it slide down her throat, and she licks the sticky remnants from her lips with a smile that tells me she is remembering something deep in her mind.

"Where did you go?" she asks after a bit.

"Go? I didn't go anywhere. Been here the whole time," I say.

"When you were holding the can of peaches. You clearly went somewhere, mentally," she states.

"Oh! That. Yeah, before I met you and Melody, I came across this old moonshiner who shared some of his White Lightning for my can of peaches that I had with me," I tell her.

"Wait, where was this?" she asks.

"Oh, I don't know, somewhere around Waynesville, I think." I know what I am saying and I'm hoping she hasn't put two and two together.

"I heard a report of them finding a body in that area, Licklog Ridge, I think," she says, thinking deeply.

"I heard that too," I say nonchalantly, trying to divert where this is going.

"Do you think it was the same guy?" she asks.

"I have no idea," I respond, hoping to change the subject. "Not to be nosy, but when did you know?"

"Know what?" she asks.

"That you were attracted to other women?" I say.

"High school. Amy Pendergast. We were at a friend's boy-girl party, and during spin the bottle, you know the game, the bottle landed on both of us, and we kissed," she tells me. "After that night, we talked about how it felt, and we both kind of liked it. So we went over to her house since her parents were not home, and we made out."

"Really?" I say, surprised.

"Yeah, I mean, it didn't seem like a big thing at the time. But some boys that were at the party saw us walking to her house, and they started a rumor around school. Now we were not in a 'relationship,' Amy and me. But the rumor made it out to be all kinds of things. Anyway, word got back to my parents and Amy's, and we were told to stay away from each other. This is the early '60s, and that kind of thing is taboo. On top of being told I couldn't be friends with Amy anymore, my parents gave me the speech on how boys and girls are supposed to be together and create a family and all the BS." Her story shows her passion and how she hates the world's perception of her and how she feels.

"What did you do?" I ask.

"The only thing I could do at the time: I obeyed my parents. I was only twelve, so I was 'confused,' as they put it. But I don't feel I was confused. Honestly, I think it is what led me to study psychology. In some way, I want to better understand why I feel the way I do toward other women and not toward men. Now, don't get me wrong, my feelings haven't changed. But being in college and meeting Melody has helped me realize that it is not bad feeling the way I do," she tells me.

Glad that I was able to deter the conversation from the old moonshiner. I feel happy and sad for Judy. This society isn't very open-minded, and I cannot imagine it is easy for her feeling how she does. For me, I don't seem to mind. Judy doesn't appeal to me in the first place, and I've come to the understanding that we all live our lives how we want. Who am I to judge? I mean, hell, I murdered a man and have a demon populating my head.

The days go on like this for about a week. We talk about everything from society to religion to politics. The more we talk, the more I realize we share a lot of the same ideologies about the world. Our connection grows, and before we know it, we find ourselves at

Monson Maine, the beginning of The Wilderness, a one-hundred-mile-or-so stretch where there are no towns, few shelters, and few make it through if they do not prepare properly. I made sure to prepare for this section as it was told to me by Mr. Clark. We spend the night going over our provisions and making sure we have enough for the next ten days. They say to plan ahead and give yourself a day or two extra as a just-in-case situation that might arise. We feel we can manage and begin the journey.

By the fifth day, we start to realize that we are running short on supplies. With the closest town for restocking being an extra two to three days out of our way, we decide to start rationing our food. Water doesn't seem to be a problem as we have passed many beautiful lakes and streams. The trip may be a bust at this point, but we tarry on as the best option we can come up with is getting to Abol Park and finding a ride to the nearest town. We haven't seen any other hikers in days. Most fall off by this point, and the southbound thru-hikers are usually well past this point.

"How are you doing?" I ask Judy.

"So far, so good. Where are we?" she asks.

"According to my map and calculations, we should be around Cooper Pond. That last mountain was Jo-Mary Mountain," I say, looking at the map. The land has been soggy and mucky when we have been in the valleys, and the climbs have been arduous steep uphills with treacherous downhill slopes.

"Let's try to find a dry area and make camp," I suggest. The last three days of straight rain make it an impossible task, and at this point, we are almost out of food and soaked to the bone.

"Okay" is all Judy musters in response.

"Now, now is the time to take her, Francis," the demon says.

"No!" I say out loud.

"What was that, Francis?" asks Judy.

"Oh, nothing," I reply, "I was looking at a spot just to realize it is boggier than the last."

"Ah," she replies.

We finally find a place that is not too bad and set up camp. It's times like this I regret thinking I could do this without a tent.

"Given our situation," Judy starts, "you can share the tent with me if you like? But just tonight, and no funny business."

"I'm too tired for any funny business," I respond.

We both crowd into the tent, and I set up my 90-degree flashlight to read like I have every night on the trail. Judy climbs into her sleeping bag, her hands under her head as she stares at the ceiling of the tent. Neither of us have said much the last couple of days, too tired to even talk. You would think after hiking from Georgia, we would be fully conditioned for this section, but other hikers we had met along the way say that this part is one of the toughest sections. But as difficult as this section is, the tranquility and views have been worth the pain, the rain, and the struggle.

Neither of us have bathed in fourteen days, and the stench in the tent is tremendous. I cannot say either of us really notice too much since we have gotten used to it to a point. I flip through the pages I have now read three times. I bought two books before my journey, *Deliverance* by James Dickey and *Jonathan Livingston Seagull* by Richard Bach. One I got because it sounded interesting, the other in hopes of helping me find answers. *Deliverance* has probably been detrimental and done nothing but driven the demon's purpose. While the one about a seagull learning to fly has left me wondering more than actually giving me guidance. After a bit, I hear Judy snoring, signaling she has fallen asleep. My gut grumbles from having little to eat the past couple of days. I look over at her, so peaceful and sound.

"Do it!" the demon's voice cries. "Kill her! You can use her flesh as nourishment and build your strength back up. Finish this adventure and complete your destiny, Francis."

I lay there trying to ignore the demon's pleas.

"We can do like last time. I can take over and just use you like I did when I killed the old man," he says. My gut grumbles again.

"I can't," I say in my head. As if I have a way to reason with the demon.

"Sure you can. Just take your shirt, shove it in her mouth, and press down. You are stronger than her. If she struggles, it won't be long, then you can start to slowly peel off her flesh so you can taste her. Go ahead. It's not bad, you know." The demon becomes more relentless.

An hour passes, and the fire I built is crackling and sizzling. A skewered piece of meat hangs above the half saturated wood. I was fortunate to find enough pieces to able to get the fire lit in the first place. Now I have a few wet pieces sitting along the edge to dry out a bit from the campfire's heat. I turn the stick I used to create a makeshift skewer. Not knowing how long it should cook for, I give it plenty of time. When I feel it has cooked long enough and my gut is screaming for nutrients, I grab the stick and take a bite. *Not bad*, I tell myself. *Could use some salt and pepper, but I ran out of those luxuries days ago.*

In the tent lies Judy's lifeless body as I reenter and cut off another piece of flesh. The protein from the meat fills me up, and I sleep soundly next to her eyeless cold body bundled up in her sleeping bag.

The next morning, I wake. As I wipe the sleep from my eyes, I look over at the carnage from the night before. It all comes rushing back to me. I scurry out of the tent and stand there.

"Jesus, Francis, what did you do?" I ask myself. "Fuck!"

"Ah, was it as good for you as it was for me?" the voice comes from nowhere. The demon has taken full hold on my existence. I crumple to the ground and wail in agony over what I have done.

"You son of a bitch, what have you done to me? Why did you do this again?" I ask through the sobbing.

"Dear Francis, I did not do this. This time, it was all you." The demon laughs at my anguish.

"No, I wouldn't. I couldn't." The events of the night flash back into my head. I climb over a log and vomit at the thoughts of what I have done.

"Oh, but you did, my perfect vessel of imperfection. The cycle is now complete. From this time forward, you will do my bidding and allow me to finish my requirements on this earth purging the wicked and filling my father's kingdom," the demon explains.

"But she wasn't wicked. She didn't deserve to die. Not like this," I say, wiping the tear stains from my cheeks and vomit from my mouth.

"How do you know, Francis? For all you know, that crap she fed you about Melody leaving her and going home was a lie," the demon states. "For all you know, she killed her over a broken heart. Also, you better get out of here before someone comes along."

The realization hits me at how right he is. I pack my belongings and clean up the best I can. I light the tent on fire to destroy as much evidence as possible, and when it reaches a point of embers, I head out.

Chapter 25

The remaining time on the trail is uneventful. I go back to my normal routine of avoiding anyone and everyone I can. I finish what I started and climb the 4,000 feet up Mount Katahdin. At the summit, I leave a memento marking my journey and accomplishment. The walk back down is bittersweet as I reflect on the entire journey. At the base again, I find someone willing to take me to a nearby motel where I acquire a room for the night. I shower, and luckily the motel has a laundry I can use. As late as it is and as tired as I am, I wash my clothes. When I get back to the room, I pass out and sleep like I have never slept before.

Late the next morning, I wake to a commotion outside. There is a police car sitting at the motel office. I don't even have to wonder if I know why they are here. I gather up my belongings, and as inconspicuous as I can, I go to the motel office. A policeman inside looks me over.

"Just hiked the trial?" the policeman asks.

"Yes, sir," I say.

"Would you mind looking at this photo? Do you know this woman?" he asks.

"No, sir. Can't say I know her," I state. "If you don't mind me asking, why?"

"She was found burned to a crisp in her tent. Looks like a campfire she built set her tent on fire while she was asleep," he tells me.

"Oh, I see. So you think I may have met her on the trail," I say, being as cooperative as possible. "I'm sorry, Officer. I met a lot of people on the trail. She may have been one of them, but I am not sure." I try to give nothing away in my reply.

"That's fine. Looks like an accident anyway. We are just trying to find anyone that might know where she is from. Thank you for your time," the officer says.

The picture was one of Judy from one of the Appalachian Trail offices. They had one of me too, as a way to track those of us hiking the trail and in the chance a hiker becomes lost or, as in this case, found dead. I pay my bill with the office manager and ask directions to the nearest train station. The officer overhears me.

"If you want, I can drop you off. I have to head back to the station," he offers.

"Why, thank you, sir. I think I will take you up on your hospitality," I reply. No room in the front of the squad car, so I climb in the back.

I laugh and say, "First time in a police car."

"That's a good thing, young man," the officer replies. "Last place anyone should ever want to be."

I think to myself the irony about how I should be sitting back here in cuffs for murdering two people. But I keep mum as the officer guides the car through the town. He stops at the bus station.

"Here you go," he says. "If you think of anything or hear anything, please call the station and ask for me." He hands me a card with his name and number for the police station on it.

"Thanks for the ride, and if anything comes to mind, I'll give you a call." I grab my gear and head into the bus station.

"Bus ticket to the Amtrak Station in Boston, Massachusetts, please," I tell the man behind the ticket counter.

"That will be fifteen dollars," the man says. I hand him the cash.

He hands me a ticket and says, "Bus 59, leaves around 7:00 a.m. tomorrow."

"Nothing for today?" I respond.

"Afraid not. Tomorrow, 7:00 a.m." He calls for the next person in line, even though there's no one there. But it signifies the end of our conversation.

Luckily there is a hotel just half a block down. I get a room and relax for the night. Luck going my way, this hotel has a restaurant and bar. I sit at the bar, have a nice meal, and put away about four beers. After the trail and all the "excitement" I had lately, four beers only melted the tip of the iceberg. The next morning, bright and early, I stand in front of bus number 59 with my ticket in hand, and right on time, we leave Bangor, Maine, at 7:01 a.m. bound for Boston.

The bus ride is a scenic four-and-half-hour ride of which I think I slept four hours of. As I get into South Station in Boston, I grab my bag from the compartment in the underside of the bus. I head straight to the restroom and then the ticket counter. Something about travelling makes me have to go. As I get in line at the ticket counter, I think to myself, What if I didn't go back to Iowa? What if I disappeared? They may eventually put things together and come looking for me. Whether it is for the old man in North Carolina or Judy. Either way, murder is murder, and I would not do well in prison.

"Next!" I hear the lady at the ticket counter call and realize it's my turn. "Where would you like to go, dear?" she asks in a thick accent to match her build.

"Chicago, please," I say. "Earliest available is preferred."

"It is an overnight rail. Would you like a sleeping compartment?" she asks.

"If there is one available on the next train to Chicago? Sure," I answer.

"You're in a hurry to get where you're going, huh?" she says slightly sarcastically.

"It's been a long five months, ma'am." I kind of chuckle, realizing the way I sound. "Yes, I am looking forward to getting home," I finish with a smile.

"It's 250 dollars. It's a shared compartment. But you'll have access to the dining car, and there is a shower available, so you can relax. Train departs from platform number 3, train number 44, at 2:00 p.m.," she tells me as she hands me a ticket. "Safe travels, sweetie," she finishes with a devilish grin.

"Thank you." I take the ticket and turn to walk away. I look back, and not sure why, but she's watching me walk away with a grin on her face and glint in her eye. Then I hear her call out, "Next!" I pick up the pace a hair and find a sandwich shop in the terminal with a table toward the back. Hopefully she doesn't have a lunch break soon.

I order a shaved roast beef sandwich, bag of chips, and a Coke. Satisfied, I sit there a bit and finish the Coke I ordered. Then about thirty minutes before my train is to leave, I head to platform number 3. I ask the attendant which car I should get in, and he directs me to one near the end of the platform. I climb on and find the room I am assigned. Placing my backpack on the set next to me, I settle in for the train to depart. Just as I hear the all aboard, I realize no one has joined me in the compartment, and I think, Yes! *I am in luck, just me.* Then the door slides open, and in comes an older gentleman who oddly looks a lot like Reverend John Luke.

I couldn't help myself. After the man came and sat down, I ask him, "I'm sorry, but have we met?"

The gentleman looks me over head to toe and says in a heavy Boston accent, "Nope, can't say you look familiar to me at all."

"Huh," I respond. "Weird!" Alarms go off in my head.

"My name is Rick." He extends his hand.

"Francis," I reply.

"I noticed the backpack. Where are you headed?" he asks.

"Home to Iowa. I returned from Nam, and with little idea of what I wanted to do when I got back, a friend suggested the Appalachian Trail. I just finished a few days ago," I tell him.

"The Appalachian Trail! Really? That's a hell of journey," he remarks.

"That it was," I say. "It is amazing how beautiful the Eastern Seaboard can be. What has you going to Chicago?" I ask.

"Work," Rick replies. "I work new deals for new locations for Sears."

"That has to be lucrative and even semi-exciting," I reply.

"I hate my job. But the pay is good, and I get to travel on the company dime. Too bad they won't pay for a plane ticket." He chuckles. "Tell me about your walk of the Appalachian Trail," he concludes.

I tell him of all the good things I got to see and do, leaving out the gruesome parts. How I crossed paths with a black bear and moose in back-to-back days but didn't see any other dangerous creatures the rest of the trip. I tell him about my elderberry experience and how Judy saved my life. I explain how something as simple as a can of peaches can brighten a person's day and bring people together. I tell him about meeting the old moonshiner, Judy and Melody, and the gentleman by Canopus Lake.

"Canopus Lake? Like in New York? Just north of the city, right?" he asks a little enthusiastically.

"Yes, that's the one. Why?" I reply.

"I had a brother who lived not far from there. He was married to a wonderful woman. Man, I can still remember the rolls she would make whenever we got together. Melt in your mouth, like cotton candy. She was so beautiful too. To this day, I cannot understand what she saw in my brother. But unfortunately, she passed away," he says, telling his story.

"I…I am sorry to hear about that," I interject.

"Oh, it's okay, that happened years and years ago. But her passing damn near killed my brother. Despite being a pastor, he took to drinking when she passed. It didn't take long, and he suffered a massive heart attack. He passed away about a year ago. Poor John, I guess he couldn't live without her," the man explains empathetically and solemnly.

"Umm…you said your brother was a pastor and his name was John?" I ask cautiously.

"Yes, why?" Rick replies.

"Oh, nothing specific. Reverend John Luke, right?" I say.

Now the man sits a little more upright in his seat and says, "Yes?"

"I think I may have met your brother, which would explain why you looked so familiar," I tell him.

"Really? Where?" he asks me.

"Why there at Canopus Lake," I respond.

"You must be mistaken. My brother John has been dead for over a year," he states matter-of-factly and looks at me like I'm some kind of nut.

"I am sorry. You are right. It must have been a doppelganger. I'm sorry," I reply and look out the window.

"Hey, listen," he says. "I get it. I served over in Korea. In fact, my brother and I both did. I know that shit they put us through can play tricks on our eyes and mess with our heads. I know you didn't mean anything by what you said. No offense taken here. Okay?"

"Yeah," I say, still a little unsure. "Again I'm sorry."

To change the subject, Rick goes on, "So did you figure it out?"

"Figure what out?" I ask back.

"Did you figure out your place in life while hiking the trail?"

"Oh, yeah, that. Yes and no. I mean, I have a degree in engineering, just not sure that is what I want to do the rest of my life. Like a part of me is telling me I am destined for more. You know?" I tell him.

"I've been there, and yes, I do know that feeling," he says.

"I just still do not know at this point. Who knows, maybe I am destined to work in the hardware store the rest of my life," I say, feeling a little down and lost again.

"It's getting late. How about some dinner?" Rick suggests.

"That sounds appealing," I say as we get up and head for the dining car.

Little did I know food on a train is not that great. The menu looks good, but the quality is subpar. I order the chicken, another meal I have not had in a long time. It came out dry, and without the sauce it's served with, it would have been inedible. But I suffer through; maybe my taste buds are off from eating granola and canned or light processed foods for so long. Perhaps my taste buds have changed when I modified my diet on the trail. I shudder at the thought and try to think of more pleasant matters, like getting home safe to Mother.

Chapter 26

After dinner, I excuse myself while I take a quick shower and prepare for bed. The sooner I get to sleep, the sooner and closer we are to Chicago. At this point, I am over my trip and just ready to be home to relax. As I lay in my bunk in the compartment, I turn on my trusted 90-degree flashlight and read a book I picked up at the train station. Another night of *Deliverance* or *Jonathan Livingston Seagull*, and I think I would have lost my mind. *Islands in the Stream* by Ernest Hemingway. I open to page 1 and begin. My mind becomes immersed in the story about Thomas Hudson. Page after page, I try to put everything that has happened to date behind me. Not sure whether it's my sheer exhaustion, the reading of the book, or the gentle sway of the train car as we roll down the track, but it did not take long before I was waking to sunlight coming through the crack in the blinds of the window. I feel oddly refreshed, more refreshed than I had ever felt before in my life. As I roll over and look over the compartment, I notice I'm alone. I climb down and get dressed. Then I check my watch; it's almost 8:00 a.m. The dining car would stop serving breakfast soon. I hurry to find I have time to get some eggs and bacon; anything would be better than oatmeal again for the 100th day in a row. Out of all the meals onboard, so far, this is the only one that tastes right. But let's be honest, how hard is it to make breakfast? I mean, I know people to have done it, but breakfast with all its options is almost impossible to screw up these days. As I am finishing my breakfast, I notice Rick returning from what must have been the observation car. I nod; he nods a simple acknowledgement of each other. After breakfast, I head back to the compartment.

"Good morning, sleepyhead," Rick says as I enter through the sliding door.

"Good morning, sir," I reply. "I hope you slept as well as I did."

"I wish. Something about the way these things rock back and forth never sits well with my biological clock," he says.

"Odd. I think I had the most restful sleep I have had the entire trip. I thought it was due to the swaying of the car over the tracks, but maybe it was just from pure exhaustion. I don't know," I explain, finding our experience being complete opposites intriguing.

"According to the itinerary, we should be arriving in Chicago Union Station around 11:00 a.m., about two hours from now," Rick notes as he reviews a piece of paper and verifies against his watch.

I settle down in my seat and open the book by Hemingway I started last night. One thing I hate about falling asleep while reading is that I tend to lose my place. I flip through the pages I think I left off at and reread about three paragraphs of the story I know I already read. I finally find a spot I think is where I left off and continue reading. Small towns and countryside whiz by the window, which is now completely open. I hit a break in the chapters and stare out the window. I think to myself as another electric pole, occasional road, or the countless trees fly by, *How many people out there are working just to survive? How many of them are doing the job they actually enjoy and love?*

As I ponder these questions, watching the world go about its daily routine while I sit here watching it go past me, Rick says, "Does the train continue to Iowa?" He asks out of the blue, much like his brother did that day at the lake. Passed away or not, I know I spoke to Rick's brother that day. Kind of unnerving, thinking about talking to a ghost, but maybe he wasn't a ghost and more along the lines of Clarence from the story *It's a Wonderful Life*.

"Umm...no. I have to change over to the bus terminal and get a ticket to Dubuque after I get into Chicago," I say.

"I see. Yeah, not too much traffic goes to Dubuque, Iowa, any time of the year, does it?" he remarks.

"No… But in a way, it's kind of nice like that. Just a little state in the middle of everything and nothing at all at the same time," I reminisce. Looking back out the window, I notice the scenery starting to change as we begin to enter the suburbs around Chicago.

"I can see why you are having a hard time finding a path for yourself. Just have faith."

That was it. It was the way Rick said "Just have faith"; it's like the words resounded in my head, much like the day I heard John Luke say the exact same thing. I smile as the buildings start to surround the train, blocking out the light, and the serene quiet of the countryside is replaced with horns honking and sirens. Time seems to slow to a halt as the conductor comes across the public announcement system, denoting our arrival.

After deboarding the train, I make my way to the bus ticket counter to purchase a ticket to Dubuque.

"The next bus to Dubuque leaves on Wednesday, sir" is all the girl said. Two days in the Windy City is not part of my plan, so I ask where the closest reasonable hotel or motel might be. She provides me an address to a Holiday Inn about three blocks away, and I head out of the station. The Holiday Inn doesn't have a restaurant attached to it, so I ask the receptionist at the hotel where I might be able to get an authentic Chicago meal. I have heard about these "fancy" hotdogs and "Chicago deep-dish" pizzas. Probably can't put down a whole deep dish by myself, so I opt for the dogs. Luckily for me being downtown, there are plenty of options, and I easily find a place that serves both. Added to my luck, they serve premade deep dish by the slice, and according to them, they have the best most authentic Chicago dog. I order one of each and a Coke. Sitting there watching the city hustle and bustle by through the window makes me think more about my plans for the future.

I have finished off Hemingway's novel, and prior to leaving the train station, I grabbed a new book, *The Exorcist* by William Peter Blatty, about a Catholic priest who extracts a demon from a little girl in North Carolina. I think, *How fitting. My first kill by the demon was in North Carolina.* Then it hits me like a ton of bricks, similar to the way that slice of pizza just slammed my gut. The signs have been there all along. The demon, Mr. Clark's suggestion to reconnect with nature, Rev. John Luke, his brother Rick—why didn't I see this sooner? I should become a minister. Tomorrow I enroll in a seminary.

Chapter 27

The sun has set behind the tall buildings of downtown Chicago. I decide to take a walk to stretch my legs and find that after a bit, I may have entered a less-than-savory part of the city. "Ladies" stand on the corners and guys bounce from bar to bar, sometimes in loud noisy groups and other times as loners who approach the girls, and they disappear inside a building or down a back alley. I don't want to look too obvious that I am from out of town and lost, so I just walk with my quickened pace in a direction I hope will lead me back to the hotel.

As I walk, a young woman approaches me, dressed in a very short skirt, fishnet stockings, bright red hair that I am sure is a wig, a black leather top that accents her not-so-prevalent chest; and she's wearing enough makeup to cover blemishes on probably three women.

"Hey, stranger. My name is Charlene. What is a nice guy like you doing in this part of town? You lookin' for something 'special'?" she asks. At first, I ignore her or pretend she isn't talking to me. Then I think about how I am lost, so I stop.

"Me?" I respond, trying to play dumb.

"Yeah, honey, you. You look like you might be looking for someone, you know, 'special,'" she says provocatively.

"Well, I'm not. The truth of the matter is, I think I am lost," I say.

"We all are, honey. Where you trying to go?" she answers, her tone has changed; as you can tell, she means well, but now I'm taking up her precious time to score a john for the night.

"I don't have any money. I have nothing to offer you," I tell her a little lie.

"Yeah, I kind of figured that already. But you look too sweet to be down here in this part of town," she says. "It's okay. Where do you need to be?" I give her the name of the hotel, and she points me in the direction I should go.

"You're very kind. Thank you," I say. "By the way, my name is Francis."

"Listen, I have a job to get back to, Francis. My kind heart is frosting over in this cold," she says.

I think about the five dollars in my pocket. Close to the last bit of money I have on my person. I hand it to her.

"Here, for your time and kindness. I lied because I didn't want to be misunderstood." Meaning, I wasn't looking for sexual favors, just directions.

"You really are sweet." Her tone is back to being all lovey-dovey, and she pecks my cheek. "If you change your mind or next time you're in town, just ask for Charlene. I'll take really good care of you," she says and sends me on my way as she turns back to her business.

"Thank you again," I say as I turn back away and head the direction she told me.

Back at the hotel, I think to myself the best seminary I can apply for at a price I can afford. Tomorrow I will go to the library and do some research. I lay down on the bed and read more of *The Exorcist*. As I read, I get the idea that going through seminary may help my other situation with getting rid of this demon. Deep in the recesses of my skull, I hear the echoing of the demon laughing at me and the notion.

The next morning, I get a copy of the Chicago transit bus routes and plan out how I intend to get to the public library on Division Street. Once I have my route planned out, I catch the next available bus, and off I go. The facade reminds me of the architecture of a prison or a school; oddly enough, both can be mistaken for the other. I walk inside and go straight for the help desk. The older lady at the counter stamping books looks up at me. "May I help you?" she says softly and politely.

"I am from out of town, and I am in transit to home," I begin awkwardly, not sure how or what specifically to ask for. "I was hoping I could find some information on seminaries in the north Midwest region."

"I would check over in the reference section where we keep books on various institutions for higher learning," she tells me. "However, if you are interested, my nephew applied to the McCormick Theological Seminary. He has been attending there for the last year or so, and according to my sister, he seems to like it."

"McCormick, huh? That sounds like a start," I say.

"It's right here in Chicago, not far from the University of Chicago," she tells me.

"Well, thank you." I turn toward the reference section. "I will keep it in mind."

I look through the various books on individual colleges and universities, everything from my alma mater, the University of Iowa, to Ivy League schools like Princeton, where Nathan is attending law school. I realize that there is no book compiled that includes all of them. I search along, thumbing through the various choices, selecting ones I know to be nearby. Nothing strikes me as a good fit. Eventually I come across a book about the McCormick Theological Seminary and open it up to find that the school caters to most Protestant faiths and is actually relatively affordable. The more I search through the pages, I find that the school is based right here in Chicago and isn't that far away. I figure, *What the hell. Might as well go look at it in person.* I return the book and stop by the main reception desk, thank the lady who assisted me, and head out looking at bus routes to get me to the campus.

After a short uneventful bus ride through Chicago, I arrive at the main hall in Lincoln Park. I go in and find an information desk.

"Hi," I say to the young man behind the counter. "I was thinking of enrolling here. Is there a way I could get more information?"

"I can do better than that if you don't mind waiting a little bit," he states. "I have someone who can give you a tour of the campus, and if you are still interested, we can set you up with an application for admissions."

"Wow. That sounds great, thank you."

Moments later, another young man arrives and takes the place of the one I was talking to.

"My name is Ralph," he introduces himself. "If you like, I can give that tour now and tell you a bit about the school."

"Sure," I reply as he leads the way.

"The school was founded in 1829 and, at that time, was located in Indiana. As the nation progressed, so did the school, and doors were opened here in 1859. In 1886, Cyrus McCormick, one of the board of trustees, had passed, and in his honor, they renamed the school in his name. I have to tell you that I heard our attendance is on a severe decline and there are rumors of us merging with the University of Chicago. But no one knows when or if that will happen. But in your situation, it only means they will probably accept you with little fanfare. Now the fall semester just started, but it should be possible to start in the new year, if that works for you," Ralph goes on and on, very informative about the history of the school.

"You seem to know a lot about the school," I note.

"I've been here for two years now. This is my last year. I graduate this coming May," he explains.

"Here we are, back at admissions," he announces. "Not a big campus, but that is kind of nice, in my opinion, as you get to know all the faculty and we tend to bond as students. It really is a good school, and if you decide this fits what you are looking for, I think you'll like it here." He shows me into the Admissions Office and walks away.

I enter the door to find a woman about my mother's age going through a pile of papers on her desk.

"How can I help you?" she says, looking up from her paperwork but not stopping what she is doing.

"I was looking to find out what it would take to apply to this school," I respond.

"Do you already have a degree?" she asks.

"Yes, in civil engineering from the University of Iowa," I answer.

"Is your diploma with you?" she asks.

"No, but I can send it or bring it at some point," I provide.

"That's fine. Fill out this form, please." She hands me a clipboard with a stack of papers and a pen attached to it.

I take the form; it's the normal general questions like name, address, next of kin, etc. Then comes the more interesting items like my faith and what degree path I might be looking to pursue. I choose the masters in divinity.

"Being that I am intending to pursue masters in divinity and this being a Presbyterian-based church and I currently am a Lutheran, will there be conflict?" I ask.

"No, it should not be an issue," she replies and goes back to her paperwork.

"Thank you." I return to filling out the form.

After sitting there for about an hour, I finish and hand the paperwork back to the lady.

"How do you plan to pay for enrollment?" she asks.

"Umm…I had not thought of that," I admit. "Do I need to pay right now?"

"No," she replies as she screens the paperwork. "But upfront payment is required for the semester prior to starting."

"I can figure that out by then," I say. "Is a check okay to send?"

"Any form of payment should suffice. Finance will send you a receipt at payment," she says. Then she hands me a form. "These are the rates for each class, and normally colleges do not provide housing for advanced studies, but we do have a small housing available for students that may require it," she tells me.

"That would be most accommodating," I say. "Is there anything else I should do or know?"

As she finishes flipping through my application, she says, "Not that I can see. The board will review your submission and be in touch with you soon."

"That sounds splendid. Thank you. Have a good day," I say as I turn to leave.

"Yeah, thank you," she replies.

I walk out of the building and check the bus schedule for the route back to the hotel. I return and freshen up prior to going to find something to eat. Being in the big city is a bit intimidating, but

I find a nice diner called the Ohio House Coffee Shop. As the city is built up around it, this quaint little gem has managed to maintain its unique stone facade and large windows inviting people in should the smell of diner delights and fresh baked goods not be enough. I ask for coffee, which I rarely do since I have a specific preference when it comes to the dark caffeinated brew. I like mine strong, no sugar, no cream; just that nutty, slightly chocolatey, even a hint of spice flavor that one gets from a well-brewed pot of java. But this cup the waitress brings me is especially delicious as I take that first sip. Missing out on a good breakfast and hearing that this is their infamous meal, I order the Deuces Wild: two eggs, two pancakes, two bacon, and two sausages. With a full belly and wide awake from the delicious coffee, I head back to the hotel. Tomorrow my bus leaves for home, and the thought of getting back is a relief as this has been an arduous but enlightening trip.

* * * * *

"This next part is the hardest for me," I say to Patricia as I pause. I finish off the bourbon in my glass and pour another long glass full, which finishes off the bottle.

"What could possibly be harder than killing two people on the Appalachian Trail?" she asks.

"The trail was nothing. The demon literally takes over in every kill. I am merely a vessel for it to achieve its goal."

"Its goal?" she asks, more perplexed than ever.

"Yes. So the way it works, or at least by my understanding, is that the demon has a set requirement of souls that it has to attain. I am merely a vessel for it to accomplish its need to fill hell with fresh souls," I tell her matter-of-factly.

"Continue," she says.

Chapter 28

The ride on the bus is uneventful. The first stop in Madison, Wisconsin, requires me to transfer buses, then the last leg to Dubuque. As I depart from Dubuque, I grab my pack and start the walk out to the house. The sun is bright; it's a bit humid in the early September afternoon. As I stride up the driveway and pass through the archway-like trees, I notice the Saratoga is parked in front of the house. I know I didn't tell Mother that I was going to be home today as I wanted to surprise her. I pass through the front door and call out, "Mother? I'm home." But there is no reply.

I poke my head into the living area and find it empty. I walk down the hall into the kitchen and find dishes in the sink, an otherwise cold appearance, like it had not been used in some time. I head upstairs, and as I reach the middle landing, I call out again, "Mother?"

A faint "Francis?" comes from my mother's room. I knock against the partially open door and step in. There I find my mother lying in bed looking drained and solemn, a plethora of pill bottles and a glass half filled with water on her nightstand.

"Mother? Why are you in bed? Are you okay?" I ask, concern and worry consuming me.

"Francis, have a seat." She pats the side of the bed next to her. I do as instructed and take her hand.

"I am glad you are home. I have something to tell you," she says weakly. "I fell ill and had to go to the hospital about a month ago."

"Why didn't you tell me?" I exclaim. "I would have come home sooner."

"That is exactly why I didn't tell you. I didn't want you to deter your plan to finish the trail and find your way," she says.

"Well, if you were sick a month ago, why are you still in bed now?" I ask.

"It's cancer, Francis." The look on her face tells me she has already come to grips with her fate and has decided to finish her days as peacefully as she can.

I have no words to say. I can see she is beyond the fight. I think at times people find loved ones that have a terminal illness and think that this time will be different. That things can be corrected or reversed. But the fact is that all we try to do is delay the inevitable, and who do we really do it for? Us because we do not want the pain of their loss or for them. Mute questions at this point. I have already experienced enough death to know the look on her face is one of coming to peace with her own existence. She has lived a good wholesome life, going to church every Sunday at the St. Peter's Evangelical Lutheran Church and teaching kids from grades 4 to 6. Her time spent doing for me and raising me, this could be debatable as to her success. Most would say I turned out okay. But if people knew the person I have become, they may not feel the same way. Life is funny that way, especially in a small town outside of a small city.

"Is there anything I can get for you?" I ask after I come out of my stupor.

"Tea perhaps. I believe Sarah has left a teapot on the stove for quick reheating," she informs me.

"Sarah?" I ask.

"Sarah Smith, Mildred's granddaughter, has been checking on me almost daily. She is a nurse, you know." She's telling me as if I automatically know these things.

"Oh, right, Mother. I guess I forgot," I say. "I'll go get you some tea."

I head down to the kitchen and turn on the burner that the teapot is sitting on. I also verified it was full of water. I grab a mug out of the cupboard and a tea bag, resting one inside the other and placing it on the counter while I wait for the water to boil. Looking through the refrigerator, I notice it's full of casseroles and premade meals. Most look like they have been there for good long minute. I check the freezer, and it, too, is full to the brim with various dishes. I shake my head and smile at the reality of how loved Mother is by the community and how my being away has left others to do my duty as her son. She has raised me her whole life and sacrificed for me, though she will never admit it. While during her time of need, I was off feeling sorry for myself. That is about to change.

I hear a car pull into the drive and the front door open a bit later. "Ms. Fleming! It's just me, Sarah," I hear a call from the foyer.

I peek around the corner of the kitchen door. A shriek from the foyer is deafening on my ears.

"Sarah, it's just me," I say.

"Francis!" she exclaims, catching her breath and balance. "You startled me! When did you get home?" She's slightly calmer now.

"Sarah? Francis?" is Mother's faint call from upstairs, quizzing about all the commotion.

I walk down the hall till I can call back up the stairs. "Yes, Mother. I unintentionally startled Sarah. I'll be up in a bit with your tea as soon as the water boils."

"How was your trip?" Sarah asks.

"Long and tiring. But needed, I suppose," I reply. "Please come in. Mother mentioned you had been stopping in to help take care of her in my absence. I greatly appreciate you doing that."

"When she had not been to church for the second week—and she wasn't taking any calls, you see—I was sent over to check on her. Mr. Clark let me in," Sarah tells me.

"Well, I appreciate you doing that and looking after her," I say.

The teapot on the stove starts to whistle, and I grab the cup with the tea bag and pour some water in. "Help yourself to a cup of tea if you like. I'll be right back." I grab the honey jar and, with the cup of tea, head upstairs.

"Here you go, Mother. Would you like me to add some honey to your tea?" I ask, setting the cup down on her nightstand the best I could, given all the medicine bottles.

"No, it actually bothers my throat at times. I find the tea by itself is enough. Could you hold it while I get myself situated and upright, please," she tells me more than asks.

"Of course, Mother," I say, holding the cup while she tries to sit up. I set it back down and reach under her arms and lean her forward, grabbing an extra pillow and placing it behind her back as I lift her into a sitting position. "How is that?" I ask.

"Much better. Tea, please." I hold it up to her lips and tilt slowly so as not to give her too much as it is piping hot.

In the doorway stands Sarah, watching with a cup of tea in her hand.

"She takes one of these and one of these at this time." She points to two of the pill bottles on the nightstand.

"Okay," I reply and extract the dosage Sarah instructed.

I hand the pills to Mother, who takes them and places them in her mouth. Then she motions for the water glass. After taking the pills, she comments, "The tea is too hot yet for my pills," with a smile.

"You two work well together," Mother comments after a bit. Sarah blushes. I respond, "Mother, you know Sarah is now married."

"Yes, well…" she trails off. "May I have my book please?"

On the other side of the bed is a copy of one of Mom's romance novels. Sarah hands it to her, and we motion to each other to head back downstairs. "I'll be back up in a bit, Mother, with some dinner. Is there anything you'd like in particular?"

"Not to sound ungrateful, anything but the casseroles in the fridge. I've had enough casseroles in the last two weeks to satisfy a lifetime," she says as she gains back some of her strength and spirit.

"Yes, ma'am." And I head back to the kitchen.

In the kitchen, I start to look again in the fridge for anything that isn't a casserole and come up empty.

"You're not going to find anything in there but casseroles. I think the entire town brought something over," Sarah tells me.

"Great." I sigh.

"I could go to the store if you like," she offers.

"No, Sarah. I appreciate it, but you truly have done enough. It would not be right for me to impose on you much further. I can go to the store and figure something out," I say. "There is one thing you could do for me, though, if you wouldn't mind, before you have to leave." I almost plead.

"Anything for you or your mother, Francis." She said it in such a way that made my eyebrows perk up, like there's a meaning behind it that I don't know about.

"Since I just returned home, would you mind writing down her daily schedule, please?" I ask.

"Of course," she replies with a smile and, if I didn't know better, a glint in her eye.

"And would you mind staying long enough for me to run to the store? I won't be long. I promise."

Sarah giggles at my request and says, "Yes."

"Again, thank you." I grab the keys to the Saratoga and expedite my trip to the store.

As I return from the store, I bring back the items I need to make chicken cordon bleu, some soup for Mother, along with eggs and bacon for the morning. In the kitchen, I find Sarah has cleaned out the fridge and posted a pill schedule for Mother, as well as some things Mother appreciates.

"Wow! You've been busy," I remark.

"Oh, it's nothing," Sarah says with a smile.

I prepare the soup to take up to Mother and cut some bread to go with it.

"I was planning to make some chicken cordon bleu, if you'd like to stay for dinner," I offer.

"I appreciate the offer, Francis, but with you back to watch over your mother, I really should be getting home to Henry," she says. Henry, her husband, was the school jock and kind of a bully. He and I never really saw eye to eye. Sarah and I dated for a short bit in high school, but when Henry laid his claim to her, I backed off and let it be. To this day, I have not decided if it was the right decision or not, but we all have a path in life and though I am still navigating my way through mine to understand its meaning, it would not be fair to bring someone else in to change their path when I still cannot figure out my own.

"I understand. Maybe another time I can repay you for your kindness," I say.

"I'd like that," Sarah says with a flirtatious smile. Then she gathers her things and starts to head out. I walk her to the door. "If you need anything, just call. Don't worry about Henry. He is used to me not being home with my schedule at the hospital and all." Sarah, despite her shyness, has always made known her attraction to me, at least in private. But now that she is married, I cannot interfere with that. I have more pressing issues at the moment. She drives away in a new Volkswagen Beetle. Everyone is feeling the crunch of the oil crisis right now and buying new more "fuel efficient" cars.

I head back to the kitchen and prep my chicken cordon bleu and the temperature of the chicken soup I heated up for Mother. With my dinner in the oven and her soup in a bowl, I take hers up to her and find she is still sitting up reading her romance novel.

"Here you go, Mother," I say as I set a lap tray across her with the soup and fresh bread. She takes a sip of the chicken broth. "This will do," she says with a slight smile. "Anything is better than another casserole meal."

I sit there a bit, knowing my dinner has a bit to cook. "Would you like your knitting?" I ask her.

"Yes, please. The bag fell and rolled away earlier, and I cannot reach it," she tells me.

I gather it up and place it on the side of the bed where she has access to it. She finishes her soup and works on the bread, sopping up the remaining broth in the bowl.

"She loves you, you know, Francis," Mother says.

"Who? Sarah?" I say surprisingly. "Mother, she is married. What is done is done," I say.

"That may be so. But she still does love you," she says.

Time for a topic change; I have no patience for discussing something I have no control over at this point. "I have to go check on my dinner," I say as I sit up.

"Oh, what did you make?" she asks.

"Chicken cordon bleu," I reply.

"And you brought me chicken soup?" she exclaims. "Now I have to wonder how much you truly love me."

"I wasn't sure what you are able to eat, so I was erring on the side of caution," I say, feeling a bit inadequate.

"Save me some and all will be forgiven," she says matter-of-factly.

I sigh as I reply, "That I can do." I head back down to find the chicken is not quite ready yet, and I fix myself some tea.

After finishing my own meal, I head back upstairs to check on Mother. Her tray is set to the side, and she is struggling to stand up.

"Here, let me help you," I say.

"I just need to use the bathroom," she tells me.

I assist her in standing and walking her to the bathroom attached to her bedroom. The only room in the house where a bedroom has its own bathroom. Kind of a good thing, given that it allows her some privacy. Knowing she is able to make the rest of the way on her own, I close the door behind her and take the tray and set it off to the side. Moments later, I hear the bathroom door and Mother standing there ready to go back to bed.

"That's better," she says as I assist her back to the bed. "Some days are better than others," she tells me. "Today was an in-between type day. Tomorrow, you can tell me all about your trip. But right now, I am tired and think I will just lay down and go to sleep."

"Okay, Mother," I say as I help her lie down and tuck her in. I give her a kiss on the forehead, straighten up a bit, and grab the tray to head out. I look back to see she has closed her eyes, and it won't be long before she falls asleep.

Downstairs I grab *The Exorcist* and settle into the high-back chair. I must have fallen asleep as I wake around 2:00 a.m. The book is open in my lap, and I am still dressed as I was when I sat down hours ago. As my eyes clear from the sleepy fog, I see a figure standing in the doorway. I know it is not Mother.

"About time you woke up, Francis." The voice of the demon immediately tells me who the shadowy figure is.

"Great, it's you." I yawn.

"You didn't think I was just going to stop coming around, did you? After all, we have a connection, Francis. I am you and you are me. There really is no difference between us," the demon explains.

"We are not the same," I reply.

"Oh, but we are, Francis. You see, I live inside of you, and without you, I cannot complete my tasks," the demon says.

"How many of these 'tasks' must you make so that I can be rid of you and live some semblance of a life?" I ask.

"Oh?" The demon, not knowing the real answer, kind of looks off and to the right. "Five, maybe ten. There is no set number per se. It is only when Father is satisfied, I guess," he says in a low, unsure tone.

"Why does God hate me?" I exclaim.

"God does not hate you, Francis," the demon replies. "No. No. No. He is just testing your will, while allowing me to fulfill my destiny, is all."

"What about *my* destiny?" I ask.

The demon moves into the light from the lamp in the room. His face is identical to mine, but somehow more evil, like a demonic, sinister version of myself. His cheekbones and brows are accentuated. His devilish smile extends ear to ear like the makeup on a clown's face, the light from the lamp striking only his most prominent features, and somehow his eyes blaze as if reflecting a flame. Yet everything about him seems hollow.

As he thrusts his face forward, providing me the first real look at him, he speaks in the deepest unearthly tone I have ever heard. "This *is* your destiny, Francis," he says with a hiss as his tongue rides the last syllable of my name. Then he's gone. Just as quickly as he thrust his face into the light, *poof*! He's gone.

I wipe my eyes as if what just transpired was a dream. I look around, and the shadowy figure is gone. The face that was inches from me a minute ago, a sinister reflection of myself, is gone. But then I catch a whiff of it—the faint smell of death.

"Shit!" I say out loud as I run upstairs. "Mother."

I get to her door and slowly open it to look inside. She is still there, sleeping peacefully. I know this as I can hear her light breathing. I roll to the side and press my back against the wall, pulling her door back closed.

"Phew." I sigh a deep sigh of relief. I thought for sure the demon had done something while I slept. It wouldn't be the first time.

I creep softly back down the stairs as I fear waking Mother would not help in her situation. As much as she will try to avoid giving me details, I intend to find out her full diagnosis. The night air is mild with a light breeze, and the moon is all aglow, so I choose to sit out on the front porch to allow myself time to calm after the visit from the demon. As I sit on the porch, I watch a few bats fly over and a rabbit hop across the front lawn; it stops occasionally to savor the dew forming on the savory blades of grass. A young fawn pops out of the woods, looking around as it stoops to enjoy the blades of grass like the rabbit. This time of night or early morning is so quiet and peaceful. I rock back and forth in the chair, where I sit just mulling everything over in my head. Am I premature in my plan to go back to school for ministry? Will I ever reach a point in my life where I am devoid of the demon now lurking in my head? Is there an end to the madness my life is turning into? As I sit there and look out over the tranquil setting before me, questions like these race through my head, but no answers.

Chapter 29

The sun crests the horizon behind the trees that form the wall like a barricade around the property. The dim light starts to overpower the moon's soft glow. The air is heavy with the pending humidity of the coming day. The small deer that was suckling at the grass scurries off back into the woods, I am sure to find its bed for the day in an attempt to avoid as much of the heat as possible. The rabbit has worked its way across the yard and disappears to the side of the house, its burrow probably near the old oak tree that stands guard over the family plots. As long as I find it does not try to eat Mother's rose bushes, it should not be a nuisance. I stand up from the chair I had been resting for the last few hours as I head inside to begin preparing breakfast.

    I grab the cast-iron skillet off the wall and give it a quick wipe with the towel hanging from the stove's handle, setting it on the burner and lighting it off with a match after setting the gas. The swoosh of the gas taking to the flame is heard, producing the brilliant bluish glow. I turn the knob to the appropriate setting and wait as the cast iron heats up, adding four slices of thick-cut bacon I purchased yesterday. As the bacon begins to sizzle, I read over the notes left on the refrigerator by Sarah, noting the pills that I must set aside for Mother at breakfast. With the bacon finished, I start the eggs. I grab two plates, placing two slices of bacon and two over-easy eggs on each. Placing both on the tray, I take them up to Mother and enter her room with a light knock. She rolls over and looks at me, smelling the savory bacon and succulent eggs with their perfectly cooked white edges and rich golden centers.

"Francis, help me sit up please," she says as I set the tray down on the opposite side of the bed. I walk around and lift her as I did yesterday, tucking a pillow behind her for support. I set the tray across her lap and take my plate, breaking the first yoke and dipping parts of the white in.

"You should have a tray to eat off of, young man," she remarks, watching me and forever being Mother.

"Yes, Mother." I continue working on my own breakfast. Maybe later I will make that arrangement. We do keep some trays in the living room from when my grandparents were alive and we would listen to the radio for something different while eating supper.

"I have to run some errands after breakfast, Mother. Is there anything you would care for while I am out?" I ask, having my the last bite of bacon.

"Given that I do not want chicken soup every meal, I think it would be nice to have some variety," she says.

"Agreed," I reply. "Anything special you want? Or more specifically things you should not have?" I ask.

"Being in my situation, nothing is off-limits," she says haughtily.

"Is that your assessment or the doctor's?" I retort.

"Mine," she says.

"What does the doctor say?" I play back at her.

"Oh, the doctors be damned, Francis. It's cancer. There is nothing anyone can do about it, and I figure I might as well enjoy my predicament the best I can. Call it a dying woman's last wish," she says all of this, as if I have no choice but to follow her wishes.

My stance and posture relax a bit as I think about the big picture and assess the reality of the situation. "Fair, I can see your points. However, I have a request of my own," I say to her.

"That is?" she hits me right back.

"No more talk of 'a dying woman's last wishes,'" I say. "There is nothing I wouldn't do for you, you know this. But the reminder of the obvious and inevitable does not make the situation any easier to succumb to," I explain.

"Alright," she agrees. "Deal. If you can hand me that pad and pen over there, I will create a list of things I would like and/or need."

I hand her the pen and pad. "I'll be back soon to retrieve your wishes," I say as I head to my room to shower and change.

Moments later, I return to find she only has a handful of requests.

"This is all you want?" I say.

"For now," she replies. "I may add more later. I don't know right now."

"Okay," I say as I take the list and head out to run my errands.

Off I go to the store to stock up the refrigerator properly—my list of items and those requested by Mother. On my way, I pass the hardware store and stop in to see Mr. Clark. The bell on the front door jingles.

"Mr. Clark?" I call out.

"Is that...?" Mr. Clark calls back. "Well, I'll be! Francis! How are you, my good man? I see the trail didn't consume you."

I laugh. "Funny you say that. There were a few times I was I afraid it just may."

He laughs with me, being the only one who actually knows what I mean.

"So how was it?" he asks. "Were you able to find what you were looking for?"

"Oddly, and after much time," I say, "yes."

"That's good!" Mr. Clark says jovially. "I knew it would help you. So tell me about your trip."

"Ah, that may have to wait for another day," I say.

"Oh, you've been home, I see." He notices the look on my face.

"Yeah..." I trail off.

"How is she?" he asks.

"Overall, I think she is doing all she can, given the circumstances," I say. "But to be honest, I have no idea. I've only been home a day, and she hasn't told me her full diagnosis yet. I'm just out getting things we need for the house."

"I know everyone in this town has been by to check on her. She truly is loved by this community," Mr. Clark tells me.

"I know." The look on my face must be speaking volumes, given Mr. Clark's reactions and tone. "I cannot sit in that house and watch her fade away," I begin. "Could you use some assistance around here?"

"I could always use help, Francis. But she needs you too," Mr. Clark says. "Tell you what. After you get settled and have a full understanding of the situation, give me a call and we can work something out. But I'm afraid you may find that your presence out there may be more required than you realize. You can't let her bullheadedness mislead you."

Mr. Clark always has a way of putting life into perspective, at least for me. I mean, hell, he is the one who convinced me to hike the Appalachian Trail to find my way. He also helped me in deciding my major in college for engineering. Summers all spent here in this store, high school through college, all up until I received the notice from the Army, and then he prompted me to talk to the Marines. He truly has been a good mentor to me. I suppose there is some truth in what he said in that I should be home more for Mother and that she needs me more than she is letting on.

"You are probably correct, Mr. Clark. I have to run these errands and get back home right now anyways. So after I get Mother under control, I will let you know." Clearly my demeanor has taken a turn toward disheartened as I say this all out loud and the realization sets in. Mother won't survive this, and I need to grasp this reality.

"Francis." Mr. Clark lays his hand on my shoulder. "You are a good man. Your mother and grandparents raised you right. This isn't easy. I have seen many struggle with cancer. I will continue to pray for you and your mother. If you find you need a break or any help, feel free to reach out to me or stop by."

"Thanks, Mr. Clark. And just so you know, you had a hand in the man I've become, and I appreciate you for it." I smile back at him and head for the door.

Upon returning home with the list complete, I head upstairs to check on Mother. She is sitting there knitting, and I see her book is not too far away.

"I am home," I let her know.

"How is Mr. Clark?" she asks.

"How did you know?" I ask. "Am I that predictable?"

She gives me a knowing look. "Don't you worry. He kept an eye on me too while you were gone."

I smile; a warmth overcame me knowing the love the people in this town have for my mother.

"I have to go put the groceries away. Are you interested in lunch?" I ask.

"Yes, please," she replies.

"How does tomatoes soup and grilled cheese sound?" I ask.

"Absolutely delicious," she remarks.

I turn and head downstairs to the kitchen. I fix her a cup of tea and her lunch as well as mine. While things are set in the kitchen, I grab a tray table and take it upstairs. No sense in listening to her bicker at me again. With lunch delivered and consumed, I ask how she is feeling.

"Oh, I think lunch gave me a bit of energy," she replies. "Want to tell me about your trip?"

"If that would make you happy," I say with a warm smile. "Give me a couple of minutes. I want to grab a more comfortable chair."

"I'll be right here. Not like I can go far very fast anyway," she says with a sly chuckle.

I shake my head and grab a rocking chair. I settle in and tell her about my trip. I tell her how arduous it was at first and how after the first day or two, my body adjusted. She asks about my back, and I tell her it has not bothered me as much as it had before. I tell her about the people I met along my journey and the majestic views. I tell her about Melody and Judy finding me naked in the stream. Surprisingly she laughs at this; my usually very modest mother laughs at me getting caught naked by two women. Interesting. I tell her about meeting up with Nathan at the Delaware Water Gap. I tell her about the man I met while resting at Canopus Lake, even the strangeness of how he disappeared into the mist.

"That is strange," she says. A look crosses her face after this part of the story.

"What is that look for?" I ask.

"Well, Francis, you haven't quite been yourself since you returned. I wonder if everything is okay," she explains.

"Oh, I think I have everything kind of figured out. I just haven't gotten to that point yet in the story, Mother," I tell her, trying to be reassuring.

"I don't mean from your trip on the trail. I mean you haven't seemed yourself since you returned from Vietnam."

"Oh, that. Like what do you mean exactly?" I ask, praying she hasn't seen the demon when I haven't been aware.

"That one night for one. Where you cried out in pain and I have caught you 'talking' to yourself. Sometimes I have heard you speak softly in a strange tone and almost like you were speaking in another language," she says, looking at me with this concern on her face.

"Oh," I say in a way that is sheepish. This is one thing I had feared, that Mother may see the demon that has taken residence in me. The question now is, Do I tell her? Or do I not tell her?

"Mother, what I am going to tell is not pleasant. I have kept it from you in a way so as to protect you. But clearly I have failed at that attempt. It is partially why I needed to go on the hike of the Appalachian Trail in hopes that I could either rid myself of the situation or learn how to control it. I may have a solution," I tell her.

"Francis, they diagnosed me with pancreatic cancer. The doctor diagnosed me in August. I had a feeling when you first mentioned your desire to hike the Appalachian Trail that things were not right after you returned from Vietnam. I spoke to Mr. Clark about this, and he agreed you seemed 'not yourself.' Of course, he explained to me the benefits of you going on this adventure and what it had accomplished for him. That, in part, is why I agreed you should go. But when I was diagnosed in August, I felt it best to wait for you to return before I told you the situation. As far as, whatever this affliction is you have acquired while in Vietnam, you don't have to tell me. I can see that it is something you clearly are struggling with." She stops me, as if she knows but doesn't want to know. Now I question if I should tell her at all as she clearly has given me a much-needed out.

"Okay, Mother. We can leave it as is. I do have a plan though, and I would love nothing more than to tell you the rest of the story," I say with understanding and hope.

"Yes, dear. Of course," she says.

"One quick question," I ask. "With your prognosis, did they give you a time frame?"

She looks down, tears welling in her eyes. "Yes, three to six months," she tells me as matter-of-factly as she can without allowing the tears to flow.

I stand and walk over to the bedside. I wrap my arms around her and give her the strongest hug I can and tell her I love her. Now I know why Mr. Clark said I would be more useful here than at the store. We share a few tears, and then I sit back up.

"I am here for whatever you need, Mother," I say as she dries her eyes with a tissue.

"I know, Francis. I think I need to rest before dinner. Before you ask, you know what would be good? A lasagna. Do you think we have what we need for that?" she asks.

"I saw it as part of your list, and yes, I picked up the necessary ingredients," I tell her. I kiss her on the forehead and softly close the door.

I prep the dinner for the night, and after placing the dish in the oven, I sit out in the living room. At first, I grab my book to read and take my mind off the conversation from earlier, but it is no use, and I break down softly as tears flow.

"Kill her, Francis," the demon says. "Just place a pillow over her head and press. You'll be doing her a favor. It's the humane thing to do, Francis."

"I cannot do that, you evil creature. How could you say that I should kill my own mother?" I reply. "How heartless are you? Oh, wait, I know that answer, as you have no heart, you vile creature."

"It would solve your problem and hers, Francis. She is in pain you could never fathom. You are actually hurting her more by allowing her to live," the demon explains.

"The only problem I have, demon, is YOU!" I shout louder than I intended, hoping I'm not disturbing Mother. "And don't you DARE use me to kill her either," I say almost as sinister as the demon within.

Chapter 30

Oddly that was enough to silence the demon. As shocking as that notion is, I realize how much time has passed, and I need to check on dinner. I remove the cover over the dish, and the cheese is fully melted on top, edges bubbling away. I leave the cover off so the top can crust. Nothing is better than that gooey browned top layer of cheese with the individual layers of cheeses and meat tucked in union under it. I step out to walk down to grab the day's mail as a set of headlights shine through the shadow of the arched wooded driveway. I pause as the old panel truck driven by Mr. Clark slowly pulls to a stop in front of the house.

I walk to the side of the truck. "Mr. Clark! What a pleasant surprise. I wasn't expecting to see you this evening."

"After our talk earlier today, Francis, I realized I had not been out here in a few days and figured I would stop out to see how you and your mother were making out," he says.

"I was just headed down to the mailbox if you care to walk with me," I offer.

"Lead the way, my good man. Lead the way."

Together we walk back down the drive, and I tell him about the conversation Mother and I had. Like a surrogate father, he places his arm around my shoulder and tells me he is there for both of us. As we head back, I tell him I have a lasagna in the oven and offer for him to stay.

"That sounds delightful. If you don't mind, I think I will head up and check on your mother," he says.

"That would be fine. I have to check on the lasagna and finish setting for dinner," I say.

With the lasagna out and rested, I cut portions as symmetrical as possible, placing each piece on individual plates. I prepare Mother's tray and walk it upstairs to her room where I find her sitting up with her knitting in her lap and Mr. Clark in the chair as they chatter away like two teenagers.

"Francis! Thank you," Mother says as I rest the tray across her in bed.

"I can bring up an extra tray and our plates to join you, Mother, if you like," I state.

"I didn't know you were staying for dinner, Clark. No. You two go enjoy at the table and talk. I have no doubt you have plenty to discuss. I can manage just fine up here by myself," she says.

Mr. Clark and I both know not to argue with Mother, and we excuse ourselves.

"Francis, this is delicious," Mr. Clark exclaims.

"Thank you. Mother showed me her method and preparations. I just followed that," I answer.

"Francis. I've had your Mother's lasagna and"—he lowers his voice to a whisper—"don't tell her, but this is better."

I just laugh. "I can assure you I will never tell her you said that. We both would get it."

We alight to the front porch after dinner. I pour an Old Forester bourbon for each of us into a set of old-fashioned glasses. We kick back and talk about old times. Stories about when my grandparents ran the store and little me running around causing chaos till my grandmother had enough aa my grandfather sat back and chuckled. Ah, those were the days. Carefree and no real worries in life.

"I remember your grandparents had a barbecue here once and your grandparents inviting me over. I think I was around twenty years old. In fact, I know I was as I had recently returned from hiking the trail myself," Mr. Clark tells me with a glint in his eye.

"I can't say I remember that." I chuckle.

"Oh no, you wouldn't. You were barely a year or two old at that point. I remember your mother sitting there holding you and rocking softly away while you napped," he tells me. "So. How was it, Francis? How is the old trail holding up?"

I proceed to tell him about my adventures on the trail, being cautious not to give away anything alarming. We laugh at the girls finding me in the river naked as a jaybird, and when I got to the man by Canopus Lake, he stops as did Mother. I'm starting to wonder if I should even include this part in my tales of the trail.

"I had a similar experience when I was on the trail," Mr. Clarks starts. "I forget where, but it was a chilly morning and I was sitting by a stream. The water was too cold to soak my feet. Hell, I would have gotten pneumonia. But I remember this old guy walked right up and sat down next to me. He asked me where I was from and where I was going. Then he told me this story, very impromptu, how he had fought in The Great War and how by the time he returned, the woman he loved had gone off and married someone else. He told me how fortunate I was for not going over there and that I should find something I loved and just let life lead the way instead of trying to force it. I thought long and hard about that old man's words. When he finished, he got up and just vanished into the mist. Strangest thing I ever encountered in life. I even got up and looked for him, but he was gone, and as he disappeared, the mist broke and you could see everything, but not him."

"Just curious. Did you catch his name?" I chuckle.

"I did. But damned if I can remember it today," he says, shaking his head. "There are things that happen in those old mountains that no one can ever explain. People go missing, people are found dead. There is a lot attached to those old mountains, a lot of history, dating, well, back before we ever came here." He pauses, as if deep in thought. "But there is a lot of peace to be found in those hills. In some ways, following that old man's advice provided me a very fulfilling life. I returned to help out your family with the store and always felt like family with you all. When your mother came to me and offered me the store, I couldn't believe it, but I also knew she couldn't run it on her own. Ah, one day, Francis, this will all be gone. I wish it wasn't so, but things change. Places change. It's just life and the world as we know it."

"I hope things do not change too fast. I kind of like life just the way it is right now. Minus Mother being sick, of course," I say.

"Here is to the past, that it may stay there, to the present, that we live through it, and to the future, that it may be brighter than ever." Mr. Clark raises his glass of bourbon toward me. We clink and drink.

"I probably should be going," he says.

As Mr. Clark pulls away from the house, I pour another bourbon and sit on the porch and watch the sun finish going down. Thoughts run through my head of the conversation I had with Mr. Clark, of him having a similar experience that I did and thinking to myself the number of places potentially haunted on the trail. Then the idea crosses my mind that maybe it is God's way of guiding those of us on the trail that are looking for answers. Regardless of the reasons, it is ironic how it all relates.

As the sun dips just below the horizon, I reflect on the conversation with Mother. She knows something isn't right, and yet I can't tell her the whole truth. Nor can I allow the demon to try and follow through with his plans. It's a hell of a pickle I have now found myself in. At what point can things change for the better?

It dawns on me, no one has checked on Mother for several hours. I down the last of the bourbon in my glass and head upstairs to check on her. As I peer in the door, I find her sleeping, her tray on the opposite side of the bed. I cautiously and quietly pick it up. As I walk out of the room, I hear "Francis?", her voice strained and soft.

"Yes, Mother," I whisper back.

"Good night," she says and drifts back off.

After cleaning up in the kitchen, I prepare for bed and now, as the sun has fully descended, decide that sleep isn't such a bad thing and lie down to drift off myself.

The following weeks become a monotonous norm, of taking care of Mother, doing odd things around the house, and occasionally stopping in the hardware store when I have to run errands. In early October, I receive a letter from McCormick Theological, reminding me that full admission was approved and I could start at the beginning of the next term. With the state Mother is in, I am not sure this will be a reality for me at this time.

"Good morning, Mother," I say as I walk in with her breakfast. "How are you feeling today?"

"I've been better," she says. "The pain comes and goes." I hand her the morning dosages and the tea I made her.

"The doctor will be by today to check on you," I tell her. He comes by once a week, given her state. When she was diagnosed, they gave her the option to stay in the hospital or to live out her days in at home. She chose to go home saying, "I've lived there most of my life, and it's closer to where I will be in the afterlife." Meaning the family plot under the old oak. She is a stubborn woman, but she knows what she wants or at least how she would like to spend her final days. Given her choice, the doctor offered to come and make weekly visits to check on her prognosis.

"Okay, Francis," she replies. Her voice is sounding weaker than usual this morning. I watch her try to eat, and I can see it is becoming more of a struggle as her body is shutting down from the cancer. Nothing is worse than watching a family member suffer through such an atrocious ailment. Given her state, I wash her down in the bed after her breakfast. Then I follow my normal routine until the doctor arrives.

At 10:00 a.m., there's a knock at the front door. Right on time. I open the door to find Dr. Mahoney—about my age, dressed in a pair of slacks, nice white pressed shirt, and a V-neck sweater vest, carrying nothing more than her records.

"Good morning, Doc!" I say.

"Good morning, Francis," he replies. "How is she today?"

"She seems weaker than normal," I tell him.

"Well, let's go see how she responds," he says, and I lead him up the stairs.

The door to her room is open, and the smell of one who is waiting for death's arrival penetrates the nostrils.

"Would you care for some coffee or tea?" I offer the doctor.

"Coffee sounds good, thank you," he replies. I usually let him do his normal evaluation to begin without me being in the way.

I return with the cup of coffee and find him finishing up.

"Mary, given the situation, I'd say you are no worse than my last visit," Dr. Mahoney states.

"The pain is getting worse," she says.

"I am not surprised," he responds. "The only thing I can do for that would be to set up an IV stand with a morphine drip to slowly administer the painkiller at an appropriate rate. Outside of that, the pills I have prescribed are about the best option I can offer. How has her diet been?" He turns to ask me.

"She hasn't been eating as much," I reply, "but I do my best to vary it up and give her choices that she appreciates."

"Yes, I am afraid that is about all you can do at this rate, Francis, just try to make her as comfortable as possible." He turns to Mother. "Well, Mary, there is not much else I can do today." He lays his hand on her knee for reassurance, that personable touch. "You keep up the good fight, and I will be back next week. Francis, I'll talk to you downstairs."

Downstairs, he tells me, "She is getting worse, Francis. If you haven't already, I would make preparations. I don't mean to seem so blunt, but with the pain increase, I would estimate she does not have much longer."

"I had a feeling, Doc" is all I can muster.

"I work with Sarah at the hospital. If you want to come by and pick up an IV stand, I can arrange for the saline drip and Sarah can teach you how to administer the dosages of morphine through the drip," he offers.

"Given her state, okay. I just want to make her as comfortable as I possibly can at this point," I say.

"That's what we all want, Francis. Unfortunately, there is not much else any of us can do. If you had not been here, I would have insisted she be brought to the hospital," he says.

"I get it, Doc. Please make the arrangements for the stand and the drip. I will be by later to pick them up and get in touch with Sarah to arrange for her assistance." Solemnly I say all this and look down to avoid eye contact as I don't want Doc to see my eyes well with the pain of losing my mother.

"Done, Francis. Give me about an hour or two, and it will be ready later this afternoon."

"Thank you, Doctor. I hope the rest of your day goes well," I say as I lead him to the door.

I stand on the porch and wave as he heads back down the driveway. Once out of sight, my body slumps. I actually have to grab the railing to keep from completely collapsing. Illnesses like this are hard not only on the patient but also on the family members. I say a quick prayer, more like a plea to God for him to take her soon so she is no longer in pain. I can only hope that he is listening.

Chapter 31

I freshen myself up, then check on Mother as I grab the keys to head into town. I go straight to the hardware store where I find Mr. Clark helping a customer. I take a seat on the stool by the counter. I think to myself how well my backside fits into the stool as I have worn a permanent impression over the years.

Finished with the customer, Mr. Clark turns to me. "Good morning, Francis. By the look on your face, I'd say you were here for a reason."

"I am and I am not sure where to start," I say. "I have a decision to make, and I am not sure what I should do."

"Given the day, I have to guess the doctor's visit didn't go well," he says.

"It did confirm my suspicions, and in some ways, I suppose it provided me the answer I seek," I tell him. "On my way back from hiking the trail, I had a few days in Chicago. With the advice and soul searching, I applied to McCormick Theological Seminary."

"You!" he says, slight shock in his voice. "You planning to join the ministry?"

"There is more to the story, but yes," I say. "There are certain things that happened while I was in the Marines, and I cannot fully explain as I myself do not fully understand them. So during my time on the trail, and more accurately on my ride home, I made the decision to go to seminary. Is it the right answer? I do not know. What I do know is that they accepted me and I have to send a payment. Now the money is not the issue. But I did all of this before I knew about Mother being sick. I cannot in good faith place the burden of her care back on anyone else as it is my responsibility."

"I think I see your dilemma," Mr. Clark says consolingly. "Now that you have received the acceptance letter, you are not sure will be able to attend the school. I am assuming you would start in January after winter break."

"Yes, that pretty much sums it up." I sigh.

"What did the doctor say?"

"I didn't mention any of this to him," I state.

"I meant what was his prognosis of your mother?" he asks.

"Oh, sorry, too much running through my head. He told me she is not getting better, if anything, it is much worse, and he doesn't expect her to be able to fight much longer," I inform him.

"It seems to me, as unfortunate as the doctors news is, you have your answer," Mr. Clark says in a tone that is both solemn and comforting. "Francis, your mother is loved by all in this town just like your grandparents were. To watch her suffer this way is tragic, given all she has provided to the community. But this is an incurable ailment. She will be better off when God's clock strikes and he accepts her into his kingdom. You know this."

"I agree. I guess on one hand, I hate to lose her, and on the other, I hate watching her in pain," I say.

"I understand," he says. "I would send the payment. I have a feeling God's plan is for you to follow through with this and he will soon relieve your burden and your mother's."

"I believe you are probably correct. You usually are," I say with a struggling smile. "I have to go this afternoon and find Sarah at the hospital when I pick up an IV drip for Mother. The doctor is prescribing morphine to ease as much of her pain as possible."

"If that is his current solution, then I can tell you from experience she does not have much longer. Very soon, God will take her," he says. The words hurt more than they should. I mean, just the diagnosis of cancer is like closing the lid of the coffin on a person's life. In time, there may be better answers, but that time is not now.

"New subject," I say. "If we keep up this conversation, I won't make it to the hospital as I won't be able to see."

"Tell me about this seminary you were accepted to," Mr. Clark states.

"Well, it primarily caters to Presbyterian, but they accept all faiths. So I can still attain my masters in ministry to be a pastor in the Lutheran church," I tell him.

"Are you planning on being here? In Dubuque?" he asks.

"I mean, I haven't thought that far in advance, but it would make the most sense. I suppose I should go Sunday and talk to Pastor Paul and get some advice," I say.

"It would probably be a good move. You may also want to consider the fact that Pastor Paul is no young man. By talking to him, you may be able to secure a position to train under him and then possibly take his place when he retires," Mr. Clark points out.

"I had not considered any of that. That is an excellent idea. I'll talk to him on Sunday after service," I say. "But I probably should get going. I need a check to send to the school and then the hospital for the supplies the doctor promised me."

"Be safe, my friend, and keep the faith. I know you have a lot on your plate, but you got this," Mr. Clark says as I head toward the door.

Chapter 32

With the check from the bank secured, I drive over to Xavier Hospital. I walk in the main reception area and ask where I might find Sarah working today and where Dr. Mahoney's office is. With visitor pass and directions, I head to find Sarah. No point in getting the equipment if I don't have the assistance I need to set it up or administer the morphine.

Sarah is working the nurses' desk of the Oncology Department.

"Hi, Sarah," I say as I approach the desk.

"Francis! Is everything okay?" she asks.

"Oh yes, everything is fine," I tell her. "Dr. Maloney stopped by earlier to do his weekly check on Mother."

"Oн!" she exclaims "That's right. He did mention something about setting up an IV drip so we can administer morphine. But you didn't have to come all the way here. You could have called."

"I was out and about running errands and figured I stop by on my way to grab the equipment from Dr. Maloney's office," I say with a smile.

"I see. Well, I was just about to go on break for lunch. You're lucky you caught me," she says. "Would you like to join me?"

"That sounds like a good idea. I will if you'll have me," I flirt back, but not too strong.

"Hope you don't mind hospital cafeteria food?" she states as we head that direction.

"After rations, I can eat anything," I state, noting the questionable rations they handed us for patrols while I was in Vietnam. She laughs.

Hospital food is never anyone's favorite food, but it is what is available. I get a tuna sandwich and some fruit, while Sarah orders a chicken sandwich and fruit. We find a table and talk about Mother and her state of health. We avoid the fact that it is the sign of the end. She offers to stop by after her shift to assist me in setting up the IV and teaching me how to inject the morphine into the drip. After we finish, Sarah directs me to Dr. Maloney's office.

"Dr. Maloney?" I say as I knock on the open door.

Dr. Maloney motions me in the office as he stands. "Ah! Francis. Yes, the IV stand and medication." He shows me the setup and says, "Here you go," with a smile.

"Thank you, sir. I spoke to Sarah, and she offered to stop by later so she can show me how to set it all up."

"Perfect!" he says. "I'll be by next week as scheduled. But if anything changes, let me know, and if needed, we can always adjust the dosage."

"Yes, Doc. Thank you again." I take the supplies out to the Saratoga and load them in the trunk. Now back to the house to check on Mother.

I return home after a quick run through the grocery store for updated items in the house. I go and check on Mother as I take the newly acquired IV drip and medicine to her room. I find her sitting up the best she can, knitting away and listening to the radio. I ask her what she prefers for dinner that night and take care of things downstairs. After dinner, Sarah comes by the house to assist and show me how to set up the IV drip.

"So now that the drip is set and her port is secured to her arm, all you have to do is change out the bags like this." Sarah shows me how to quickly connect and disconnect the IV solution. "Then to administer the morphine, you open this cinch, and you can use it to adjust the flow to be more or less depending on the recommended dosage by the doctor. Since Dr. Mahoney has it set for 5 mg, then we set it here, and you should not have to worry about it again until the bags are empty," Sarah explains as she shows me.

"That does not seem all that difficult," I say.

"Thank you, Sarah," Mother says as I can tell the morphine is kicking in. Her eyes start to glaze over like the guys did when we gave them morphine shots in the field during the war.

Sarah and I venture downstairs.

"Sarah, I cannot express my gratitude enough," I say to her.

She looks back at me with a glow about her, one I have seen in women before but cannot place the understanding of why they get it. It makes her seem more beautiful than I can remember.

"Francis, I would do anything for you," she says. "And your mother, of course. She has always been so kind to me," her tone shifts and picks up a bit.

"Sarah, I..." I pause. I become lost for words. "I...I truly am sorry," I say finally.

"Sorry? For what?" She looks back at me with this look. I look away because if I don't, I may do something I might regret.

"I don't know." *Oh, I know*, I think as I stare off past her.

"You have nothing to be sorry for," she says this as if she knows exactly what I am talking about. "But I have to get going." She gathers up her things. I reach for arm and grasp it. I don't want her to leave. I want to wrap her up in my arms. She lays her hand on mine, the one that is holding her arm.

"Francis," she says with a knowing smile. "I know. If things were different."

I release her and slump. "I...again I am sorry. I shouldn't..."

"Francis, it is okay. But I have to go home to Henry," she says.

I shake off my ignorance of the reality. "Yes, yes, absolutely. I...I don't know what came over me. Thank you again for your assistance with Mother and showing me that." I smile and open the door for her.

"Francis," she says. "There are things I would like to say to you too. Right now is not the time. I am here if you need me again." She smiles and walks out to her Beetle.

If only she knows how much I want and need her. I was a damn fool for not fighting for her more in high school. But what if I had? I still would have gone off to Vietnam. I would still be the same as I am today, and who knows? Maybe through college, we would not have lasted. Oh, I don't know. I walk over and pour a shot of bourbon. I sling that down and pour myself another very long pour.

Chapter 33

The week goes by, and as Sunday comes, I think about what Mr. Clark suggested, in talking to Pastor Paul. For the first time in many years, I prepare to go to church. Before going, I make sure Mother is okay and situated. I let her know my intention.

"Francis." She smiles at me. "I am glad you are finally going back to church. Say hello for me."

"I will, Mother." I lean down and kiss her forehead.

I find my spot in the back of the church. I try to remain inconspicuous, but too many recognize me.

"Francis?" a voice asks.

"Hello, Mrs. Smith," I say. "How are you today?"

"I am well," she replies. "It's nice to see you back. How is your mother?"

"She is holding on. I hate to say she has been better, but given the circumstances, she is doing as well as can be," I say.

"We understand that. We will continue to pray for her," Mrs. Smith replies as she sits down.

Me too, I think in my head.

"Francis?" Pastor Paul asks.

"Pastor." I stand and shake his hand.

"It is good to see you," he says. "How are you, and how is Mary?"

"Mother is as good as can be expected," I reply. "In fact, if you have time, I was hoping to talk to you about something?" I ask.

"Will after service be okay?" he responds.

"Absolutely," I answer.

"It truly is a blessing to see you this morning, Francis," Pastor Paul says.

"Thank you, Pastor." I smile in return and sit back down as he continues his rounds of the congregation.

The service is typical: affirmations, donations, sermon, and benediction. During the prayer portion, a special note is made of my presence and Mother, given her condition. Most of it, I feel numb, I cannot lie. But it is a good feeling knowing that people love my mother. I sit through the service thinking to myself what the hell possessed me to choose the ministry. But as I sit there, I am reminded of all the good people in this town and congregation that truly care. As things wrap up, I sit and reflect waiting for the masses to file out. As the sanctuary clears and all that is left is but a few small groups chatting, I head toward the main door where I know I can find Pastor Paul.

"Ah, Francis," he says as I approach.

"Pastor Paul. Good service. It's nice being back," I say.

"You asked to speak with me?" he asks.

"More along the lines of advice," I say.

He looks around. "I think enough have filed out that I can afford some time," he says with a warm smile. "Here, let's go to my office."

As we head in, he motions for me to have a seat. "What can I do for you, young man?" he asks.

"After I returned from Vietnam, I have been struggling with figuring out what my purpose is in life and what I would like to do," I tell him.

"Didn't you go to school for engineering?" he asks.

"I did," I reply. "But I just do not feel the same passion for that anymore."

"I see," he says as he hangs up his robe and shawl. "So what are you thinking now?" he asks.

"Funny thing. I applied to McCormick Theological Seminary in Chicago," I say.

"You did?" he says with surprise.

"I did," I say solemnly.

"I am a bit surprised. If I may, what brought this on?" he asks.

"After returning, I was struggling with what I should be doing and where I needed to be in life. I spoke to Mr. Clark about my dilemma, and he recommended I walk the Appalachian Trail to help me find myself," I begin to tell the story. "I started the hike thinking I would receive a sign from above. But nothing manifested itself."

He laughs. "Yeah, God rarely sends an angel down to direct us."

"So I have learned," I reply. "But in more subtle ways, God, I feel, did speak to me…" I proceed to provide the *Reader's Digest* version of my venture.

"In a way, you feel God is directing you toward the ministry," he states.

"That's the best answer I have been able to come up with," I reply.

"And how can I assist?" he asks.

"To be honest, I am not sure," I start. "After talking to Mr. Clark, he suggested I speak to you in hopes to get some advice."

"Clark has always been a faithful servant of the Lord and this community," Pastor Paul replies. "Well, is it okay if I tell you a bit and ask you a few questions?"

"Yes, sir. Absolutely."

"When I first started, I wasn't sure why either. For that part, we can bypass, because in time, you may start to realize why you were chosen," he tells me. "But in all of this, it is about leading the flock or congregation. In that, you have to apply yourself because they count on you as the minister."

"I can understand and appreciate that, Pastor," I say.

"To be honest, Francis, your desire to do this has taken me a bit off guard," he continues.

"I can understand that also, Pastor," I say, trying to be humble. "I do have a concern though."

"What's that?"

"Well, I have sinned. I have had to kill people. Is that…okay?" I ask, afraid at this point to give too much away.

"Francis. We have all sinned. Though yes, the killing of another is the deadliest of sins. The one thing you should remember is this:

God forgives us all. That is why he sent his only son to die to on the cross for our sins. You doing your 'duty' in Vietnam is something God can see, and provided you pray and ask for his forgiveness, he shall. God knows our flaws, and he knows we are imperfect," Pastor Paul says.

Pastor Paul offers to pray with me and help me in asking for atonement for my sins. Afterward, he offers for me to guide me through the learning process and agrees to take me on as an assistant pastor after I finish the seminary. I thank him and show my gratefulness for his approval. I leave as he has other obligations and I have to be getting back to Mother.

Chapter 34

The month of October is not easy as my entire life is consumed with caring for Mother. Aside from ensuring she takes her medications and is fed, I basically am left to watch her fade from this physical existence on earth. Each day is a continuance of the day before, it seems. As much as I love my mother, it's hard to watch her deteriorate. I'm going mad. My drinking is getting worse as I find it is the only outlet to drown the pain and dreariness of being in that house. I no longer have to worry about the nightmares as most nights, I am awake tending to Mother.

The beginning of November comes, as well as a letter from McCormick Theological Seminary stating that my payment has been received. They also include a notice that I should receive paperwork in the coming weeks with introductory information for students as well as my first-semester classes. The news of going back to school is underwhelming at best as my duty to Mother has not ceased.

Then on a blistery cold night, I'm sitting in the rocking chair I had set in Mother's room and am awakened by the sound of her weak voice.

"Francis," she says, barely audible.

Wiping the tiredness from my eyes, I sit up in the chair. "Yes, Mother."

"Come here please and sit with me," she whispers.

If the house wasn't deathly silent, I would never hear a word she's about to utter.

"I met him, Francis," she says. "He came to me."

"Who, Mother?" I ask, realizing I myself am whispering back to her.

"Your affliction," she says. An odd way to describe the demonic spirit attached to me, and I could only assume that is who she's referring to as I know of no other affliction.

"My affliction, Mother?" I say, hoping I'm wrong and that it's just the morphine talking.

"Yes, dear. The demonic spirit you brought back with you from the war," she starts. "I don't have much time left, so I just need you to listen. He visited me before you went on your adventure. At first, I thought it was you just standing in the dark. But the voice speaking to me was yours but not yours. I understand why you had to go. I also now know why this has happened to me. For he has visited me again. He told me that you must be alone and therefore I had to die. He told me there was no way he could ever convince you to kill me yourself and that this was the only way he could get you to comply."

My eyes are like saucers at this point, tear-saturated saucers as wide as they could ever be without popping from my head. Rage sears through my very core. I want to strangle the demon, but to do so would be to strangle myself and that, minus hanging, is impossible to do.

I just sit there turning a dark sinister red, but not that of the demon but of my own hatred for what this entity has done to my mother, the old man, Judy, Melody, and not to mention, me. I feel helpless and destroyed. As if the last several months of caring for Mother and watching her die slowly isn't enough, NOW to find out that this bastard attached to me is the cause. It is almost too much to bear.

"Mother," I say, tears soaking my cheeks, my chin, and hands as they hold hers. "I do not know what to say. I am so sorry to have brought this on you. On this family. It is all my fault."

"Francis," her meek voice says as she squeezes my hand. "It is not your fault. I have known for a long time. I did not mention it to you after your return because I was afraid you would not return or do something drastic. This would have happened no matter what." She pauses as if to catch her breath, but it's probably to gain her strength.

"It's odd also that when he told me, he even apologized. But it's all going to be okay. Because he is not the only one to visit me."

I wipe the tears from my face and look at her in surprise and worry. Another demon or, God forbid, the devil himself would just be the icing on the cake, and I might completely lose any control I possibly have left.

"Michael came. You know the Angel Michael, the one who cast Lucifer out of the kingdom of God. He himself came to me and told me a story of how this demon came about. Then he told me the demon's purpose and how he could not possibly hurt me. Michael told me God allowed this cancer to happen so that I may enter his kingdom and not be subjected to the demon's doings."

"Mother," I say. "You should rest. Clearly this is the morphine talking, and you are too weak to speak of such things."

"Now you listen here, Francis Isiah." Her voice is no longer meek but full of her old self. "I know what I heard and what I saw. I know about the demonic spirit attached to you. I knew well before the morphine. I have not much time left, but I want you to know I will be going to heaven. Michael the angel has assured me. But, Francis, I also know this demon is not going away and will most likely be the death of you." She sighs and tears well in her eyes. "But I made a deal, Francis. I offered something they could not refuse, and no matter what you do for the rest of this life, you have a place in God's kingdom. You will be with your father, your grandparents, and myself. But you must give in and give the demon his due, and for the love of me and God and heaven above, you must not get caught. Just do your tasks and all will be well. God has already forgiven you, and he has a plan to destroy the demon. But only if you follow the deeds set forth."

At this point, I do not want to defy my mother, and yet this is the craziest thing I have ever heard in my life. My mother is telling me to give in to the demonic spirit and legitimately kill people. To top it all off, it is in the name of the Lord. What in hell is going on?

Later that night, Mother falls into a peaceful sleep, never to wake again. I sit in the rocking chair and slowly glide back and forth, the words told to me racing through my head one minute and creeping by the next. It's as if my mind cannot completely ascertain the knowledge it has received. I softly weep tears of pain and joy. It truly is an odd feeling one can have when a loved one passes, especially a mother. You weep for their loss and you weep for joy in knowing they are no longer suffering. You weep for all the things they have done for you, and you weep knowing you have to commit the highest of sins. It is the right side of wrong, and yet it still has to be done.

I spend the following week aligning the preparations deemed by Mother for her passage to heaven and her earthly flesh to be placed beside Father's. As I cater to her wishes, I do so in an impenetrable fog. The tasks laid before me reside on the cusp of absolute insanity, and I am left with no choice. As per Mother's wishes, I am to complete my divinity. In doing so, I am to return here and continue the grace she bestowed upon those in the town. All while "filling" hell with souls unworthy of God's grace. Complete and utter insanity, there is no other way to view it.

After Mother's tribulation of passing, I start the plans of undetectability for my own fate.

* * * * *

"I am sorry to hear of your mother's passing," Patricia says. Her empathy is starting to shine as she realizes the full scope of the trauma this man has endured through life. It does not give him the right to kill, but she is starting to understand that his plight is not of his own doing.

"Thank you. It was many years ago in this house," I tell her.

"Let me see if I understand this correctly so far. You supposedly are possessed by the demonic entity while in Vietnam. Then you come home confused and unsure of where or what your life is purposed for. So you embark on the adventure of hiking the Appalachian Trail where you try to get a grasp on life and your purpose. Right so far?"

I sigh as I think back on the whole thing. "Yes, that's correct."

"Now during this trip, you don't really get any direct answers except through a supposed ghost and later his brother that steers you to want to go to seminary and become a priest. Right?" she says.

"A pastor," I correct her. "But yes, that is the gist of it so far."

"In what world did you think this would play out to be a good thing?" she asks.

"Well." I think for a minute. "You have to understand I truly have no reason to kill anyone. Everything I have done is to stop the killing. All I want is peace. I hate what this entity has brought me to become," I try to explain.

"Why not just have an exorcism? Have a pastor or priest remove the demon," she states.

"Because it would not end there. As my mother told me, this is part of my destiny," I state.

"It seems to me that you enjoy having this demon control you in killing people."

"I pray every day for that to not be the case. Although I have been doing this for so long I truly have not been able to find a way to make it end," I say. "You don't believe me, and that's fine. If I was in your shoes, I wouldn't believe me either. But I swear this has all been the truth."

"If I arrest you, then I can send you to jail and this all ends," she says.

"No, it would not end there," I say. "It would only give the demon more opportunity to kill."

"They would put you in solitary," she says.

I laugh. "Solitary will not confine this demonic spirit. All that would happen is, he would transfer to someone else, and I would rot in jail for crimes I cannot be held accountable for," I say.

"But *you* did the killing," she exclaims.

"I have only been a vessel for the demon. He takes control and manipulates me like a puppet," I explain.

"Ugh. Francis, you are frustrating. There are ways you could have dealt with this, and you choose not to address those options."

"I understand why you may think that. I assure you I have spent years trying to find the right answers to allow me the peace I seek so badly," I try to explain.

"Francis, as I look about this room, it does not seem to me that you have ever had any intent in finding peace. Nor does it appear to me that you intended to ever stop killing," Patricia points out.

"Yes. I followed the words of my mother and figured out ways to go undetected. I did this so that I could hopefully one day find a way to be rid of the demon and find my peace," I reveal. "I think I have finally found a potential solution to the killing and finding my peace," I remark after the silence that engulfs the room.

"What is that?" Patricia asks.

"If you will allow, let me finish my story, and I will reveal my plan to end this all," I say, looking her over.

"Okay, I'll keep listening. Under one condition: You release me from these bindings," she demands.

"I cannot do that. But if you give me a minute, I will return with a solution to afford you more comfort," I offer. Before she could protest, I leave the room and head upstairs for a fresh bottle of bourbon.

I grab a strap off of the table and take it over to her chair. I secure one arm to the chair and release her bindings, thus freeing one hand for her. This risk is immense as it means she now has the opportunity to free herself. However, as long as I remain in the room, she cannot without my knowing. I reposition her seat so that she now has access to the glass of bourbon I refill for her. I take a long swig of my own glass and continue with the next part of my story.

Chapter 35

It's January 8, 1973, first day of classes at McCormick Theological Seminary. I received my schedule in the mail from the school before Christmas. With everything complete and covered at home, I pack my bags yet again for another addition to my life's adventures. This one no different than any of the others as I have no idea what to expect. I settle into my dorm room the night before and meet my roommate, Bill Horace. Not a bad guy, he says he hailed from Indiana.

Class lineup is pretty standard: one on faithfulness, intro to biblical studies, church history, and Christian ethics. I take to the first instructor, Pastor Moore, who teaches faithfulness right off the bat. I guess the thought is, we are pretty faithful given our newly chosen studies and career paths. But with Pastor Moore, it's different, like he could tell it is easy for one to say they believe in God and are faithful in all aspects. But most of the time, it is just something people say so that they "blend" in. In some ways, I can relate to this and his way of presenting the material for the class.

One thing I do appreciate about the way things are structured is that as students, we are assigned mentors. Now I am not sure if this is because it is a smaller school or the fact that they understand we all struggle in one fashion or another with our own personal understanding of faith or that people have a misconception of religion in general. But it is a nice touch, and for me, I'm fortunate enough to have Pastor Moore assigned as my mentor.

The first assignment is one I can relate to, a paper defining the different religions around the world and how we assimilate to our particular faiths. For me, it's simple. I grew up in a Lutheran-based home; we went to church every Sunday. As a child, I was expected to be seen and not heard and follow the lessons in Sunday school to learn about Jesus and God through the printed word in the Good Book. I did this "faithfully" all through grade and high school. It's not like I had a choice. My mother and grandparents attended without question; therefore, so did I. Now I realize this does not define my own faithfulness to God or my religion. The reason being is, during my time at Iowa, I can't say I was perfect in attending church every Sunday. But that did not change my outlook on religion.

I am also not ignorant of the fact that there are other religions and different cultures that believe different things. I may not completely understand other religions and their beliefs, but hey, that's what this class is about: affording me the opportunity to learn and understand different walks of life. The one thing Pastor Moore stressed the first day is, we are all different, have different backgrounds, different life experiences, and we are all viewed the same in the eye of our Creator.

As I begin my research on faiths I know little about, my unwanted friend pays me a visit.

"Ah, it begins," the demon says.

"What beginning is that?" I ask.

"The truth. The truth that as much as you study and learn about your God, the more you will realize I am still here and you cannot be rid of me. There are only two ways you can be rid of me, Francis: meet my requirements to fill hell with fresh souls or die. But if you die, I only find another to fill my needs," the demon explains.

"My goal is to find a way to be rid of you for good," I respond.

"Then kill yourself. That is the easiest way, Francis," he replies.

"No, I have no intention of killing myself," I say.

"Then go… Go kill people to fulfil my destiny. All you are doing here is prolonging the agony and inevitable," he says.

"I won't do that either." This last statement I must have said loud enough for others to hear me in the library as I got the finger over the lips ("Shhhh…") and queer looks by other nearby as if to ask "Is this guy okay?" I bury my head further in the book I'm reading and say in a much softer tone, "I will find a way to be rid of you and even possibly rid the earth of you if I can."

The demon, at first, just laughs at me in response. "No one on this earth can banish me or prevent me from fulfilling my task, Francis," he finally says through fits of laughter.

As I embrace my new path in life, I say, "Through God, there is always a way, and I intend to find it."

"You will only find yourself conforming to my way, Francis. It is expected," he says, now more demanding and sterner.

"And who expects me to conform? I feel I have done well to hold you at bay as long as I have," I retort.

"Oh, yes. Francis, you are the savior!" saturated with sarcasm, the demon replies. "Like you prevented me from killing the old moonshiner or Judy. Yes, Francis, you are doing so well. You stopped me from killing your mother, but she was terminal anyway, and even then she was pure of heart and soul. The other two were pure evil and had places in my father's kingdom."

"You leave her out of this!" I say out loud. Much too loud as it would seem as I see what I can only assume is the librarian walking my way. I grab up my things hastily and leave before I am told to leave. I see her stop as I walk out, with her hands clasped across her midsection, fingers hooked into each other like an old schoolteacher.

I head to the courtyard where, for a January, it is chilly but not entirely unbearable. I sit on a bench with my satchel of books next to me and place my head in my hands. How am I supposed to disguise the demon inside of me if every time I study or write a paper, he surfaces and terrorizes me? Then it strikes me; something he said hits me.

"Why was Judy a candidate for your father's kingdom?" I ask.

At first, there is silence.

"Oh, I see," I say to what appears to be no one but myself. "If I have questions, you cannot be bothered to answer them."

"Poor Francis. Judy was not innocent," he says finally.

"How is that?" I ask.

At first, I think I am crazy to be indulging this monster. But if his purpose is to use me to fill his father's kingdom with evil souls, I feel I have a right to know their supposed crimes.

"Francis. Melody did not go home, you blind fool. Judy killed her in a fit of rage," he says.

"You're lying. I don't believe that."

As the words leave my mouth, a paper appears on the bench next to me, and a wind blows, revealing an article titled "Female Hiker Found Murdered on Appalachian Trail." I grab the paper and turn to the news article.

> *On New Year's Day, the body of young woman found stripped naked and stabbed multiple times was found in Greenbrier State Park, Maryland. Police say the body was found along a creek bed that is adjacent to a side trail for the Appalachian Trail. The unidentified victim is another number added to the yearly body count of missing or murdered associated with the trail that runs from Georgia to Maine.*

"That does not say it was Melody," I point out to the demon.

"Keep reading," he says.

> *A pair of khaki shorts, plaid flannel shirt, and a white tank top were found about a half mile away next to a green backpack with the initials* MJ *embroidered on the flap. The victim was badly decomposed and clearly had been there for several months according to police. They are asking for any information that can be provided to the identity of the blond, green-eyed victim.*

My jaw drops. I am completely flabbergasted at the information in the article. I hate realizing the demon is correct. How could Judy kill Melody? I mean, she loved her, right? Then I am reminded of that night in Hot Springs; they were arguing outside my room when I was on the phone with my mother.

"You agreed to come," Judy's voice exclaims.

"I know, Judy, but this is too much. I never fathomed the extent of this journey," Melody says. "And you ran off Francis, the only person I truly enjoyed talking to out here."

"Oh, I see," Judy says. "So I bore you."

"In a way, YES!" Melody screams.

"Well, I am sorry I am such a BORE. You didn't seem to mind when I gave you orgasm after orgasm," Judy retorts.

Melody pauses. "You are missing a key factor in my sexual desire: a penis!"

"I KNEW IT! I knew you were not committed to this relationship," Judy slams right back.

"It is NOT that I am NOT committed to this relationship. It is the fact that YOU are impossible to be around, let alone live with!" Melody screams.

"Now do you remember, Francis?" the demon asks.

"Yes." A massive pit forms in my gut as if I was just punched. Tears well up in my eyes, both for the knowledge of Melody being murdered and my connection as I killed Judy.

"You see, Francis, the people you kill for me are truly evil and belong in my father's kingdom," the demon states, almost in an empathetic tone.

"Murder is still murder," I state. "If I get caught, the judicial system is not going to care what the reason is. Not to mention how it will be viewed when I stand before St. Peter and answer for my entrance to heaven."

"Oh, Francis. I can take care of that. I'll make sure you have a place in my father's kingdom," the demon says, and I can almost see the smirk on his demonic face in the tone of his voice.

"Francis?" a voice from across the courtyard says. I turn, and Pastor Moore is standing there.

"Francis, why are you sitting out here in the cold?" he asks.

"I started coughing in the library and had to leave," I say.

"So sitting out here in the chill of the night is going to make your cough better?" he says, looking at me like I've lost my mind. Little does he know, I have. "And who were you talking to?" he asks.

"Oh, I work out problems in my head by speaking them out loud." As I utter the words, I realize how crazy I *do* sound and drop my head in disgust with myself.

"Do I need to take you to the infirmary?" Pastor Moore asks.

"No, sir. I promise I am fine," I say, hoping he buys my answer and decides to go or at least stops quizzing me.

"Okay, Francis. Would you care to join me?" he asks.

"Sir?" Not sure where this is going, I'm a bit worried.

"Well, I was just on my way to my office, and to be honest, out of all the students in my class, you seemed the most intrigued and, at the same time, the most out of place. Besides, I am your mentor, and I intend to make it a point to get to know all those I am mentoring on a personal level," Pastor Moore states, expressing that it's less of a request and more of an order, so to speak.

"In that case, I suppose I have little choice," I say with tight lips and raised eyebrows.

"I'm not going to scold you, Francis. Just get to know you." He laughs.

Chapter 36

I follow Pastor Moore to his office. It's not much of an office, more like a converted closet really. There is a small desk with a wood swivel chair, papers, most likely reports, scattered across the top of the desk illuminated by a green desk lamp. Stacks of books line one wall and a single chair just inside the door. I think to myself, *At least I can make a quick exit if required.*

"Have a seat." He motions to the chair by the door as he takes his at the desk. He opens the bottom drawer and pulls out a bottle of Jameson Whiskey and two glasses.

"Care for some?" He hands me one of the two glasses with about two fingers worth in the bottom.

"I guess so." I take the glass. "Thank you."

"Francis, how old are you?" he asks.

"Ummm…" I look up and to the right as I truly cannot remember.

He laughs at me. "You don't remember how old you are?"

"Twenty-nine," I say. "My family does not put much stock into birthdays, and honestly I do not track the years."

"I guess that's fair," he says. "So tell me something about yourself, Francis."

"Let's see, I am from Iowa. I applied here to get my master's in divinity. I am twenty-nine years old, but we covered that," I start.

"Oh, come on. I can get all that from your student record. No, I mean tell me about yourself. You are about six years older than most of the students. Why?" he says with a sly grin on his face.

Great, I think to myself, *what do I tell him? "I went to Nam, a demon possessed me, I hiked the Appalachian Trail, killed a few people while looking for a purpose to my life, and decided I'd become a priest"?* I want to just scream.

I sigh deeply. "To be honest, I have been dealing with issues for the past year or two and have not had real direction. I graduated from the University of Iowa with a degree in engineering. Upon graduation, I received a draft notice from the Army. But before I could report for that, I went and talked to the Marine recruiter. Based on my degree, they enlisted me to join the Engineering Battalion, and after my training, I was shipped off to Vietnam. While on patrol one day, a booby-trapped body blew up, disintegrating my sergeant and riddling me with shrapnel, some of which I still carry inside me to this day because it is inoperable. Having no clue what I wanted to do with my life and knowing engineering wasn't for me after all, I made the decision to hike the Appalachian Trail on the advice of a family friend. This was supposed to give me guidance and help me find a path to follow in life and it did and it didn't as I was and perhaps still am confused. Anyway, I was here for a few days last fall and applied for the divinity program. After applying, my mother died of cancer, and I kept my appointment here. Why? I haven't a freaking clue. I am still trying to figure that out." I took a breath and downed the two fingers of Jameson in the glass. Pastor Moore just stares at me in disbelief or shock or something.

"Holy shit, Francis." Now I am the one wide-eyed as I just heard a pastor curse. "I think you can honestly say you have been through hell and back," he concludes.

"Sir, to be frank, and in no way disrespectful, I live hell every day. If you want someone to admit how lost they are"—I raise my hand—"I am right here."

"If you don't mind, I'd like to share a bit about myself with you. Although I cannot say I have dealt with the same trials you have. I feel in some way I can relate to portions of your story," he says.

"If I can have another two fingers of that Jameson, I'll sit here all night," I reply.

He chuckles, grabs the bottle, and pours three into my glass.

"I finished seminary at Princeton University in 1962, just before all the Vietnam War crap started. With a mountain of debt and the idea that I also love my country, I applied for a chaplain's position in the Air Force. Of course, before my commission was up, we started that whole thing over there, and I applied for a second go round. Of course I went. I was assigned part of the Ban Me Thuot East Airfield. Now, I'll admit I cannot associate my duty or time over there to anything you would have done or seen in the trenches. But during my time there, we supported Special Forces, and what those guys came back and told us, not to mention some of their own, was ungodly. I can only imagine how you feel."

At this point, I take just a sip of my whiskey listening to his background and story. Maybe this is why I can relate to him so well. Granted he wasn't involved in direct combat, but I know a lot of those air bases over there got hit regularly; it was no parade for anyone who served. "After I resigned my commission, I returned here to the States expecting to just walk into any church and be the pastor. But that didn't happen either. I did some odd jobs here and there. I heard about this opportunity to teach here, and I applied. This is now my second year here, and due to my situation, I am not married. They offered me an apartment within walking distance. So I am able to stay late and help mentor students like yourself." At this point, he pauses too and takes a long swig from his glass. "So what would you like to take from your experience here at McCormick?" he asks.

One question I dread, given my true purpose for coming to the seminary. I have not thought of another reason to provide yet if I was confronted with this situation. I sit there with a blank stare, like a deer on a dark road suddenly illuminated by headlights. I try to sidetrack the question.

"I guess because I grew up in the church and I felt that with all the crazy stuff I have seen so far and been through, this might grant me peace."

Wow, that sounded better than I intended. I applaud myself. Now I wonder if he bought it. Pastor Moore just looks at me like he is trying to size me up. Maybe my ruse isn't convincing enough.

"I am not sure how much peace being a minister will afford you, as you do realize that your congregation will be coming to you for guidance, advice, and counselling," he says finally, still watching my reactions.

"I understand that. But I suppose with it being their issues and I am jut acting as a confidant and a voice of reason, I can then ease my own pain through helping them and ultimately provide me solace and my own peace," I respond, hoping that all made sense and it helps cease his questions like this. He just sits there with his arms crossed and twirling the Jameson in his glass.

He finally says after absorbing my statement, "We can discuss this further in the future. I think your mindset may change or develop as you get further in your studies."

Little does he know that my entire mindset, though obscure, is to find a way to rid myself of the demon inside of me and, if possible, rid the world of the demon. I cannot see my overall mindset of that changing. But for now, I am in the clear and will have to develop a better answer in the future as I can be assured this won't be the last time I am asked.

Chapter 37

It's been three months since I started my classes at McCormick Seminary. My adjustment at the seminary has not been easy. After Mother passed, I have had to figure everything out on my own. Here, I know no one, and though everyone has been nice and accommodating, I am still left to ask myself if I made the right choice. There is one professor I have that I feel a bit of a connection to, Pastor Moore. But he is my instructor; I cannot expect him to be a friend, not yet. If I was to be seen with him now, it may be seen as favoritism, and I do not want that.

The only person outside the seminary that I know is a street hooker named Charlene. I cannot say that a student of theological studies should associate with a prostitute. But I wonder, I wonder if part of my mission might be to understand how someone like that enters or gets caught up in that life, and maybe if I can understand what leads them to that type of profession, maybe I can find a way to lead them out of it? It sounds ambitious as women in that profession rarely talk too much about themselves and just stuck on doing what they have to obtain cash from a john. Hmmm...I wonder to myself. Then I conclude there is only one way to find out.

I start out for the corner where I met Charlene. My walk through the streets of Chicago are interesting at best as there are people milling about to get their needed items, headed home from work, some may even be headed to a night job. I am just another person to be ignored. As I make my way through the streets, I note various places of interest: a deli, an Italian eatery, a shoe store, little convenient stores on each corner, and if not, there is a bank.

As I get near the corner where I met Charlene, I feel a pang of fear and anxiety. Will she even remember me? What do I say? Will she even agree to talk to me? I decide if I see her, I will ask if she would like to join me for a bite to eat. Wow, it sounds like I am going to ask a hooker on a date, like a real freaking date. I must be insane. I look around as I get closer and don't see her. *I'm such an idiot. This was a stupid idea*, I tell myself. Then I hear a voice, her voice.

"Hey. What you looking for?" calls out Charlene.

"Me?" just like last time, I play dumb, but this time, I truly am dumb for thinking this might work or was a good idea.

"Yeah, you," she replies. "I like tall men. Is there something I can interest you in?"

"Umm...sure, would you like get something to eat?"

"Oh, honey. You are in the wrong part of town. Wait..." She recognizes me, the lost out-of-towner. "I know you, don't I? Yeah, I do. What are you doing back down here?" She lightens her spiel and changes her tone to be softer and accommodating.

Sheepishly I look at her and ask—hell, I've come this far, right?—"So I actually did come here to see if you might like to get a bite to eat."

"I don't know. I have to make money to pay the rent, you know," she says.

"Yes, I get that. Look, I'll pay you for your time and the meal. I'll explain over dinner if you agree to join me," I say, practically pleading.

"I never met such a lost cause as you. Damn, I forgot your name," she says.

"Francis. Honestly, I am not sure I even provided it when we first met. Charlene, right?" I answer.

"Yeah, you remembered little ole me. You remembered. You really are sweet, aren't you?" she says in a joyous tone.

"I have this uncanny ability to never forget things. It actually can be annoying at times," I tell her.

"Well, I have a place where we can go," she says.

"That works," I say.

"Okay, let's do this. Fifty dollars for the hour, and you can buy me dinner there, deal?" she offers.

I feel it's a little steep, but it's this or another night of no one to talk to. "Sounds fine with me. I accept." And I pull out some cash and hand her fifty dollars.

"Okay, Mr. Lonely Heart Francis, let's eat." She turns in the direction of the little restaurant she told me about earlier.

"So did you come back to Chicago just to see me?" she asks.

"Not exactly. I applied for college here and was accepted," I tell her.

"Oh my gosh, big college boy. Which college? University of Illinois? DePaul? I got it, Loyola. You look like a Rambler," she says proudly.

"Actually, McCormick Theological Seminary," I say meekly.

"Seminary? Isn't that where they teach the Bible? You going to be a priest or something?"

"Yeah, something like that," I say.

"I think you have your priorities jumbled back here, talking to me and you want to be a religious type," she says.

I laugh. "Well, I signed up the day after I met you. They accepted me, and I started in January. Although everyone has been really nice, I feel like an outsider. So I decided to come here and talk to someone I actually knew. Crazy idea, I know," I say.

"I agree you come off a bit crazy. But I like your company so far. Here we are." She points to the door of the restaurant.

I catch on quick and open the door to usher her in.

"You are a bright boy," she jokes.

"I have my moments," I say.

"Table for two?" the maître d' says.

"Yes, please. Umm, a quiet spot preferred," I answer, and we are ushered to a small table toward the back.

The maître d' gives Charlene a look thinking I didn't catch it or wasn't paying attention, and she just gives him a glare. We are seated and handed menus.

"Why did he look at you like that?" I ask.

"Oh, that's Lil' Jimmy. He has that name for more than one reason. Anyways, this is my cousin's place. They all know me here, and even though my cousin would prefer I didn't stop in on a night I'm 'working,' it'll be fine," she explains. Moments later, a rather large guy walks up to our table.

"Charlene. I thought I asked you to not come here dressed like that." More of a statement than an actual question.

"Francis, meet Tony, the owner of this establishment and my cousin. Tony, before you embarrass yourself, I'll talk to you in the back, okay? Okay." Charlene stands up and grabs her very large cousin's arm and drags them to the back, leaving me there to wonder if I really did make a mistake.

Charlene comes back a few minutes later. "Sorry about that. Tony can be overprotective. But everything is fine I took care of it. Do you know what you want? The ravioli are to die for, and Tony has his own sauce he makes just like his mama's." She speaks so fast I can't get a word in edge-wise.

"Whatever you think is best," I say.

The waitress comes over. "A bottle of Chianti Pinot Noir, *per favore*," Charlene tells the waiter.

Charlene looks at the scared look on my face as the wine list had that as the most expensive bottle. "Oh, don't worry. I told Tony you were my new boyfriend and I didn't have time to change. So he offered a bottle on the house. Since he embarrassed us, I figured I'd make him pay for it." My look of fear didn't disappear as I am thinking to myself Tony's a big guy and could rip me apart despite my training. "Don't worry, he can afford it," she finishes.

The waiter brings us two glasses of water and then a bottle of the wine with two glasses. After pouring a snifter glass, which he hands to me to approve, he proceeds to fill the glasses.

"May I interest you both in an appetizer?" he asks.

"Yes, the calamari," Charlene states without consulting me. Luckily I come prepared that I'd have to pay by washing dishes.

"And have we decided on our meals for the evening?" he asks.

Charlene looks at me then at the waiter. "Yes, two ravioli meals, please. And tell Tony no skimping."

"Of course. I will have those out shortly," he says and disappears into the back.

"So a minister. Why?" Charlene asks me. At this point, I am slightly unsettled as the last moments happened in such a blur and I have to reacclimate myself.

"That's a long story," I say.

"It's your time," she says with a smile.

As I start, the waiter brings us salads and a basket of fresh baked bread. I tell her how I went to college for engineering and then off to Vietnam. After I returned, I wasn't sure what I really wanted anymore, and then about the Appalachian Trail, granted this is all the *Reader's Digest* version. Then I tell her how while on the trail, I, or more accurately during the train ride from Boston to Chicago, how I alighted on the idea of becoming a minister. Of course, I leave out the reasons behind my choice. As I ramble on, I notice she actually is interested and is treating this like a date of sorts. Not sure if she's acting the part or truly is interested, but it's better than sitting in the dorm.

"How about you? Not to sound rude, but how did you happen on…" Not sure how to word it, but luckily Charlene takes over.

"Becoming a 'working girl'?" she finishes my thought. "It's a story as long as yours, but to put it quick and straight, I made some bad choices, and though the world looks at it differently, I don't mind it. I get to meet interesting people, like yourself, and it beats working here dealing with asshole customers that tip for shit or my jerk of a cousin."

"So no drugs?" I ask, being direct than I normally would be.

"No, never touched the stuff," she says bluntly. "I mean, I smoke cigarettes, but that's it."

"And the…" I start.

"The sex?" Charlene interjects. "Believe it or not, most of these guys just want a hand job or blow job. Don't get me wrong, it's not glamourous, but I make enough to get by. Am I a good Christian girl that is all prim and proper? No. But you knew that. Which makes me wonder, why? Why me?" she asks.

"To be honest…" As I start, the waiter brings our meals out. "You were nice to me. Like I said, this hasn't been an easy move for me. Especially since my mother recently passed away."

"Oh my gosh. I'm so sorry. I didn't know your mom passed," she says empathetically.

"It's okay. Yeah, after I returned from the trail, I found out she was diagnosed with cancer. She passed away this past fall," I tell her.

The meal turns out to be one of the best Italian meals I have ever had. You can tell the sauce is fresh and homemade. The ravioli is obviously handmade also as the texture is soft and pillowy. Not knowing what to say at this point, we chat about the meal and not much else. We opt to skip dessert, and the waiter brings the check. Not as bad as I thought, and just as Charlene promised, the wine is on the house. Curiosity killed the cat, as they say, and I ask an almost night-killing question. But I refrain.

"I have a feeling we are over the hour time limit," I mention.

"It's okay," Charlene says. "I have enjoyed myself, and it's fun to give my cousin Tony a hard time. Plus you have been good company."

"Thank you. I guess my mother raised me right," I say.

"Would you like to come back to my place? No extra fee," Charlene offers.

"Umm. You know, I appreciate that offer. But I would like a rain check if that is okay. Instead, I was hoping maybe we could do this again sometime. Maybe a little more formal or less impromptu," I counter. As attracted as I may be to Charlene, and she is attractive, I don't know if I am ready to reveal my condition to her or anyone else yet. Along with that, I kind of want to see her more often and see where this goes.

"You really are a sweet guy, Francis. Okay, we can do this again. But if we are going to have an actual date, you have to do this right next time and pick the place," she says.

"Okay," I say and smile at her as she smiles back. We walk out with the bill compensated. I walk her back, and we part ways.

"Francis," she says as I start back toward the seminary.

"Yes."

She is facing me. I walk back toward her, and she reaches up, grabs my neck to pull me closer, and gives me a kiss on the cheek. She hands me a piece of paper. I look at it.

"My number, so you can call me for next time. Have a good night," she says then walks away.

I respond with a sheepish grin on my face, "You too." Perhaps too soft for her to hear as I turn again and head back down the street.

I think to myself on the walk home about the evening and all the questions I wanted to ask but refrained from. Some things just do not add up as to how people end up where they do in life, and these questions have always intrigued me. Perhaps the next meeting with Charlene will grant me the time and the courage to ask her these things. I know what she told me, but I feel like there is more to it than that. Maybe it comes down to the fact that I really do like her and just want to know more about her.

"She will be perfect, Francis," the demon strikes. "A street hooker who gives sexual favors for money. If I didn't know better, Francis, I'd say you are finally catching on to your part of the plan."

"I am not going to allow you to kill Charlene," I reply.

"You are right, Francis. I won't kill her." He says, "You will."

"Not that either," I say.

"Oh, I see," the demon replies a little gleefully now. "You want your way with her first. That makes sense. Yes, you have sex with her, then kill her. It will emphasize her sins, and you can get revenge when she laughs at your decrepit state," the demon says, referring to my injuries from the blast.

"You really are a bastard," I say out loud as a passing couple turns to stare at me then picks up their pace. *Great*, I think, *now people think I am insane, walking down the street talking to myself like I have Tourette's or something.* The demon just laughs in my head as I hurry back myself. Hell of a way to finish what was a good and reasonable evening.

* * * * *

"So you have felt love, outside of your mother," Patricia states.

"In a way, yes. But it is never long-lived," I say.

"What about Sarah?" she asks.

"I could never bring Sarah into the life I live now. It would make her an accomplice. Besides, my path is set. But it will soon come to an end," I state.

"How will it end, Francis? If you kill me, they put you in jail, and you have already noted that is not an option," Patricia points out.

"Because everything must end. It is only a matter of time," I say.

Chapter 38

"Francis!" I hear a voice call to me as I walk out of the classroom.

"Yes, sir," I reply as I spin around to address Pastor Moore.

"You seem chipper lately. Things are going well? Are you finally settling in and adjusting to school?" he asks.

"Yes," I reply "I think so. Nice lesson today. I enjoyed it."

"You enjoyed listening to me discuss how individual religions are drawn to their homage?" he asks. "I have a hard time believing that. It seemed to me that you were distracted and your mind was elsewhere."

I laugh. "Yes, I met someone. We had dinner last night. Nothing really, just a nice meal, and I feel we connected."

"Good for you, Francis. I am glad that you are putting yourself out there. I know it is not an easy thing for you to do," Pastor Moore relates.

"It does beat sitting around here doing nothing but studying" is all I can come with as a reply as my mind is solely on Charlene and when I might see her again at this point.

"Are you still able to do our weekly meeting?" Pastor Moore asks.

"Yes, that is always on my schedule," I reply. "I have to get going, Pastor. Is there anything else?"

"No, Francis. I'll see you at our next session," he says. I head out.

Pastor Moore and I have a regular mentoring session once a week to cover my progress, life in the school, and overall well-being.

I have grown fondly accustomed to these weekly sessions as we have developed a bond of sorts. I realize he does this with all the students he mentors; however, my respect for him has grown through these sessions into more than just a mentorship for me.

As the week goes by, I find it harder and harder to concentrate on my studies. Now not to worry, I am not slacking in any way, but every free chance I get, I find myself thinking of Charlene. I cannot find the reason why she has captivated my mind so much. Maybe it is the exotic ideal that she is not the normal type of women most men become attracted to. Perhaps it is her profession that has captivated me about her. Regardless of the reason, she is all I can think about when not studying.

I look at the time and realize I have little time before my weekly mentoring with Pastor Moore. I head to his office and find the door closed, which is odd as I cannot think of a time it has ever been closed. I knock.

"Come in," a voice calls from inside.

"Pastor Moore?" I say as I slowly open the door.

"Ah, yes, Francis. Please come in, have a seat," he says.

"Everything alright?" I ask. "I am not used to your door being shut."

"Oh yes. I was just reading a letter from an old friend," he says. "So how are things?"

"Things are not bad. I am keeping up with my studies," I say.

"Are you now? And this woman you have?" he asks.

"Oh, that. Yes, well, that is just something new. I cannot say it will be a distraction toward my goals here with school," I say.

"Francis." He gives a chuckle. "You are the most distracted I have ever seen you since you started here."

"Yeah, okay, maybe she has been occupying my mind a bit more than I realized. Is it really that noticeable?" I ask.

"I cannot speak for anyone else, but I have noticed. Then again, I know you, or at least feel I know you, better than others here in the school," Pastor Moore replies.

"I can agree with that," I state. "To be honest, aside from you and Charlene, I cannot say I associate with anyone else."

"Charlene. So that is her name," he notes.

"Ah, yes." I did not realize I had said it out loud.

"Is there more to this story?" he asks.

I had to think for a moment. "We met a while ago, and, well, I was feeling couped up and needed some fresh air. And as it turned out, I found myself near where I met her. We 'bumped' into each other again, and I offered to take her to dinner. For now, that is really all to the story per se. I can't say I know too much about her," I tell him, hoping he won't pry too much into the situation. I am not sure how well "dating" a prostitute as a student of the Bible will be received.

"Okay. We can talk about other things then if that is okay." Pastor Moore eyes me over again like he can tell there is more to this than I am letting on. He is getting good at reading me, which is scary as there are things that I cannot divulge or am afraid to tell anyone at this time.

"I have a question," I say in hopes I can steer the conversation for once.

"What is that, Francis?" he asks.

"How does possession work? Like demonic possessions?" I ask.

"It depends on the circumstances. What brought this on?" he asks.

"Oh, just something I came across in my studies for Christian ethics," I say.

"Possession of a demonic spirit is something that can happen. Granted, it is rare, and one has to be careful as real ailments can be misleading and be seen as a possession of demonic origins when in reality, they are true medical conditions," he explains. "There are references in the Bible toward the exorcisms of demons by Jesus in both Mark and Luke. There are also references to the disciples performing or cleansing of demonic spirits. However, I cannot think of the exact references off the top of my head at this time. You follow the Lutheran doctrine, correct?"

"Yes," I answer.

"If I am not mistaken, there is a Lutheran ritual for exorcism in the pastoral handbook of the Lutheran church, as you will also cover some of this subject in later classes. But in general, the overall perception by the public and in the eyes of most religions is that those possessed by a demonic spirit cannot be held liable for their actions. It's a duality in the eyes of the world, I guess you might say. Though the possessed individual may do or say things that is considered wrong or unholy, if they are truly possessed, then the demonic spirit is credited as being the true source of the evil and not the individual. Therefore, in the eyes of the church, again in most cases, the possessed are not liable. Now, how the courts may see it, that's another story, and I am no lawyer. I would think that in a case like that, it would have to be proven, and proving someone is legitimately possessed in the eyes of the court would be as hard to prove as, say, some who claim insanity." Pastor Moore's explanation draws more questions, but here again, I have to be careful of the level or distance I take this so as not to reveal too much about my own situation.

"How can one tell they are possessed, or how can someone tell IF someone is truly possessed?" I ask.

"Again, that depends on the situation and the individual. A person possessed may develop or display a sudden change in behavior. They might not. They will most likely experience strange horrific dreams as demonic entities tend to expose themselves in the late hours of the night while the individual sleeps and is less aware," he tells me. "But here again, you have to be extremely careful as mental illness and even some physiological ailments can be misinterpreted as a possession and vice versa. Take epilepsy or Tourette's, for example. These are real medical conditions that to the unknowing can be mistaken for something else like a possession. Did something happen in Vietnam, Francis?" Pastor Moore looks at me with grave concern as he asks this.

"I am not sure," I say quietly. "I mean, no, no, I don't think so. I have rough dreams sometimes, but I do not think it is from possession," I say this with more emphasis, almost as if I needed to convince myself.

Pastor Moore has an uncanny way of reading me and seeing things I try to keep hidden.

"I appreciate the information. I really was just curious," I say.

"Is that part of your reasoning for following this path? To become a priest capable of performing exorcisms?" he asks. "If so, it's a noble path to undertake. It involves a lot of study and patience. It is not for the weak of heart," he says.

I think about that last part a little bit. "I actually haven't thought about it. I just came across something in my studies and was curious," I say.

"Well, if you would like to know more about the topic, I can arrange for you to have a meeting with Reverend Chavez. He teaches a lesson in one of his classes about the subject, and he actually has had to perform an exorcism. He is the closest thing to an expert here at the school that I am aware of," Pastor Moore tells me. At this point, I feel I need to get out of there.

"I appreciate that. For now, though I think I will stick to the basics of this semester. Don't want to get too far ahead of myself." I laugh. "But if anything changes, I will let you know, and we can arrange something."

Pastor Moore eyes me warily. "Okay, Francis. I think that is good for this week. If you need anything, you know where to find me." I stand and grab my belongings as I turn toward the door to leave. "And, Francis, I am here to assist you. In my eyes, our sessions are no different than, well, let's say a confessional. What you tell me here stays here," he says.

"Thank you, Pastor. I will keep that in mind, I promise," I say and leave.

After I leave, Pastor Moore turns back to the letter he was reading.

Pastor Peter Moore,

> *I truly appreciated your letter to me about Francis Fleming. I am pleased to hear that he is doing so well in seminary. I am also very pleased to hear that he has such a knowledgeable and concerned mentor to guide him.*

LAWRENCE NEWTON

In reference to your questions about his character, I am hard-pressed to be able to answer them completely. Yes, I knew Francis his entire childhood as his mother and grandparents ensured he was raised in the church. He was a sweet and caring boy growing up. But once he went off to college, my connection with him strayed a bit as I rarely saw him during those years. Then of course he joined the Marines and was sent to fight in Vietnam. After he returned to Asbury, he maybe came to service once or twice. Then according to his mother, he went off on an adventure to hike the Appalachian Trail at the recommendation of another partitioner of mine, Clark Knowles, who worked for the Fleming family for years before taking over their hardware store here in town.

I spoke to Clark about why he suggested this trip to Francis, and he told me that Francis was struggling a bit upon return from Vietnam. Clark suspected it was involving the injuries Francis sustained in combat. I do not have many details on that experience. You will have to ask Francis. I did not find any of this odd as I am sure you have experienced this, like many of the men who have served and returned from that war who are physically, mentally, and emotionally traumatized. But Francis did come talk to me after his trip, rather suddenly and even a bit out of his character, given I had not seen him for many years and he told me he had applied to McCormick Seminary and wanted to be a pastor. Knowing the family and how he was as a child and young man, I found it a pleasant surprise, and I believe he will make a fine pastor for the Lutheran church.

Francis did make a statement during our conversation that at the time I dismissed, but given your letter and the nature of the letter, I have garnered it further thought and prayer. He said, "Well, I have sinned. I have had to kill people. Is that...okay?" Something clearly happened to the young man in Vietnam. I am not sure what, and I am not sure I am much assistance at this time to figure it out. But I also am curious like yourself as I did agree to take Francis on as my assistant pastor to complete his training following seminary.

I can also tell you his mother was a true saint recognized in this town. Francis was very close to her and cherished her. She also came to me once concerned about Francis and his well-being, but at the time, we associated it with his time in Vietnam. I can tell you her passing was hard on the entire town and especially on Francis. But after her ascent to heaven, he didn't miss another Sunday at church until he left for seminary.

I pray reading this does not set off any alarms or change Francis's current path. I still feel he will make an excellent leader in the Lutheran church. We all have to hurdle the rocky path to able to guide those that are struggling on their own paths. I feel whatever Francis is dealing with is a passing thing and this will only make him stronger.

Yours in Christ,
Pastor Paul Gunther

Chapter 39

It has been a few weeks since I last saw Charlene. I call the number she gave me; butterflies build in my gut as this is outside my norm.

"Hello?" The voice on the other line is clearly Charlene's.

"Charlene?" I say.

"Yes."

"This is Francis," I say.

"Oh! Hi. How are you? I was beginning to wonder if you were ever going to call me," she says.

"Yeah. Sorry about that. Things have been a little busy for me with school and all," I tell her.

"It's okay," she says.

"I was thinking that I have a break in school coming up and was wondering if you would be available for that date we talked about?" I ask.

"Gee, Francis, I don't know. I mean, you took this long to call..." She pauses.

"I see," I start to say. "I just got busy. I am sorry."

"I am just messing with you, Francis. I would love to go on a date with you," she says.

"Oh, good. Great. What night are you free?" I respond.

"I don't know, Francis. I have such a set, busy schedule," she says, giving him a hard time again.

"You're messing with me," I say, starting to catch on. "How about this Friday?"

"Friday is no good for me. Kind of a big night, if you know what I mean." I do, and I cannot say I like that part of this arrangement.

"Yeah, okay. I understand. Well, how about Sunday afternoon?" I offer.

"That works for me," she says. "Where would you like to meet?"

"How does Buckingham Fountain sound?" I ask.

"That works for me. Time?"

"Let's meet at 5:00 p.m. I figure we could go for a walk and then eat," I say.

"I can do that. Where did you find for us to have dinner?" she asks.

"It's a surprise," I say. It really isn't; I just haven't settled on a place yet. But I can by Sunday.

"Well, I have to go, Francis. I will see you then," she concludes.

"Great! See you then," I say "Goodbye."

"Talk to you soon." She hangs up the phone.

Sunday arrives, and I head to the fountain. I find a nice place nearby that I hope she likes. It's a little wine bistro that serves tapas. It is a nice afternoon as the temperature is not too hot but not chilly yet. I sit on the edge watching others walk by people on roller skates and the occasional jogger. I see a woman walking toward me, and as she approaches, I realize it is Charlene. She is wearing a pair of bell bottom jeans and a leather vest with tassels over a shirt that flares at the wrists. I hardly recognize her as I stand with a beaming smile and walk toward her.

"Well, don't you look handsome," she says, eyeing me over.

"This? I just threw this on," I say. Truth is, I spent an hour trying to decide what I wanted to wear for this date. I finally settled on slacks, a turtleneck, and a blazer.

"So where to, Mr. Dapper?" Always the smart-ass Charlene.

"I thought we could walk around the park and chat for a bit. I found this little wine bistro that serves tapas for us to have a nice quiet place to sit and talk. If that works for you?" I say, looking her over and trying not to stare. She smells so good, and the sun, as it slowly drops in the sky, beams off her face. This is the first time I have seen her in daylight, and it suits her well.

"Lead the way." We turn and start to walk toward the lakefront.

We chat about the past couple of weeks to start, then talk about my time on the trail. How I went to college for engineering and then was drafted into the war. She tells me how she tried community college and how things didn't work out when she met her husband.

"Wait, you are married?" I ask.

"Heavens no. Not anymore," she tells me. "No, I caught him cheating on me, and I killed them both." Shock covers my face as she tells me this as if this is normal behavior. "Oh, it's okay. I was arrested and then let off on a technicality," she says, reading my shock. "You have nothing to worry about."

I stand there a bit, absorbing the information she just blurted out and understanding the full scope of the situation.

She continues to move the conversation along and hopefully bypass my current vibe. "After that incident, it was hard for me to find work. I helped out Tony at the restaurant waitressing for a bit. But I always felt like the customers were talking about me and pointing at me. It kind of led to my current profession as my customers now could care less about my past."

"I understand," I say as calm and rationally as I can.

We continue walking and talking about the current state of affairs in the world. I tell her about the spirit I met on the trail and how I met his brother on the train. I explain how this helped me find my way to applying for seminary. Basically, we talk about anything but her killing her husband and his mistress.

We proceed to the wine bistro and enjoy a few tapas as well as a bottle of wine or two. As the sun is setting, we decide to walk back around the park some more before we call the night.

"Francis, she is perfect. She killed two people and got away scot-free," the demon resounds in my head. I do my best to ignore his ploy.

"It's getting a bit chilly," she mentions.

"Here, take my jacket." I slide out of it and go to drape it over her shoulders. I look around, and no one is to be seen. At this point, the demon sees his chance and takes over, wrapping my arm around her neck and dragging her to a nearby bush completely out of view.

THE DEMONIC SAVIOR

The next morning, I wake and think of what happened the night before. I remember meeting with Charlene and our walk. I remember the bistro and the tapas. I see my jacket is hanging on the back of the chair by my desk in my room. But I cannot remember how I got home or any other part of the night.

I decide to call Charlene to ask how she is but realize it is early. With the next week off from school, I decide to drive back home and check on how things are.

Chapter 40

Returning from break, I see a newspaper lying about in the quad.

"Girl Found Strangled in Hyde Park." The title catches my eye. It isn't uncommon that people are murdered in a city like Chicago. But being that I was just in Hyde Park on the date with Charlene, I feel this one warrants my attention. I also realize I have not spoken to Charlene since that night.

> *A jogger found a young woman, about twenty-five years old, strangled and mutilated in Hyde Park. Suspect unknown, and the nature of the killing is yet to be determined. The young woman was found wearing bell bottom jeans and a leather vest. Any information pertaining to the investigation should be directed to Chicago Police Department's Homicide Division.*

The realization of that night hits me, like I ran into a brick wall. I look around to see if anyone has noticed me or my reaction. I proceed to my room and weep. I know it was Charlene. I know I'm the killer. I could barely stomach the thought that I killed the only person I had connected with in this town.

"Yes, Francis. It was us. Don't you remember? She told us she got away with killing her husband and the woman he was sleeping with," the demon resounds in my head. "She had to die."

Remembering what Mother had told me just hours before she passed, I try to console myself with the knowledge that this is my fate in life. I wish I could go back and stop her from telling me at all. If she had never told me, then the demon would have no reason to kill her. But no, no, she had to tell me, leaving the demon to take over once again and leaving me the burden of another on my conscience.

"Look in your closet, Francis."

There in what appears to be a doggie bag from the restaurant is a pair of eyes, Charlene's eyes. I shake my head in fright and disbelief. Why? I do not know. This is the nature of my life from here till the end of me: being the vessel that allows the demon to extract the eyes from his victims as a way to ensure their passage to hell, the kingdom of his father.

As Pastor Moore finishes the lecture and releases us for our next class, or whatever is on our schedule, I walk up to the podium where he stands.

"Francis. You don't look so good. Is everything alright?" Pastor Moore asks as he looks up from his notes at me.

"I would like to talk to you at your earliest convenience, Pastor, please," I say in a strained voice.

"Absolutely," he replies. "I have time this afternoon around 4:00 p.m. if you can meet me in my office at that time."

"Yes, that will work just fine. Thank you, sir," I say, and I head out for my next class. As much as I want to skip the rest of my day, I cannot change my routine so as not to lead to suspicion.

Later that afternoon, I arrive at Pastor Moore's office. I find the door cracked open, and I knock lightly on the frame.

"Come in, Francis," I hear Pastor Moore say. "So why the change in schedule? You look pale and distraught. Is everything okay?" he asks.

"I…I killed someone, Pastor. Please forgive me," I meekly say.

"Francis," he says in a fatherly, comforting tone as he stands and embraces me. "Francis, we all know. We all understand. There are things we are all made to do that goes against God's will. Believe me when I say he will forgive you, my son."

As comforting as his words are, I begin to sob. The news or verification that I had killed Charlene has been overwhelming.

"I know not where to turn, sir," I say. "I feel like I should not even be here. Like I am a blasphemy of my own existence."

"I can assure you, Francis, you are not a blasphemy," Pastor Moore says, ushering me to sit down.

"I am not sure you understand, Pastor. I killed people. The sin of all sins," I say as I try to pull myself together.

"'In whom we have redemption through his blood, the forgiveness of sins, according to the riches of his grace.' Ephesians 1:7," Pastor blurts without missing a beat. "Jesus died on the cross to forgive ALL of man's sins. Including yours, Francis."

"Yes, Pastor, I know," I say.

"He is the only one who knows the truth, and he is the only one you need to convince in your salvation. 'But the Lord stood by me and strengthened me, so that through me the message might be fully proclaimed and all the Gentiles might hear it. So, I was rescued from the lion's mouth. The Lord will rescue me from every evil deed and bring me safely into his heavenly kingdom. To him be the glory forever and ever.' *2 Timothy 4:17,*" Pastor Moore recites by heart, almost as if he knew this day would come and had this all prepared.

"Amen," I follow, knowing the verse well.

"Francis, I have something to tell you. As part of my plan to mentor you to the best of my ability, I reached out to Pastor Gunther," he starts. An expression of surprise spreads across my face as I have no real idea what may have been said between them. Good? Or bad?

"He told me you had not been attending church the last few years. Some was explainable as you were in college, then Vietnam, then the trail. He admitted when you came to him after applying that you had chosen this path but assured me that God has a reason for choosing you and that he and I, and I believe you too, should take solace in that fact alone. We as mere mortals cannot understand or grasp God's plan for us. All we can do is make choices as those 'forks' in the road are presented to us. I feel God placed a heavy burden on you. I cannot say why. But I have all the faith in the world that you will soldier through this rocky road and be forgiven by the Lord," Pastor Moore tells me.

I think about all of this for a bit. Considering what just happened, I have severe doubts that this is all part of God's plan for me. I highly doubt God's intention is for me to be his executioner regardless of the reasoning behind the killing. The only thing that makes some semblance of understanding is that this burden was involuntarily thrust upon me, and now I am left to accept the burden and follow through with the path ahead me. I think of it like I was given an option of a fork in the road and, instead of being able to choose the other option, was blocked off with Do Not Enter signs—thus eliminating any chance of me being able to choose the righteous path. Perhaps I have it all wrong. Perhaps the only way God is able to steer me down a path of righteousness is to force me to undertake this path that is littered with death and remorse.

Pastor Moore lays his hand on my shoulder. "Francis?" he asks.

"Sorry, Pastor, I was just taking in all that you just said," I reply, coming out of the fog. "Why me?" I ask.

"Though we can never be sure, Francis, I think the answer is another question. Why NOT you?" he says.

"I can give plenty of reasons why it shouldn't be me. I didn't ask for this. I don't want this burden. I just want to live a free and happy life," I say.

"You do not want the ministry?" he asks.

That's when I realize what I said and that I was talking about the burden of the demonic entity and Pastor Moore is thinking I was referring to my choices of being at the seminary. Now I have to backtrack and cover.

"Oh no, Pastor. I meant, why am I the one who had to kill? Why did God force such a burden on me that I have to commit sin in order to be one of his chosen in teaching his word?" Phew, I hope that's enough.

"I see. That, Francis, is again one of those questions none of us can answer. The only way you can get the answers to those questions is through prayer. 'Therefore, I tell you, whatever you ask for in prayer, believe that you have received it, and it will be yours.' Mark

11:24. It won't be spelled out for you. You may not even know that God has listened and granted your answers. But I assure you God is listening. As long as we continue to accept that and accept God into our hearts, our souls will be nurtured and are safe. Your sins will be forgiven, Francis. You must hold on to your faith."

As Pastor Moore says all of this, I am reminded of what Mother said that last night: *"You must give in and give the demon his due, and for the love of me and God and heaven above, you must not get caught. Just do your tasks and all will be well. God has already forgiven you, and he has a plan to destroy the demon. But only if you follow the deeds set forth."*

"Thank you, Pastor Moore. I understand. I will continue to pray on this and await God's answer," I say. I start to gather my items and prepare to leave.

"Francis, before you go. I read your last paper. Very inspiring. I caution though: Do not let this 'bump' in the road deter you from why you are here. You have a very bright future ahead I see in the ministry." Pastor Moore's words of confidence provide me some peace that I am able to appreciate.

That night, I create a prayer that I recite nightly and sometimes daily as a way to hold the demon at bay long enough for me to finish my time at seminary.

Dear Lord,

I have sinned, as you are well aware. I want to be your disciple as I spread your word to those who do not know you. But I cannot do this alone. As you are aware of my affliction, I ask for your assistance in ensuring I remain at peace until I fulfill your desires. Please, Lord, watch over and hold the demon at bay until I finish my studies. Please, Lord, keep me from sinning and allow me the chance to be your humble servant.

Amen.

THE DEMONIC SAVIOR

From that night forward, I do not hear from the demon inside. My remaining time at seminary proves to be as peaceful as one could hope. I continue with my studies and earn high accolades for my insightfulness and knowledge. God truly is listening. But I know this is short-lived. As much as I want to believe that I could continue to just pray after seminary and God would hold this affliction at bay, I know it is not possible.

Graduating seminary comes much sooner than I ever anticipated, and though I never forget the demon lurking inside me, it proves to be some of the better years of my life. At least some of the most peaceful. I venture back home and am appointed to be Pastor Gunther's assistant until his official retirement when I take over all duties of pastorship in the church I was raised.

But after my graduation from seminary, it does not take long for the demon to rise and take hold of me once again. By this point, I have established my methods and the room in the house, each step meticulously thought out to prevent detection. Every piece of the process becomes mechanical in the way I would execute the movement. Every minute detail is painstakingly considered to ensure nothing is available to lead to me as being a suspect. I purchase a vehicle specifically to make sure I'm inconspicuous. I dress so that no one would suspect me. I ensure everything is indetectable.

* * * * *

"It appears to me you found a way to subdue the demon, if he truly exists," Patricia notes.

"I did, but it was only temporary. I could never subdue him long enough to not become who I am. He would have destroyed me before I could," I tell her. "And believe me when I say he is real."

"So where is HE?" she exclaims.

"Careful what you wish for, Officer Patricia Sutton." I give her a stern glare, reminding her she is not in a position to challenge me for I am all that holds the demon back.

"Frankly, I think you are full of shit, Francis," she challenges back. "I think you hide behind the church to be the real demon and not that you are possessed."

Luckily for me, I contain the rage. But the demon is screaming in my head to kill her.

"Challenge ME! Who does she think she is?" I hear him calling out, enraged beyond any other time I can think of. It takes everything I can do to subdue him and not kill her. She is my only hope for salvation.

Chapter 41

"Where did she go?" Lieutenant Rivera asks.

"I don't know. One minute she was there, the next she's gone," Officer Janowski replies.

"Why? Why do all these college kids have to be out tonight?" Lieutenant Rivera responds. Then he says into the radio, "Car 2, do you have a visual?"

"No, Lieutenant," a voice on the radio responds. "It's like she vanished."

"Do we have all the cars' plates that have come by?" Lieutenant Rivera asks.

"We have all those that came from this end," the radio calls back.

"I have all the ones you and I wrote down," Officer Janowski remarks.

"Let's hope we can trace all of these on our lists," Lieutenant Rivera says. "I do not see how she just up and disappeared. I knew we should have had more eyes. Damn budget cuts."

* * * * *

Chris and I have traveled to five cities over a two-week period. Each police department we speak to is forthcoming and willing to help. After we presented our findings that these were not isolated incidents, they agree there is a potential unsub out there doing this. Though given the lack of evidence and just a myriad of victims that all fit a specific modus operandi, we are just throwing darts at a board without actually aiming. He could strike anywhere, anytime, and we have no idea how to track it. So each city performs training specifically to keep the lookout for this unsub. Each city establishes task forces with undercover female officers set to closely match the description of the other victims.

It's toward the end of our trip that I receive a call from Chicago PD asking if we could stop in before we head back to Quantico.

A sergeant walks in. "Special Agent Bedford?"

"Yes," I reply.

"You have a call from Chicago," he says and leads me to a terminal.

"Special Agent Bedford," I answer.

"Nate?" I hear John Beaumont's voice on the line.

"Hey, John!" I say. "What can I do for you?"

"We set up that task force like you suggested, and our undercover is now missing," John says.

"Missing? How could she go missing?" I ask.

"We don't know. We placed two to three female officers out on the street to pose as close to the MO description as possible. We had two unmarked patrol cars standing by to assist and oversee the operation. Lieutenant Rivera was in one of the patrol cars with the team. One minute she was there, and the next she was gone. The guys watching the street said they had a crowd of college kids block their view for just a minute, and after they cleared, Patricia was gone." John's voice is clearly upset, I can tell over the phone.

"Alright, John. We were supposed to be headed back today, but I'll call headquarters and work something out where we can stay and help you. Chris and I can be there tomorrow," I tell him.

Chris and I arrive at Chicago PD headquarters and are showed upstairs as before. We are directed to the Vice Division and into a room where Capt. John Beaumont, Lieutenant Rivera, and a cadre of officers are sitting awaiting our arrival. The entire division is complete chaos, as to be expected when one of your own goes missing.

"Where are we at?" I ask as John extends his hand to me.

"Nate, I wish I could tell you. We had two unmarked cars at either end of the street keeping an eye on the situation. Each car was writing down plates of all vehicles in and out, and both had eyes

THE DEMONIC SAVIOR

on her location. A huge group of college kids walked around her location, and then she was gone," John Beaumont provides the most up-to-date information.

"So what car was she talking to?" Chris asks.

"We are not sure. At that time, there were five cars in the area. We are running the plates now," Lieutenant Rivera tells us. "It's crazy. It is like she just vanished in thin air." He is clearly taking this hard as he is the senior officer in charge.

"Okay," I say. "Let's get a list of the plates and see what comes up. Each plate, we will investigate and talk to the owners. Clearly it has to be one of them," I say.

"The plan was simple. Every john that approached her and she picked up would be taken around the corner for questioning by the team, and then she would return to her post to await the next one," Lieutenant Rivera explains the plan.

"That's not far from the way we would have run it either, Lieutenant," I say, trying to reassure him that this is not his fault. If this guy wanted to get caught, he would have been sloppy, and we would have had him by now. But he is not sloppy, and thus why we are out hunting him. But at least it confirms the suspicions of Chris and me. This is a true unsub that has to be caught.

"Sir." A uniformed officer hands Lieutenant Rivera a sheet of paper. "The list of plates and owners."

Lieutenant Rivera looks over the list. He hands it back to the uniform. "Write these down on the board in the conference room."

The conference room is where the detectives from both Vice and Homicide are poring over ideas, theories, and all the evidence. The room is a standing-room only, and every table is littered with papers, photos, and pads. The board at the front of the room is covered in ideas; a roll-around writing board is brought in so the uniform can add the list. As each vehicle with description is added to the board, I glance over occasionally to see the progress. About halfway through, one name and vehicle catches my attention.

Francis Isiah Fleming. Brown Town and Country. Dubuque, Iowa.

I nudge John. "See what I see?" I say to John.

He looks back at me. "What the hell is Francis doing in Chicago?" John asks.

Francis Fleming, a buddy from our unit in Vietnam. The same guy who nearly lost his life in an explosion that killed our sergeant. The same guy who I met and had lunch with on his trek of the Appalachian Trail. *It can't be*, I say to myself. But it makes no sense as to why he would be on this list. What the hell is he doing in Chicago?

I ask John to join me in private.

"John, is there somewhere you and I can talk?" I ask.

"Yeah, Nate. Let's go to my office." John leads the way, both of us knowing what this is about.

We enter the office and close the door.

"You saw what I saw," I say.

"I did," John replies.

"What's the probability he is in Chicago the same night you are doing a stakeout?" I ask.

"Close to a million in one," John replies.

"How do you want to play this?" I ask.

"I have no jurisdiction in Dubuque, Nate," John points out.

"No, but I do. Especially if this is legit and the entire case is across state lines. Then it automatically becomes an FBI case," I say.

"We cannot go in there guns blazing. I mean, he is one of us," John says. "I have an idea."

"I'm listening," I reply.

"Why not you and I take a road trip and talk to him? I mean, he might not even be the person we are looking for," John points out. "Maybe he was lonely and just happened to be in Chicago. Who knows."

"I want that to be the case, John. Truly I do," I say as I take a deep breath.

Chapter 42

As day breaks over the horizon around the house, no light penetrates the solitary kill room Francis created in the basement of the old house. No birds chirp as the deathly silence engulfs the entire property. A light breeze sways as a storm begins to form on the horizon just west of the sleepy house. Francis and Patricia sit in the brightly lit room just staring at each other.

Patricia breaks the silence, "That is a hell of a story, Francis. But I still see flaws in your entire process. Things that you could have done to stop the demon."

"Perhaps, but as I have tried to explain, the ability to place the demon at bay always turned up fruitless," Francis starts to explain. "As much as I want peace for myself, I also wanted to see the demon banished back to hell where it belongs. That is the one thing I have not been able to accomplish or determine how to do. Until now."

"I empathize with your predicament. However, I feel you could have just done yourself the favor by ridding yourself from the demon and not being the victim in your own body. What do you mean 'until now'?" she says.

Ignoring her last question, Francis offers, "I don't know about you, but I am hungry. Would you care for some breakfast?" The complete change in topic takes Patricia off guard.

"Yes, you know, something to eat would be nice," she responds.

Francis leaves Patricia unattended in the room as he heads upstairs to cook breakfast. Patricia realizes what he has done and immediately begins to use her free hand to remove the strap around her other hand. Within no time and her hands free, she unties the bindings on her feet. She looks around the room. The table with the assortment of knives is appealing. But due to his size, she is unsure if she can overpower him. She thinks to herself. *He drugged me. There has to be something around here that I can use to subdue him.* She eyes the medicine cabinet laid in the wall. She finds the vials of sedative and a fresh syringe. She fills the syringe and waits for him to return.

The smell of freshly sizzling meat filters down to the room. He left the door slightly ajar when he left, and Patricia can hear him scraping the pan as he flips the eggs. Her stomach growls as the realization that she hasn't eaten in hours and had nothing but bourbon takes effect. The clinking of silverware on plates, then his weight on the creaking boards of the stairs outside, alert her to his approach. She slides her hand back into the loose cuff and positions her feet to appear still strapped to the chair. In her free hand, she holds the syringe with the sedative.

Francis enters the room. "Here you go." He places the plates on the metal dissection table.

"Do you expect me to eat one-handed?" Patricia asks.

Without a word, Francis walks over to her and leans down to remove the strap around her other arm. At the same moment he realizes she is already free, Patricia drives the needle into his arm, and the pressure of the liquid immediately plunges into Francis's muscles. Just as he goes to react, the sedative takes effect, and he slumps to the floor, the needle still protruding from his arm.

Patricia takes a deep sigh of relief, slumping in the chair herself. *Now what do I do?* she asks herself. She knows he will be out for a while and eats the breakfast provided, then removes both plates from the table. She lifts him up off the ground like a sack of potatoes and hoists him onto the table. She straps him down just as he had done to each of his previous victims.

Patricia then goes and looks through the house for a way to call out. But in each room, she finds no phone. *Who lives these days without a phone?* she asks herself. The entire house is filled with Francis's family memories. A picture of his mother hangs over the fireplace in the living room. She finds a picture of his father, though looking at it, she first thought it was Francis himself until she realizes the date on the back. His mother's bedroom with the IV stand and drip is still positioned next to the bed. It is almost as if nothing has changed in the last decade. Based on the layer of dust in several rooms, it seems as though no one has bothered to clean either. Everything is just left to decay as time passes by.

Patricia then sits and thinks, a debate roaming through her head on what to do. She can sit there and await the cavalry, so to speak, as she is sure by now, Chicago PD is fervently looking for her. She looks around the room again. She thinks the tools used by Francis to kill and dissect his victims are an appealing sentiment to what she could do, which is kill him the way he killed his victims. But she is an officer of the law now, and she cannot allow her emotions to take hold of her. If she did, she would be no better than him. Then she sees it. A placard on the wall. Discreet and almost nonexistent as she has overlooked it throughout each of her searches.

The diagram shows various circles positioned around what appears to be the layout of the house. One room, apparently the room she was in, holds the most of these circles. She follows the diagram to where one might be, and she finds a wire protruding from the ceiling. She follows it to the other end and finds where it disappears into the ceiling again, and another follows to yet another location in the ceiling. This continues until she finds that each circle on the diagram shows the exact location of where these wires disappear and reappear. The thought hits her. In Francis's story, he said he was educated as an engineer, and in the Marines, he was trained in demolition and explosives, thus how he was injured. He prewired the entire house to disintegrate should he ever be caught.

A moan comes from the table behind her. "You bitch!" The demon has awakened and realizes the situation it is in. "Do you know who I am?" the demon demands. "These chains, these restraints cannot hold me."

Patricia grabs the K bar off the table. "No, I do not know you." She knows clearly that the voice speaking to her is no longer Francis.

"I am Alastor, demon of possession," Alastor states. "I was sent here by the lord of hell, Lucifer himself, to fill his kingdom with fresh souls." He lurches and flings all of Francis's mortal being against the straps that bind him to the table.

"So Francis wasn't lying. You truly are the one behind all of this," Patricia states.

"Of course I am. You do not truly believe such a pathetic being as Francis is capable of killing people. No, he is a mere patsy," Alastor claims. "I! I am the true rebirth of the lord. Taker of all sinful souls."

"And these, these jars up here, do they belong to you?" Patricia asks as she picks up the first jar she sees and holds it above the demon.

"Yes. They belong to me, the eyes of the sinful souls I have sent to my father's kingdom," Alastor replies.

"Hmm… So what would you do if I destroyed them?" Patricia asks. Alastor becomes frantic. She can see the demon try to escape the flesh of Francis. "Oh, look at you. So powerful, yet you cannot escape the flesh that binds you," Patricia taunts. "It is not the restraints. It is Francis that binds you."

"You pathetic miser. I know you. I know your past. I know even your future," Alastor begins to relax as he knows the struggle is pointless.

Patricia twists off the top of the jar in her hand and smells the rubbing alcohol–based solution. She pours some on the flesh binding the demon. An evil and devilish look of her own spreads across her face.

"Yes, Patricia. Do it. Set him aflame and set me free," Alastor pleads.

"Patricia, no!" Francis's voice overpowers the demon. "There is holy water in the cabinet. Coat the knife in it, then plunge it in my chest. When you are done—"

"Don't listen to him, Patricia. That holy water trick will not work." Alastor takes back control as they struggle internally.

Patricia is beside herself. She sees why Francis kept saying that just exorcising the demon would not be enough, why he needed to find a way to send Alastor back to the kingdom of hell from which he came. She sets down the jar with the eyes. She goes to the cabinet and looks for the holy water. She grabs it and sets it on the table. She grabs all the jars of previous victims' eyes and smashes them on the ground. Francis's mortal body starts to flail around as Alastor screams in demonic tongue, cursing her and her belligerence. She then grabs the bottle of holy water and, with the K bar in one hand and the bottle in the other, is poised above the body of Francis strapped to the table.

Francis works his way past Alastor, "Do it, Patricia. It is the only way. Soak the knife and plunge it into me. Then flip the switch by the front door, just like the diagram says, and run clear of the house."

"Nooooooooo!" screams Alastor as she soaks the K bar, tosses the bottle, and with two hands grasping the hilt, thrusts it into Francis's chest. Just before the tip of the knife penetrates Francis's flesh, the demon's hand breaks free, clasping her arm.

It felt like an eternity. Vision after vision of death. She sees the battle of heaven and the Archangel Michael drive out Lucifer. She watches Cain kill Abel. Every major battle known to man flashes before her eyes as well as the most notable killers of all time: Jack the Ripper, Lady Bluebird, Ed Gein, and even all of Francis's victims. The last image she sees is one of her own doing.

The knife penetrates Francis's torso, and the hand goes limp and lets go of her arm, but the transfer is complete.

"Now you know, dear Patricia. I will never be sent back until my destiny is served." The now softened voice of Alastor is heard in Patricia's head. "Now you will be my vessel. I can assure you, as you just caught a glimpse, my story is much more interesting than the one Francis told you." Alastor laughs a haunting laugh as he sinks back into the deepest recesses of Patricia's mind.

Patricia knows she cannot explain what has happened here. She rips the placard off the wall and heads upstairs to find the trigger for the devices. As she nears the front door, she finds a single switch covered, and looking at the placard, she figures this has to be the trigger. She reads over the placard, which denotes she has approximately three minutes to get clear of the house before all goes up in an intense fireball. She casts the placard back into the center of the hallway, flips the switch, takes a deep breath, and runs like hell down the driveway.

As she reaches the end, she hears the first pop, then the next and the next. She walks back through the arched trees lining the drive and, at the end, stops to watch as the intense fireball, once a house, licks her face with its immense heat.

Epilogue

John and I bring Chris into John's office.

"Chris, we know one of the potential suspects," I tell him.

"Which one?" Chris asks.

"Francis Fleming. The brown Town and Country that is on the list of vehicles," I tell him.

"Nate, that creates…" Chris starts.

"We know, Chris," John interrupts.

"How likely is it that he is the subject we are looking for?" Chris asks.

"Enough that we want to leave immediately to talk to him. But he is in Dubuque, Iowa," I say.

"What do you two propose?" Chris asks.

"The three of us go and talk to him. If it appears that Francis is involved, then we can remove ourselves, and you can take the lead. But the longer we wait, the less our chances of protecting one of our own," I say.

"Okay. Let's go," Chris states.

We gather our belongings at the station and go to the rental car that Chris and I had acquired. At this point, protocol be damned; we have a fellow officer missing, and each of us want to find her alive. On our way out, John passes the reins to Lieutenant Rivera, and we leave Chicago headed for Dubuque, Iowa.

Three hours later, we arrive in Asbury, Iowa, the little suburb of Dubuque. We stop at the local police department and identify ourselves.

"Officer Jones. I am Special Agent Nathan Bedford, this is Special Agent Chris Bennett, and Captain John Beaumont of the Chicago Police Department. We would like to talk to the commanding officer of this police department," I say.

Officer Jones is taken aback as I am sure this is not a normal day. But before he could respond, a large man steps out from an office.

"Gentlemen, I am Sheriff Hansen. May I ask what this is about?" Sheriff Hansen says.

"Sheriff, if you don't mind, can we talk in your office?" I ask.

"Sure, right this way." Sheriff Hansen motions for us to come into his office.

We provide all the details from the beginning. How Chris and I noticed a link among various cases through various cities. How we established training in each police department and set up individual task forces. Then how last night, one of Chicago's own came up missing during a stakeout. We proceed to tell him that one vehicle stood out from the others belonging to Francis Isiah Fleming.

"Pastor Francis? You're kidding, right?" Sheriff Hansen replies in astonishment. "I've known Francis my whole life. Hell, his family owned the local hardware store till they sold it to Clark Knowles, who worked for them for years."

"Sheriff, we only want to talk to Pastor Fleming. We find it odd that his vehicle was 180 miles from here last night, and one of our officers is now missing," John says.

"Alright, gentlemen. Quite an entourage you have here, two FBI boys and a captain from Chicago. But with one of our own missing, I get it. I'll send a patrol car out with you all so we can all stay in the loop. I assume you have the address since you have his plates?" he concludes.

"Yes, Sheriff, and we appreciate your cooperation," I say.

As we turn onto the road leading to Francis's address, we hear explosions and a massive fireball over the tree line. Each car hits the gas and barrels up the driveway. Our cars stop short of Officer Patricia Sutton standing in the middle of the drive watching the house burn intensely.

To Be Continued…

About the Author

Lawrence Newton is a retired US Navy veteran, enabling him to have circumvented the globe. He is also an informal master of the culinary arts, which has brought to life unique flavors to his line of sauces. His other interests include exploring more culinary oddities in the kitchen as well as extensive travel with his wife and family. Lawrence is a budding prolific author that uses his writing to delve into the human psyche where others have not dared to enter.